The Inked

by

Kristina Streva

The Inked Series

The Inked

Cover Art by *Diana Carlile*

The Wild Rose Press, Inc.
PO Box 708
Adams Basin, NY 14410-0708
Visit us at www.thewildrosepress.com

Publishing History
First Edition, 2022
Trade Paperback ISBN 978-1-5092-4381-5
Digital ISBN 978-1-5092-4382-2

The Inked Series
Published in the United States of America

The beast dove forward in a sharp motion, a missile aimed at its target. At full speed, its nose slammed into the front of the boat, causing it to splinter even more.

The sisters' screams echoed through the water as a siren call as pieces of the ship were propelled in different directions. Yuri grasped her sisters firmly, pulling them to the other end of the boat. Their bodies trembled as the beast forced his wide, grinning mouth into the hole he had just created. His jaws chopped only inches away from Yuri's face as she gulped in his hot breath, sour on her tongue, the rotten flesh of spoiled meat. She sobbed as each tear dissolved into the sea as if it had never existed. One minute there, one minute gone, just like her mother that Yuri wished was still there to protect them. The anchor that had been weighing heavily on her chest had finally made its way to rock bottom, pulling any hope of survival with it.

"I'm sorry I couldn't protect us," Yuri wept, hugging her sisters tightly. She shut her eyes as the beast's teeth continued to chomp away at what was left of their shelter. Its sharp, serrated teeth scraped at the wood. Yuri tucked her head down to her chest. Soon, it will be over.

Just then, the sound of a horned trumpet echoed through the water.

The beast thrashed its head back as pieces of the boat splintered around it. Its beady eyes glanced one last time at its missed supper before retreating.

Dedication

I dedicate this book to my family and friends who believed in me sometimes more than I could believe in myself. Special shout out to my Father Paul, Mother Vita and Brother Vincent. I love you all.

Chapter 1

It was a cold March day on the coast of Denmark, the kind that left your face frost-kissed when you breached the ocean surface, breathing out a silken mist upon the air.

Yuri and her sisters, Britt and Tanis, liked to make a game out of who could race to the surface the fastest. But it was a relatively pointless challenge as Yuri would always win, being so petite and agile; her long silvery gray hair would flow behind her in its own rhythmic dance as she gracefully propelled herself to the surface.

It was at moments like these that she imagined she was one of the merfolk.

She pictured herself with one long, beautifully jeweled and sequined fishtail that would sway back and forth, reflecting the light that poured in as she got closer and closer to the surface, seeing shimmering images of the sky and puffy clouds as she neared the top. This was not her reality, though, despite how badly she wished it were true. In place of a beautiful, bejeweled tail, she and her sisters all had eight long tentacles that would move like charmed snakes as they swam.

Tentacles were nothing by comparison to glistening fishtails.

The writhing, squirming elongations possessed no beauty about them at all.

"How did you manage to win again?" Tanis laughed as she broke the surface. "You cheat!"

They laughed. Then Yuri suddenly stopped laughing. She stared instead.

Beads of water dripped down the thick and jagged scar that ran across Tanis' left eye. The droplets lingered a while, settling momentarily into the fissures of her old injury before running down and pooling on the curve of her cheek like an open canal. Yuri's mouth twitched into an ungainly forced smile as she averted her gaze from her sister's puckered skin.

She wanted to *always* look the other way, but this was her sister. And a sister deserved for her to *not* dislike looking at her face. A sister deserved positive, unconditional regard. Yuri only wished she were not so flawed herself that she could not deliver that degree of love toward Tanis.

This was awkward—and this was all too horrible and painful, having to always look the other way when the scar on Tanis' face seemed to again wish to sear itself into her mind.

An unwavering sense of guilt set in as it always did when she looked at her sister's marred skin. To see her this way was enough to break her heart and spirit. But at a certain angle, the scar lines melded into normality such that Yuri could imagine just smooth pink skin, unblemished.

But always, she knew it was there. The scar, the reminder, the fears since laid to rest.

Tanis had only been fourteen at the time and a naïve girl with an untainted view of the sea, a hopeful blank canvas ready to be painted with all her life experiences.

And painted she soon was—only not the way anyone would have hoped. Painted in blood.

Yuri blamed herself for not being more stringent. Had she done a better job at warning Tanis about the merfolk, maybe she never would have ventured into their territory that day.

The ocean breeze ran across Yuri's body as if it was the whispering winds of guilt.

And Athena never would have cut Tanis' eye with the sharp edge of a shell.

She shuddered for a moment before regaining her composure.

"I guess you'll have to train harder to be faster than your old sis. At least you beat Britt this time," Yuri retorted with the faux smile that she had grown accustomed to wearing, like an unwanted gift from a relative—ready to be discarded the first moment no one was looking.

It was necessary to keep the illusion of happiness for her sister's sake.

"Where is Britt, anyway?"

Tanis spun around and then dove back down into the dark ocean, her inky black tentacles pushing away the water around her, helping her glide down effortlessly.

Her younger sister was right; Britt hadn't reached the surface yet. Blood rushed from Yuri's face into her limbs as her chest grew heavy like an anchor digging deep its metal fluke.

She lunged into the water after her youngest sister, crying out, "Tanis! Stop! Please!"

Her heart pounded against her ribs, drumming to the beat of her fear. *Boom-boom. Boom-boom.*

Tanis' electric blue hair danced behind her in the distance, seemingly beckoning Yuri to catch up with its long wispy ends curling like fingers, summoning.

Come on. Come on!

"Tanis!" Yuri screamed as water rushed around her eight swirling tentacles.

She propelled herself forward to catch up to her sister, who by now had managed to cross over into forbidden territory and had stopped in front of an enormous formation of towering boulders.

The large stones formed a tight circle around the open enclosure.

They looked akin to mighty guards protecting treasures inside.

"Over here," Tanis shouted back toward Yuri.

Yuri tightened her fist into a stiff ball, helplessly watching her sister swiftly disappearing into the entrance of the enclosure. Its tight opening seemed to swallow her whole like the long winding gullet of a predator. One moment, its jaws were wide open and beckoning to receive her, tempting and tantalizing. But the next, she was gone away into the dark and seemingly endless labyrinth, following after Britt, swimming through tunnels and voids, panic-stricken.

But if Britt had somehow disappeared, what if Tanis simply did too?

The enclosure might swallow and devour them both!

Tanis, please, slow down! Tanis, turn around—and swim back! she silently hollered. At the same time, another part of her was willing Tanis forward. *Find Britt! Save Britt! Tanis, go!*

There was no easy solution; both options bearing

too much risk, too much potential loss.

Yuri gulped in the salty ocean water through her gills, still following Tanis, letting the narrow entrance consume her too.

Human rubbish shamefully covered the seabed inside, a scattering of accrued metallic parts, timber, plastics that could no longer find buoyancy since they were now filled to the brim with mud and sand, and all manner of other rotten detritus. It was as if some vast sailor's ship had exploded there, leaving behind the remains of its broken corpse lying on the floor, an eerie graveyard of bygone times.

But the plastic was especially vile—because it would never disappear. The plastic was the enemy of everything that lived—or tried to—in the ocean's swirling depths.

Yuri now gripped her chest tightly; the anchor was back again. She knew all too well about the threat of humans. Her mother had warned her about them when alive.

"I heard Britt's voice. She's over here somewhere!" Tanis shouted, waving her arms frantically from the other side of the enclosure. "Britt's here, over here!"

Yuri carefully maneuvered her body across the scattered remains as if expecting the objects below to pull her deep into the seafloor like a sand striker leaping out and snagging its prey.

Her sister was up ahead, hovering over Britt, who had been caught in the fierce jaws of a hideous metal contraption. Blood and ink oozed out of her tentacle that its razor-sharp steel teeth had pierced. The water surrounding them immediately became a dark cloud of deep red, and Yuri swished her arms back and forth to clear through the murky haze.

As the blood dispersed, Yuri's body tingled with a familiar sense of dread.

The taste of iron lingered on the tip of her tongue, just the same way it had during one of her mother's excursions. As the eldest, her mother had expected her to protect her younger sisters, to always be the sensible one, the one who looked out for them both and kept them safe and together.

They would often journey to the surface in a group just so her mother could teach her how to protect her sisters from the land dwellers everyone had seen and feared.

It was during one of those excursions that Yuri had witnessed just how dangerous humans could truly be. A loud bang had echoed from one of the large, docked ships, and Yuri held her hands to her ringing ears. Her mother's frail veiny arms pulled her back under the water as a trail of hazy red surrounded them. Her eyes widened as the corpse of a man heavily sank down into the sea, leaving the tip of her tongue scorched with his metallic taste. The man's eyes stared wide toward the surface, seeing nothing at all. They were already glassy, a milky white, his spirit departed along with most of his body's bright red blood as it pumped free in the final throes of his heartbeat.

Now, her sister leaked a similar red in the water, causing a flurry of mixed emotions and panic inside Yuri's mind. Soon, Britt could bleed out.

"Tanis, quick, pull one side of this trap, and I'll pull the other! I think we can pry it open," Yuri said, digging her tentacles firmly into the sand, gripping for

Yuri's hands shook as she grabbed both her sisters' arms. "We need to hide, now."

This time, no one argued. No one breathed.

Up ahead was a cracked wooden rowboat that had been flipped upside down. Its sandy gray bottom was split wide at the seam, showing a large zig-zagged cavity that had caused its demise.

"Over there!" Yuri pointed to the broken rowboat as she swam ahead of her two sisters.

The beast hovered over them, its beady eyes tracing the water like deep black holes looking for anything it could consume. It opened its wide jaw, revealing long pointed teeth as if it was grinning.

"We have to lift the boat to get under it," Yuri whispered to her sisters while grabbing the edge of the damaged vessel.

Her sisters rushed to her side to help, each digging long, slender fingers under the edge of the ship. It was heavier than they had hoped. This often seemed to be the way of things. Like the roots of a tree, it had dug its way into the sand after years of being abandoned and had gradually become a part of the seabed. Their forearms strained as they pried it up. Slowly, it started to peel itself free of the wet sand.

"Get in," Yuri said, holding the edge of the boat up so her sisters could crawl under before tucking herself in as well. Her arms throbbed, mimicking her beating heart. *Boom-boom. Boom-boom.* She struggled to lift her limbs; they felt as heavy as branches as she pulled her sisters into a tight embrace and peeked out of the crack.

The heinous beast's long, pointed nose had caught a whiff of something in its surroundings, and it began to circle down progressively closer to their ship. The water rippled around its mighty tail as its proboscis steered down toward the sisters' hiding space, aimed at its target.

Tanis gasped, "Britt, your tentacle is bleeding again!"

Britt grabbed her tentacle with her hand and bit her lip, letting out a tiny whimper. She sounded afraid now, sounding her own age for a change. But this tone was still not one the sisters wished to hear. It meant she was suffering, at least in her own head. She was scared. It meant she was being the young one again, the vulnerable one, the child—the one Yuri really needed to worry about. But for real this time. No petulance, just horror.

And it was too late.

The beast dove forward in a sharp motion, a missile aimed at its target. At full speed, its nose slammed into the front of the boat, causing it to splinter even more.

The sisters' screams echoed through the water as a siren call as pieces of the ship were propelled in different directions. Yuri grasped her sisters firmly, pulling them to the other end of the boat. Their bodies trembled as the beast forced his wide, grinning mouth into the hole he had just created. His jaws chopped only inches away from Yuri's face as she gulped in his hot breath, sour on her tongue, the rotten flesh of spoiled meat. She sobbed as each tear dissolved into the sea as if it had never existed. One minute there, one minute gone, just like her mother that Yuri wished was still there to protect them. The anchor that had been weighing heavily on her chest had finally made its way to rock bottom, pulling any hope of survival with it.

"I'm sorry I couldn't protect us," Yuri wept, hugging her sisters tightly. She shut her eyes as the beast's teeth continued to chomp away at what was left of their shelter. Its sharp, serrated teeth scraped at the wood. Yuri tucked her head down to her chest. *Soon, it will be over.*

Just then, the sound of a horned trumpet echoed through the water.

The beast thrashed its head back as pieces of the boat splintered around it. Its beady eyes glanced one last time at its missed supper before retreating.

Chapter 2

Kaleb, the son of King Oasis, sat on his red and gold chariot. Large black seahorses adorned with golden paint pulled it forward as his army followed behind, saddled on their seahorse steeds. With each command from the King's son, they drummed their fists on their armor made from reinforced turtle shells, all stunningly painted and garnished in sequins and gold.

A few days ago, King Oasis had proudly declared that there would be a competition between him and his twin brother, Neo. A beast had been terrorizing Atlantis, and whoever brought him the head of this creature would take the throne and the enormous bounty that came with it.

"Forward! We can't afford to lose the trail of this beast!" Kaleb shouted as he lifted a long golden horn to his lips and blew.

His army moved forward in unison. He trailed behind them in his chariot, gripping his long-pronged golden trident in one hand and horn in the other. Kaleb was on the hunt, much like the monster who had hunted the occupants of Atlantis. Just last week, two more children had gone missing, and now that his troop had moved forward, he could search the area for survivors.

His eyes carefully scanned side to side, above, and then finally to the bottom of the seabed. To his left, he spotted a damaged boat flipped upside down with a large, jagged hole in one side. He tightened his grip on the trident, swimming down toward the dilapidated rowboat. Silver strands of hair stuck out of the damage in the boat's side, looking like kelp waving in the current.

"Hello?" His body crept forward hesitantly as he cleared his throat. "By order of the King Oasis, reveal yourself!" Kaleb's voice bellowed through the water.

The rowboat stirred as the head of a young girl tentatively made its way out of the hole. Her pale body followed, embellished in a purple laced corset that ended where her long black tentacles protruded. Kaleb's mouth dropped open. Now, Yuri swayed before him. His wide eyes traced her body up and down.

What...what is this girl doing here? Oh!

"Do you mean to harm me?" Yuri asked, cutting through the silence, her tone sharp as a blade.

Kaleb's mouth curved into an amused smile. *She's bold.* He had not seen her kind very often—they stayed hidden. This was new to him.

It was for a fair reason they hid away since his people hated hers, after all. Despised them with great passion. He ran his hands through his light-brown hair and then down to his chiseled jawline.

What if my father had found her? He shook his head, refocusing mossy green eyes on Yuri as he studied her.

Her hair was beautiful, and much like that of the mermaids he had grown up with, it was long and flowed behind her in the water as she moved. Yuri's eyes met his, and he held her gaze, staring at the stunning icy-blue that looked back at him. He traced her pale complexion from her face down to her skinny arms, now held bent and stiff against her hips.

"Do you not know who I am?" He wore a cocky smile that hollowed into dimples at his cheeks.

Yuri's brows furrowed. Her sharp glare stabbed at his ego, causing his dimpled smirk to retreat from his face like a wounded soldier. "Honestly, I don't care who you are. Answer the question. Are your intentions to harm me?" Her eyes darted to his pronged trident.

Kaleb's grip loosened on his weapon as he stooped toward the seabed, his eyes remaining focused on Yuri's icy-blue scowl. He opened his palms, letting the trident roll out of his hands and onto the sandy seafloor. Inching back, he straightened his arms, outstretching his hands high over his head. "No, I don't wish to harm you. Do you wish to harm me?" He wiggled the fingers of his empty hands.

Yuri crossed her arms over her puffed-out chest. "That entirely depends on you," she sneered. Her nostrils flared.

The once-retreated smirk returned to Kaleb's face. *How could such a small and petite girl have so much attitude? This girl is feisty!* As his heavy trident sank deeper into the ocean floor, he lowered his hands and tapped awkwardly at his sides. His armor clung to his broad, muscular chest as he gestured in a proper bow. *I might as well introduce myself properly.*

"I'm Kaleb. My father is King Oasis of Atlantis. My troops and I came out here to hunt the beast that terrorizes these waters." Kaleb paused for a response that didn't come. He waited.

His stomach knotted at Yuri's silence. It twisted like the ends of a fishing net. Her deep-blue eyes stared off to the rowboat in which she had emerged. "And you are…" His voice trailed off as her eyes returned to him. Her plump pink lips parted to reveal unexpectedly sharp pointed teeth.

"My name is Yuri. I don't mean to be on your people's territory. I came this way looking for my sisters, and we were attacked—most likely by the very same beast you are hunting. I suppose it was hunting us… Anyway, we would be grateful if you were to kill it."

A sense of pride rushed over Kaleb. She had confirmed that he and his troops were on the right track. He bit down on his lower lip, fighting the upward curve of his mouth.

"Is something funny?" Yuri huffed.

Kaleb shook his head back and forth as he forced his face into a firm stare. "No, of course not. But it's quite impressive that you are still alive. You certainly don't want to become dinner for that thing. Where are your sisters?"

Yuri's hair fell forward into her face as she bowed her head, looking down at the seabed. Kaleb's stomach churned again, causing him to twist uncomfortably. *Have her sisters died?* "You are awfully quiet," he said softly, tilting his head.

"My sister is injured," Yuri responded reluctantly. Pain crossed her face like a fleeting shadow as their eyes met. She did not seem very sure of herself now. She seemed worried, bearing the weight of the world.

She pointed to the broken boat from which she had emerged. "Tanis…Britt…You can come out now."

Kaleb froze, his arms falling stiff at his sides as his widened eyes watched two more of *the Inked* emerge from the tattered rowboat. The youngest had long blue hair that flowed like her sister's and an innocent doll-like face with a button nose. It gave away her youth. However, much like a cracked porcelain doll, she carried a scar across her eye. Her painfully thin arms were wrapped around the other sister, whose angular face scowled at him. One of her tentacles harbored a deep cut, and as Kaleb stared, she pushed back short pink hair to better reveal glowering brown eyes and an array of sharp teeth.

"Hello, ladies!" Kaleb said, tapping weaponless hands at his sides as his eyes gazed back and forth between the two sisters.

Yuri swam in front of Kaleb, blocking his gawking view, her tentacles moving around her like irritated serpents ready to bite. "Your satchel," she said, pointing to the golden bag tied to his chariot. "Does it have any medicine in it? I mean—I mean, my sister, she needs something."

"Uhh, right," Kaleb responded, doing a backstroke toward his chariot. His navy-blue fin fanned the water as he kept his eyes focused on all three sisters.

The satchel had been packed in the morning by Ella, his childhood caretaker. She had raised him and his brother since they were children as they had never even known their mother, who had died during childbirth. Even though both he and his brother were well in their twenties, Ella still worried and cared for them—maybe in a similar way to how Yuri too took care of and worried about her own younger siblings. *Old habits die hard*, as people said. It did not matter how old "children" became—they always needed to be looked after, at least in Ella's eyes.

"There should be something in here to help your sister," he said confidently, unclipping the satchel from his chariot. He was sure Ella had packed beyond the essentials. She usually did. Kaleb dug his fingers into the over-packed bag and pulled out item after item. *Rope, fish, knife, kelp, more rope, fish, bottle… Hmm, let's see.*

"Wowza," Britt scoffed under her breath, causing Tanis to nudge her.

"It's best not to offend someone trying to help us," Tanis whispered back.

The ridged edges of a Scotch bonnet shell brushed across Kaleb's callused fingers. He pulled the shell out of his satchel, holding it up in front of him. It had been stuffed with a healing potion made from aloe, blowfish gills, and red sand. "Here we go," he said, twisting it around in his palm like a prized trophy.

Yuri reached out her arm, opening the palm of her hand. Her long red nails adorned her skinny fingers, which extended toward Kaleb. "Well, aren't you going to give me the potion? You did spend about ten minutes looking for it, after all. Not sure why you would waste your time if you were not planning on helping us after all that effort," Yuri chastised, dropping her extended hand to her side.

Britt hissed from behind her, "He's wasting our time. Let's go!"

Yuri cranked her neck toward her sister, thick and wavy brows furrowed over her side-eyed glare. Britt huffed, crossing her arms over her chest in defeat. That glare meant *shut up*.

"So?" Yuri said, readjusting her gaze.

Kaleb tossed the shell up and caught it again in his

palm, running his thumb over its ribbed grooves. "If I give you this, what do I get in return?"

"What exactly do you want?" Yuri hissed, placing her hands on her hips.

"Well," he said, taking a deep gulp and shifting his eyes to the seabed. "I'd like to get to know you. I haven't encountered your kind very often, and certainly never had a conversation with one." His face flushed into a light pink, similar to the rosy petals of a blooming flower. He hesitated as he looked back up at Yuri's now seething expression.

"You think we are something to be examined?" she said, raising her voice. "We aren't objects!" Her tentacles flared out, mini sea serpents ready to strike.

Kaleb's hands lifted in retreat. "No! Not at all!"

"Well then, what is it?" Yuri's voice chopped through the water.

"Look, I think my people misunderstand you and your sisters," he said, dropping his hands to his sides, opening himself up even more to her harsh gaze. "Maybe eventually, I could get them to see what I see. That would be nice, wouldn't it?"

Yuri placed her hands back on her cocked hips. "Nice? Why would that be nice," she snarled.

Kaleb winced at her words; his pained expression caused Yuri's furrowed brows to arch into temporary peaks. She appeared to be thinking deeply as her arms fell to her sides and for just a moment, her face softened, reminding him of the beautiful angelic portraits that hung in his father's castle.

However, it was short-lived as Yuri crossed her arms back over her chest, regaining her composure. "And how do you propose we 'get to know each other' when your people hate mine? Should I pop over for brunch next week?"

"Since that isn't an outright *no,*" Kaleb said as a grin returned to his face, "We can set up a discreet meeting place. Somewhere we won't be seen."

Britt lunged forward from behind Yuri, dragging Tanis' tiny frame with her. Veins bulged at the sides of her scowling face. "She certainly will not!"

Kaleb tumbled back against his chariot, catching himself with his palms. His eyes darted to his trident still lying on the seafloor.

"Stop, Britt! You need the medicine! Don't do this!" Yuri rushed in between Britt and Kaleb, extending her arms, a self-appointed referee.

Kaleb straightened himself, rising tall. Britt flashed the pointed ends of her sharp teeth as Tanis tugged gently on Britt's arm, corralling her back.

"That's enough!" Yuri shouted, gliding toward Kaleb. The closer she came, the closer Kaleb moved to meet her as if a magnetic force pulled him in. "That's close enough," Yuri said, extending her arm. Her palm faced up as she wiggled long, red-nailed fingers. "You give me the shell, and I'll agree to meet you. ONCE." She managed to make it sound as though the benefit would be all his. But if he did *study them* as he had intimated, that could be to their advantage too. Well, possibly.

Kaleb traced the blue veins extending through her arms and into her outstretched hand. Her skin was fair, smooth, and unblemished. "Okay, deal," he agreed. It was better not to press his luck. And for some odd reason, he desperately wanted to help the peculiar three—even if they were rude and ungrateful at times.

He held the medicine shell in front of him and reached out his hand, placing the grooved shell into Yuri's soft palm. His fingertips grazed across her cool, pallid skin as he pulled his arm back. The contact sent shivers down his spine as both he and Yuri quickly pulled away from each other, averting their gazes to the seafloor. They appeared to have crossed over an unmarked line.

Yuri's face flushed a rosy red as she turned to her sisters. "Here, put this on her wound," she said, tossing the shell over to Tanis. She deftly caught it—somehow, without chopping off her finger on its sharp edges.

Tanis quickly obliged, doing exactly as Yuri had requested and roughly digging into the shell's contents with her fingers before smothering the contents over her sister's wound. The thick red substance's effect was immediate, hardening instantly around Britt's tentacle.

Yuri took a deep gulp of seawater before turning back to face Kaleb. "Thank you," Yuri said, trying to push out a warm smile that merely escaped as a grimace. Kaleb nodded, accepting her forced gratitude as genuine. "Okay, let's get the details of our deal over with," she said, exhaling water from her gills.

"Well," Kaleb said, running fingers through his sandy-brown hair, down to the back of his neck.

Yuri's eyes squinted as she tilted her head. "Well, what?"

A shadow of uncertainty cast over his face as he dragged the end of his navy-blue finned tail across the seabed floor, making circles in the sand. "Well..." He hesitated nervously, then said, "Why don't I meet you on your territory. Tomorrow?"

Britt huffed loudly from behind Yuri in protest letting bubbles pool from her nostrils. "All right," Yuri said, ignoring her sister. "There's an old rock formation on the eastern border that protrudes out of the sea. It's close to the coastline. Once you cross into our territory, head for the coast. You won't be able to miss it. We can meet there tomorrow at noon."

Kaleb's mouth twisted up into a curved smile. His dimples pinched at his cheeks. "Looking forward to it," he said, jumping back into his chariot.

Yuri's eyes rolled up into her head as she spun around to face her sisters. They glowered. "Let's go home."

All three sisters swam away from Kaleb's golden-red chariot, their black tentacles waving behind them as if they were saying goodbye. The farther they got, the smaller they seemed until they completely vanished out of Kaleb's view. He inhaled the salty seawater, blowing it out of his nostrils. Had he imagined the whole thing? "Onward," he said, pulling the reins.

Chapter 3

Yuri's long hair cascaded like a waterfall over the edges of her sea kelp hammock. As she lay there, she stared up at the dark cave ceiling of her home, the pointed edges of its long skinny stone peaks hanging down above her. It wasn't much, but her family had turned this underwater rock burrow into a home. It was well hidden, away from the surface and sunlight, camouflaged by a dark moss-like algae that grew in the ocean depth. It felt safe to Yuri, and more importantly, felt like home.

She turned her head to face the entrance of the cave and looked out past the long vines that draped over its wide mouth in the style of a curtain. The dilapidated remains of a makeshift kelp swing hung in the distance. As children, their mother had set up the swing for them to play on. She would watch them from the entrance as they swung up so high that they felt like gulls, rather than sea-dwelling castoffs. As they jumped into the soft moss, their mother would shout, "Be careful!"

Yuri sighed, turning her head back to the ceiling. She dearly missed her mother's voice. When their mother had gotten sick, she'd spoken less and less and then, in the end, said nothing at all. It had been hard to know, for a while, whether her taciturn state was because she had lost all ability to communicate vocally or whether it was that everything had been said. They assumed the former since she would often seem to speak with her eyes or with her smile, or with her soft and warm touch upon their bodies or their hair.

"Breakfast is here!" Britt shouted from the entrance, holding an assortment of dead fish by their tails. "Okay, I have a mackerel, a cod, and a small Steelhead trout," she said, swinging all the dead fish onto a table made from a filed-down boulder.

Tanis swam down off her hammock, scrunching her nose up in disgust. "Pass on the mackerel," she said, grabbing the tail fin of the codfish. Her jaw cranked wide open, revealing tiny, sharp, serrated teeth. She tilted her head back, dropping the fish headfirst into her gullet, penguin-style. Her teeth tore at the flesh and scales like a woodchopper, spitting out the bones.

Britt grabbed the remaining two fish, dangling them by their tails in front of Yuri's face. They swung side to side. "Mackerel or trout?" she asked. "You are spoilt for choice."

Yuri reached up, grabbing the trout out of Britt's extended hand. Its scaled body slipped through her fingers as she raised it to her lips and opened her wide jaw.

"It's a good thing I like mackerel!" Britt laughed, gulping down the leftover fish and plopping down on her hammock.

Yuri dug her long red fingernails in between her teeth, picking out the fish bones. It was almost time for her to meet Kaleb, as promised. She lifted herself, stretching her arms over her head as she maneuvered her way to the opening of the cave.

"Where are you going?" Tanis asked, her head peeking out from her hammock.

Britt was toying with the cleaned fish bones, balancing them on her fingers, when she looked up to see Yuri by the entrance. "Wait, you aren't actually going to meet up with that merman?" she asked, tossing the fish bones to the floor and jumping out of her hammock. "That's stupid."

Yuri inched her body further toward the door. "Yes, I promised him, and you should know that I always keep my promises." And besides that, her blood boiled. It was only to save Britt's life that any kind of a return favor was needed. Britt, yet again, did not appreciate what had been done for her. Typical Britt. Not that Yuri resented having to see the stranger a second time. For some odd reason, she was quite warming to the thought of it.

She looked down at her pale hand, which had briefly touched Kaleb's the other day. Her body tingled again, remembering the way he had smiled after it happened and how they'd jolted away from one another, the same way as after a sudden jellyfish sting. Despite pretending to be tough, she couldn't deny that she found him both handsome and charming. She couldn't remember ever feeling that about anyone before.

"Seriously, don't go!" Britt shouted as she dashed past Yuri.

She spread her tentacles over the exit to form a kind of umbrella, then knotted them together to try and prevent their unfastening.

Yuri shook her head. "Britt," she said, placing her hand on her sister's shoulder. "A promise is a promise. Kaleb held up his side of the bargain for you, and I need to hold mine." She really wanted to say, *and I only owe him the meeting because of you!* But it seemed almost as though Britt must have had that same thought simultaneously. She retracted her tentacles, looking down at where her nasty wound had once been. Her inky black flesh was smooth and unblemished, not even a scar visible.

Yuri pushed past her sister, finally making it through the opening of their cave. She took a deep gulp of water and looked out past her mother's dilapidated swing set. Her path forward was marked by small colorful stones that her mother had also placed like breadcrumbs so very long ago so that she and her sisters could always find their way back.

As she glided forward, Tanis sprung up behind her. "Be careful, Yuri!" She locked her into a tight bear hug.

Yuri tapped her youngest sister's hands gently. "I'll be back before nightfall, I promise."

As Yuri swam down from the cave, Tanis gripped Britt's hand tightly. Together, they watched Yuri fade away from their home.

Chapter 4

Kaleb's bedroom was adorned with gold much like his chariot, while long red drapes in an opulent but not too thick fabric were half-drawn across the windows to allow just the right amount of light to pour in from the ocean surface. When the light managed to cascade through the curtains in the early morning, it created patterns inside his room. Most décor in the kingdom had been taken from the humans. Occasionally, a shipwreck happened unprovoked, but most of the time, it was the work of the mighty King Oasis with his eye on some treasure or other.

A long golden antique standing mirror his father had gifted him leaned against the right wall, next to a stained wooden dresser. Kaleb's green eyes peered back at him as he fidgeted with his hair, admiring himself. He hummed his father's anthem in his head. *With his mighty strength, he darkens the sea, to protect and provide for his kingdom-to-be.*

"Ah! There's my better half," his twin Neo said, opening the door and barging into his room like a conquistador.

Kaleb pointed to the door. "You do know that's there for a reason, right?"

Neo balled his fists and danced around Kaleb, taking a few playful punches, anything to annoy his brother. They were identical in appearance, from their sandy-brown hair to their navy-blue tails. It was as if Kaleb's reflection had jumped through the mirror itself to tease him. "Yeah, so I can open it and annoy you," Neo retorted, jabbing his fist at Kaleb's arm.

Kaleb dodged his brother's punch and maneuvered himself to the old dark-stained wooden dresser where his golden winged cuffs sat nestled on top.

"Who are you dolling up for, then?" Neo rushed forward, grabbing one of the cuffs off the dresser and holding it over his head.

Kaleb shook his head in the style of a disappointed parent scolding their child. He reached his arm forward, extending his hand toward Neo. "Give it back," he said firmly.

"Hmm, I don't know," Neo said, swimming to the other side of the room, dangling the cuff into Kaleb's view again and relentlessly teasing. "Maybe Athena? I know she's been eyeing you." He tossed the cuff up high, easily catching it in his palm.

Kaleb's nostrils flared as he lunged forward, punching Neo in the arm. The cuff dropped out of his brother's hand, and Kaleb scooped it up before his brother had another chance to clutch at it.

"Athena? Really?" Kaleb said, snapping one of the cuffs onto his left wrist and plopping himself onto his bed. "She's not my type. If I'd been interested in Athena, I would have made a move by now, don't you think?"

"Not necessarily, no. Perhaps you believe she has the eye for me instead!" Neo teased. That was unlikely since they were more or less identical.

"I wouldn't choose a woman who chooses you," said Kaleb, seemingly serious. He was *not* serious, of course. But still, his brother's teasing was at the wrong moment. He was in a rush.

"Ouch," Neo said, rubbing his punched arm. "Honestly, brother, you are so picky. She comes from royal blood and is the most attractive mermaid in all of Atlantis." He paused. "Plus, Father chose for you to be wedded to her for whatever reason," he said through clenched teeth. "Something I really cannot begin to understand."

Kaleb looked up at his brother's pressed lips. The faint glimmer of the green-eyed monster lingered in his gaze.

"If you are into her, you should court her and become betrothed in my stead," Kaleb said, clipping on his other cuff and swimming to the doorway. "She doesn't need me to marry a prince. Either of us will suffice. Plus, with her strawberry-blonde hair, light blue eyes, and matching tail, she's more your type anyway."

"What's that supposed to mean?" Neo sneered, blocking the entrance with his body.

Kaleb snorted. "Nothing. It's just that I find her to be..." He paused for a moment, thinking carefully on his words. "Ordinary."

Neo let out a sarcastic laugh.

"Athena? Ordinary? She's the daughter of a noble, and the most popular mermaid in Atlantis. Honestly, I don't even know why Father considers you better suited to marry her!"

The former good humor between the two was fading.

"You said that already, just now. But anyway, there is a myriad of possible reasons. Perhaps it's because I knock when entering a room—and don't block doorways," Kaleb responded sarcastically, gesturing with his hands toward the door. "Can you move?"

Neo folded his arms, leaning his back against the grooves of the doorframe. His tail stretched across to the other side like a barricade.

"Just tell me where you're going," Neo huffed. "You better not be hunting for the beast outside of designated times. We agreed when we would go. And the rules state—"

Kaleb pushed his way through his brother's barricade, now fully annoyed. "I'm not a cheat, Neo. I don't need to cheat to win the throne. I'm just going for a ride to clear my head."

Neo glowered as Kaleb swam down the long red corridor they had once played in as children. Its vibrant bright red had faded over time much like the relationship between him and his brother, it had become tattered and stained with years of neglect.

Chapter 5

Kaleb ran his hands across his giant black seahorse. Its nostrils huffed giant bubbles in the water as he lifted the straps over its head, saddled it with his reins, and nestled himself onto his chariot. He had received vague directions from Yuri on where she intended to meet him.

Big Boulder...Can't miss it. The sun was rising in the east, and he tilted his head to admire the glimmering light expanding across the ocean surface. *Plenty of time in case I get lost.*

"Onward," he said, loosening the reins. His giant seahorse growled as it pulled Kaleb's chariot forward with ease. Ocean water flowed through his hair like gusts of wind through a grassy knoll.

The closer he got to the border that divided his people from Yuri's, the colder the water felt against his face. He shivered as he crossed over into her territory. He had never been on this side of the ocean before, and while it looked fairly similar to his side, it lacked the golden finesse and hoopla of Atlantis. He saw no castles filled with man-made items, no sea creatures lavished in gold, and no king to abide. He watched as a consortium of crabs shuffled past him, their vibrant blue shells huddled against one another similar to a formation of shielded soldiers. He chuckled to himself as they passed right by him, unaware of his presence.

They don't know I'm royalty.

Up ahead was an enormous boulder extending from the far depths of the sea. Its tip breached the ocean surface in a shape similar to the fin of a whale, hiding its massive size under the waves, waiting there to catch unsuspecting vessels.

Kaleb scanned the area while swimming to the tip of the humongous rock's peak. *This must be it.* His head bobbed in the water as he placed his hand against the dried edge of the boulder. It felt warm against his palm from soaking in the sunlight. Perched in the distance was a picturesque glistening pink sand beach, sloping down into the sea. A white rowboat was docked on its shore, matching the white and blue striped lighthouse that sat farther inland. He watched as a cloud passed behind its tall structure and marveled at its beauty. *Does Yuri want to share this with me?*

Yuri had been watching Kaleb from a distance, keeping an eye on him. His light-brown hair was wet and weighed down on the sides of his face. He looked quite bedraggled and, she thought, perhaps just a little bit flustered too. Under the water, his navy blue fishtail swayed back and forth as his chiseled chest held steady against the current. She traced the golden cuffs on his arms right up to his muscular bare chest.

A plump white seagull landed on the tip of the boulder and screeched at Kaleb, nipping at his head with its hooked yellow beak. "Get off me, you stupid bird!" he shouted, attempting to whack the crazed attacker with his hands.

Yuri swam up behind him, laughing as her pale face emerged out of the water, leaving her hair clinging to the back of her neck. "A mighty prince taken down by a poor old seagull!" she teased him without mercy.

Kaleb jolted, swinging his body around to face her. She pushed her upper body against the boulder, resting her hands and forearms across its warmed surface as her lower half dangled discreetly in the sea, the way a giant sea serpent might. From this view, Kaleb thought she could have passed as one of the mermaids. Her silvery gray hair tumbled down her back and over her delicate top made of pink seashells. The seagull nestled its fat white-feathered body into the crook of Yuri's arms, appearing as though settling into its nest and planning to stay there for some time yet.

"Friend of yours?" Kaleb asked, amused, keeping his distance from the squawking bill.

Yuri scratched the top of the seagull's head, causing its watchful eyes and hooked beak to shut. "Kind of. I found him caught in a sailor's net a few years ago and helped him out," she said, lifting his plump pillowed body to reveal only one webbed orange foot.

Kaleb inched his neck forward, tilting his head to get a closer look. The seagull lunged toward him, its wings flapping vigorously toward his eyes as it squawked at him.

"He doesn't like men. You probably remind him of the sailors," Yuri said, placing the seagull back between her arms. It circled, pecking at its tail feathers before settling down again.

Kaleb laughed, nodding his head. "Yeah, I can see that." His dimples pinched at his cheeks. Still, he was impressed by how she had befriended the wild bird.

Yuri's mouth curved up into a half-smile as they swayed there in the water, staring at each other for just a moment. She quickly averted her gaze to the ocean as she cleared her throat, pressing her lips into a firm line. "I hope you didn't bring me here just to ask me about a seagull. Our deal is just today, so you should probably make it count," she said, looking past Kaleb's shoulder toward the lighthouse, intentionally avoiding his eyes.

"Yes, of course," Kaleb agreed, fidgeting with the cuffs on his arms. He took a slow, deep breath in. *Just ask her, you coward.* "Why do they call you and your sisters, *the Inked*, sorceresses of the sea? Do you do dark magic or something?" Kaleb asked, letting the words exhale with his breath.

"HA!" Yuri snickered, throwing her head back. "Now, that's funny!" She let her body sink into the water, dipping in her sun-dried hair. The silvery strands darkened the moment they touched the water.

"Why is that funny?" Kaleb asked, watching the beads of water drip from the tip of her darkened hair down to her bare stomach as she pushed back out of the water, placing her arms back around the gull now fast asleep.

"Ah, maybe because the only creature with any magic in this whole damn ocean is your father, the mighty King Oasis," Yuri replied, appearing as though she found this image tiresome.

Kaleb pushed his back up against the boulder next to her as he stared out toward the lighthouse. His elbows rested behind him as a plane buzzed overhead, leaving a trail of white through the clear sky. He always knew his father wielded powers. After all, he was able to darken the sky and cast storms over the seas, but Kaleb had never known where that magic came from. Neither he nor his brother had inherited any special powers.

"Hey." Yuri snapped her fingers in front of Kaleb's face. "You still with me?"

Kaleb turned to face Yuri, leaning his right shoulder against the huge rock.

Even in his relaxed state, he looked like a chiseled sculpture of a Greek God and she couldn't stop her eyes from searching him.

"My father was just born as 'the mighty' name that he is," Kaleb replied, shrugging his shoulders. "He can't exactly help that, can he?"

Yuri watched as the beads of water pooled on his collar bone and then dropped down to his chest like rainfall. She forced her eyes back up to his, which stared back at her like emerald gems from his tilted head that hung over her. He was so close she could see the hint of dark stubble that loomed on his jawline.

"You don't know, do you?" she asked, swimming around to the other side of the boulder's peak.

"Know what?" he asked, blocking her path with his statuesque body. His green eyes reflected the light from the sun as he stared at Yuri, hoping to pierce through her tough façade. But that could require some time—if it were achievable at all.

Yuri leaned her back against the warm boulder. Her shoulders relaxed as she took a deep breath in. "Well," she said, turning her head to face Kaleb. "You never heard of the Pauper's Magic Dolphins?"

Kaleb's face twisted into a deeply dimpled grin. "The children's story?" he laughed.

Yuri shook her head. "The thing is, Kaleb, it's not a story! No wonder your people fear us; they just don't know the truth," she retorted as her body stiffened like a coiled snake ready to strike. "And I had hoped that by asking me here today, you wanted to hear about it. Sorry I was mistaken."

For some reason, she had taken offense at his mention of the fairy tale. Kaleb threw his hands up into the air. "Whoa! Why are you getting so heated? Maybe we are thinking of different things."

"Perhaps we are," Yuri said, uncoiling her tentacles. She sucked in a deep breath, preparing to be more patient and to try again to talk to him in a decent manner. She gazed at him, her lips lacking a smile now. "Then what is the story you were thinking of?" she asked at last.

"Well," Kaleb said, lowering his hands to his sides and looking out toward the lighthouse. "My caretaker Ella used to tell me a story before bed about a pauper and his magic dolphins." Yuri's piercing blue eyes widened as he turned to face her. He cleared his throat which had become dry and hoarse.

"The story went like this. Back before Atlantis existed, there were no mermaids or mermen, only primitive animals and the ancient monster ruling them.

"It was a giant octopus with long black tentacles and a taste for men, and it could swallow ships in a single bite, leaving no trace they had ever existed. One day, a pauper's wife fell ill, and he needed to sail across the sea to get her the care she required. The pauper loved his wife and was willing to risk his own to save hers. However, on his journey, the monster appeared.

"And around his sick wife swam three magical dolphins which fueled the monster's powers over the sea. He begged the monster for mercy, and it offered him a deal to cure his wife in exchange for his servitude. The pauper saw no other choice but to agree and, with his agreement, the monster lifted the pauper out of the boat with its giant tentacles, placing him into the sea.

"The magical dolphins swam circles around his legs, creating a vortex of bright illuminating light. The pauper squinted, temporarily blinded. When he regained his vision, however, he was not the same. In place of his legs was a long, fishlike tail. It seemed his legs had been taken in the bargain, though he did not see this coming.

"For an entire year, he spent his days at the monster's service under the sea and was forbidden from seeing his wife or having any contact with humanity. One day, while the monster slept in the darkness of its cave, he crept in and stabbed the monster in the eyes with a sharpened spear.

"The monster, now blinded, screamed out in pain, while the pauper fled with the magic dolphins. According to the story, he then convinced his wife to live in the ocean with him. And so it was that with the help of the dolphins, she became the first mermaid.

"Together, they created Atlantis."

"Well, that's some story," Yuri screeched sarcastically as she crossed her arms over her chest.

Kaleb tilted his head quizzically. "Then I'm sorry. I don't understand why you would be so upset over a simple children's story. You seemed to take some offense to it, but it is harmless."

Yuri's face lit up, and she spat out, *"Harmless?* Harmless! Perhaps it's because your children's story is a mockery of my people's history! Perhaps because it's poisonous!" She turned away from him, refusing to talk anymore. She had believed he wished to find out about her 'people' but really, he was here to mock her species like everyone else did.

Kaleb reached his hand out instinctively to comfort her. He placed it on the back of Yuri's right shoulder. She slumped her body down into the water, causing his hand to fall.

"Please don't touch me," she snapped, turning around to face him. Her light, icy-blue eyes darkened into the eyes of a stormy winter's night, cold and fathomless.

Kaleb met her dark stare, his face tight and worried. "I didn't mean any disrespect," he said, scratching at his chin as though he might find a solution there. He paused for a moment, dropping his hand back down to his side. "I came here to learn more about you. If my story is wrong, maybe you can tell me the correct version?"

Yuri's face seemed to soften with Kaleb's words. Her dark eyes lightened slowly like storm clouds being blown away in the passing wind. She opened the gills on her neck and took a deep breath of fresh air, exhaling out through her nostrils. The crisp air always comforted her; she was glad she could breathe both water and air, unlike a fish.

"The supposed monster in your story was the victim, and the pauper was not," she said, turning to face Kaleb whose steady eyes were focused on her. "She was the great ancestor of my people and the protector of the sea for many of the original creatures that dwelled there.

"Men would come by with their nets and spears and try to slaughter thousands of sea creatures, but she would protect them with the powers provided to her by the dolphins.

"You see, the three dolphins had appeared to her one day, offering her a great responsibility. She was to protect the ocean from man, and when she was no longer able to perform that task, they would choose a new protector."

Kaleb listened intently, nodding his head as Yuri continued.

"One day, a pauper showed up in a small rowboat with no spears or nets. He anchored his boat in the center of the ocean and called out for *my* great ancestor. When she appeared, she looked upon the sad-looking man with mercy. Her massive size towered over his boat, and yet he had come unarmed. He told her that his wife had just recently died, and it was too painful for him to continue his life on land. He wished for a new life, a life beneath the sea.

"My ancestor thought that perhaps he could help form a dialogue between mankind and the sea, so she agreed to his request—on one condition. After a few years of living in the sea, he would return to land to be an advocate for the sea creatures and help stop the violence and wanton pollution of mankind," Yuri said, pausing for a moment.

Kaleb replied, quickly filling in the gap of silence. "And then what happened?" This was definitely a different story from the one he had been told. Of course, maybe this story would set off her ire again.

Yuri pointed to Kaleb's blue fin that swayed just under the surface. "And then she turned his two legs into a fishtail much like yours."

Kaleb scratched at the back of his head. He was

going to have to broach the subject of her anger yet again. "This is the story that annoys you? But to me—and maybe I am just slow to understand, in which case, forgive me, Yuri—but it sounds like a win-win." It was hard to put all this into words without risking her great irritation and upset tone.

"I'm not done yet," Yuri snapped, running dry of patience at last. "Can't you ever just listen?"

Kaleb lifted his hand, pretending to seal his mouth with an imaginary zipper. But she was a strange one. She asked couldn't he *ever* just listen—but they had only just met one another, so what was this "ever" meant to be about? He probably could not win no matter what he said right now.

Yuri sighed and continued. And Kaleb shut up finally, trying to attune his ears to what she was really saying.

"He spent several years living in the sea as promised. My ancestor even grew something of a liking toward him as she taught him the ways of the ocean. Eventually, it came time for him to hold up his end of the bargain and leave for land again. But he had grown so fond of the sea and had no intention of keeping his promise. So, while my ancestor slept, he crept silently into her cave and pierced her eyes with a spear. With her blinded, he stole her three magic dolphins and left to build the underwater kingdom that you now call Atlantis.

"However, there was a price to pay for all his thievery. A curse was placed on the firstborn child of every founding family in Atlantis. Instead of a beautiful, jeweled mermaid tail, every firstborn would have long, dark tentacles just like mine. The pauper brought all these imperfect children back to the cave, where he had left my ancestor blinded. Yet despite being blind, she cared for the abandoned children and *their* children until eventually, she died of old age. My mother's great grandmother was one of the original children born from the curse."

Yuri teared up, choking on her words.

"And now, your people cast us out as if we are not the product of your people's greed. You call us *the Inked,* and you fear us when we are the ones who should fear you! My sister, Tanis, wandered onto your people's territory as a child, and you know what they did to her?"

A harried look washed over Kaleb's face as Yuri continued.

"They held her down and slit her eye open with the sharp edge of a shell. Just some stupid merchildren already filled with hate against our kind," she sobbed. "They would have been happy to kill her. They just saw her as some ugly creature anyway, something not deserving of love."

Kaleb reached out again, placing his hand on her shoulder. She quivered under his touch as he ran his hands up and down her arm, trying to comfort her. Her skin felt warm and smooth against his palm as he watched her deep, icy eyes water up with tears. Instinctively, he pulled her body into his with force, embracing her in a tight hug. She felt small and fragile in his embrace, not like a monster or *an inked sorceress,* but a girl who'd been forced to be strong for way too long a time.

Yuri's head was pressed up against Kaleb's bare chest. His steady heartbeat, akin to waves hitting against the rocky shore. The smell of musk and sea salt lingered on his skin as his tan arms squeezed her tightly. She tilted her head to look up at his face. Yuri was much shorter in stature, and Kaleb's striking emerald eyes gazed down upon her. His sandy-brown hair blew back gently in the wind as he bit his bottom lip. She tried to reach up, and he tried to lower himself. Somehow, it would have felt more reassuring if they had been better able to look into one another's gaze.

Yuri's face reminded Kaleb of a Victorian painting he had once found on one of his explorations, something of which his father markedly disapproved. Her skin was extremely fair, and, in the sunlight, it glistened with a dewy glow, as did her sun-kissed hair. He watched as her plump, pink lips parted, and something primitive came over him. He grabbed the back of her head, his fingers intertwining with her long, silky, gray strands as he pushed his lips up against hers. She did not struggle—but neither did she really return the kiss. His soft lips kissed Yuri with such force that it left her temporarily stunned. As she shut her wide eyes, his hands traveled to her waist. He gripped his fingers around her hips, pushing her against the boulder as he continued to kiss her with a starved sense of passion that needed to be quenched.

Caw, cawwwwww! The plump seagull awoke from its slumber and squawked frantically, spreading its wings over the top of the boulder. Yuri pushed Kaleb back with her hands as she sank into the water and somehow slipped out of his grasp. It was possibly accidental, possibly on purpose. From Yuri's standpoint, it was most certainly the latter. She would not allow herself to fall for a merman, no matter how charming he was. Her sisters needed her, and she couldn't afford such pleasures, especially forbidden ones. But still. She liked him. She was drawn to him. And this was awkward, or potentially would be.

The seagull flew up into the sky as Yuri sank down only deeper into the ocean, becoming a shimmer in the waves, leaving a wake, and then growing into a ripple.

He could barely even believe she had been there with him, in his arms. Perhaps she had not. Perhaps he had dreamed her—like the fairy tale that had maddened her so.

Kaleb bobbed in the water, staring at the boulder blankly. One moment, she was there, and the next, she was gone. He placed his hand on the water's warm surface and smiled. This wouldn't be the last time he saw her; he was sure of that. He would find her again, no matter how hard he had to search or how long it took. Kaleb turned to face the lighthouse. The sun was setting behind it, the sky blazing in orange and red.

It really is the most beautiful sight.

Chapter 6

Neo watched in the distance as his brother fawned over one of *those creatures.* He had followed his brother all the way from the kingdom, stealthy stalking him. His fingers ran over the blade of his knife holstered around his waist as he watched his brother kiss the filthy *Inked* creature. Why would his brother even choose to mingle with sea filth when he had an entire kingdom of beautiful mermaids throwing themselves at him?

Neo pulled the knife from its sheath, staring into its reflective metal surface. He grinned back at his devious reflection. If it were up to him, they would all be exterminated. *When I'm finally King, I can rid the ocean of this primitive filth.*

He ran his index finger over the tip of his sharpened blade, accidentally cutting through his skin. A small amount of blood dripped into the water, reminding him of the bloodshed during previous hunts for the beast. If Kaleb and his appointed soldiers were able to rid the ocean of the beast before he could, there would be no doubt that his brother would get the throne.

Neo shoved his hand into the water, placing the knife back into its sheath as he let the salty ocean clean his wound. He watched as *the Inked* girl swam down into the sea, leaving his brother bewildered and looking on, bearing an expression of confusion.

His face twisted into a dark grin. *Father will have to choose me now.* As Yuri sank deeper into the ocean, Neo followed her like a predator lurking in the murky water. Yuri's inky black tentacles waved behind her like sea serpents and disgusted him. *She has to have enchanted my brother. Why else would he be interested in such a malformed creature?* He pulled the reins back on his seahorse, prompting it to stop, and watched as Yuri disappeared into the side of a mossy cave hidden in the depths.

Neo pulled his golden armor off, throwing it onto the moss-covered seabed. While pulling out his knife once more, he brushed his hair back with his fingers, parting it to the side as his brother often did. He loosened his lips while staring at his reflection in the blade, twisting his mouth up into Kaleb's typical cheeky simper. *This should do.* He pulled off his sheath, tucking the knife back in and discarding it next to his armor.

"Excuse me?" Neo said. His neck poked through the long hanging kelp curtains as he pushed them aside with hands.

All three sisters turned to face him as if ballerinas spinning on cue.

"You invited him here," Britt shouted. Her lips pulled up over her sharp teeth as she glowered at Yuri.

"No! I didn't!" Yuri's brows furrowed as she screamed back.

She crossed her arms, moving forward toward Neo. "Did you follow me here?" she scoffed, her long tentacles flaring like Medusa's head.

Neo cleared his throat, pushing his whole body

through the kelp curtains and into their home. *Got to nail this performance.* He opened his palms toward her, bowing his head down. "I didn't like how we left off. I wanted to apologize and hopefully get another opportunity to get to know you."

"Hell no," Britt shouted, swimming in front of Yuri. "It was a one-time deal, buddy!"

"Britt, just stop," Yuri said, gently pushing past her sister. As she got closer to Neo, she inhaled the water around him. He smelled slightly different than she recalled. Not of musk or sea salt, but otherwise clean like the fresh scent of a newborn. She traced him up and down with her eyes, observing the same navy-blue tail and stark chiseled chest she remembered.

"Where are your cuffs?" she asked, noticing his wrists were bare.

Neo rubbed his right hand against his left wrist. "Oh, uh…I must have left them at our meeting spot," he said, throwing on a faux cheeky smile. "Maybe you can help me find them tomorrow?"

Yuri sighed as her sisters scowled and huffed in the background like the low growl of dogs before they attacked. "You know where to look, so just go find them yourself," Yuri responded, waving her hand toward the exit.

"Well, listen," Neo said, grinning and leaning his body against the side of the cave as Kaleb had done against the boulder. "If you don't agree, I'll just stay here until one of your angry sisters comes and attacks me."

Britt responded, "No problem there," swimming forward and baring her teeth.

Yuri stretched her arm out like a barricade, pushing

her sister back. "Fine," Yuri said reluctantly, nodding toward Neo.

"What do you mean by *fine,*" Tanis peeped. Her wide eyes darted back and forth between Yuri and Neo.

Yuri turned to face her sisters now.

Britt was nodding in agreement, a scowl drawn across her face.

She pulled both her sisters into a tight huddle as Neo remained leaning against the entrance, tapping his hands across its mossy sides.

"Listen, it's fine. If he meant to harm me, I probably would already be dead. Maybe this is good for us. Maybe he can help his people see us as something not to be feared? And perhaps we shouldn't fear him either," Yuri said, squeezing both her sisters' shoulders tightly.

Britt pulled away, breaking her sisters' huddled circle. "Do what you want," she screamed, storming out of the cave and pushing Neo aside as she scowled at him.

Tanis remained by Yuri's side, gripping at her sister's arm. "Are you sure he's safe?" she whispered, glancing over at the back of Neo's neck protruding out of the cave entrance as if he were gazing into the night's sea. He tapped at his sides as he whistled.

"I promise," Yuri said, kissing Tanis on the forehead.

Neo watched from the corner of his eye, feeling a pool of disgust building in the pit of his stomach. He shook his head, forcing his mouth into a grin.

"So, same time tomorrow?" he called out to Yuri as though arranging a romantic date.

"Okay," Yuri said, trying to hold back the grin

forcing its way across her face. Despite trying to hide her excitement, her heart raced like marlins zipping through the sea. She couldn't help but feel elated over the potential to be alone with Kaleb again.

"Looking forward to it," Neo said, giving her a wink before leaving.

As he gathered his armor and traveled back to Atlantis, he thought about his brother and how he could kiss such a low-level creature. His stomach twisted into knots as he inhaled the water around him, water which still carried the squid-like scent of *the Inked*. He couldn't wait to get home and cleanse himself of the experience, but first he had to put the proper preparations in place. Soon, he wouldn't have to worry about these disgusting creatures touching his brother. Neo would bring them to his father's attention, and the throne would be his.

Chapter 7

Kaleb woke up the next morning, still enchanted by his brief kiss with *the Inked* girl. He lay in his bed staring at the blank white ceiling, picturing her hovering over him and her hair draped down over his face like a canopy. He could still feel her lips on his, like the lingering tingle of citrus.

He had dreamt that he was King of Atlantis, and Yuri ruled by his side on a golden throne. It was their wedding day, and the merfolk of Atlantis cheered and spun around in a synchronized dance, bedecked in colorful masks made from sea glass and shells.

But it was just a dream.

He stretched his arms over his head, arching his back as he lifted himself off his bed, causing the sheets to crinkle around him. Today was the day of the third scheduled hunt for the beast that had been terrorizing their home. He pushed aside the long red curtains, peeking out to see the faint glimmer of sunlight pooling into the ocean depths. Kaleb had gotten up early to prepare himself and his soldiers. He reached for the large golden trident kept tucked under his bed next to his armor. Its three prongs glimmered at freshly sharpened peaks, thirsty for blood.

There was to be a hunt every three days until the beast was caught and beheaded. Usually, on the mornings of the hunt, Neo showed up to taunt him while he dressed in his armor, but today he just hadn't come by. Kaleb scratched his head, staring at his shut wooden door and expecting his brother to barge in. But there was just silence. *Odd, perhaps he slept late or is already at the stables…I had better hurry.* He fastened his armor at his waist, and wrapped his hands around his trident, taking a deep gulp of water as he opened his bedroom door to reveal the long red corridor.

Kaleb glanced back at his unmade bed that had held dreams of Yuri between its sheets before swimming down the passageway which opened out onto a large, marbled foyer. An enormous double door embellished with golden gems was mounted tall at its exit. Two guards kept post at each side wearing matching red emblems of the King holding his trident across their chests.

"Gentlemen," Kaleb said, nodding to the guards as he swam through the doors.

Both guards bowed as he passed, nodding their helmeted heads toward the floor.

Behind the castle was a huge wooden stable with a salvaged steel roof that hung over the seahorses. Kaleb counted each of them in their stalls, all in place except for three.

He looked to the left of the stables where four golden chariots remained untouched. He scratched at his chin. *Did Neo leave already? Surely, Neo wouldn't have left for the hunt with only two mermen and no chariot?* He shook his head, saddling his seahorse to his chariot. *Perhaps he's forgotten today's another scheduled hunt?*

Kaleb's troop began to show up, swimming in formation to the stables, like the legs of a centipede moving in unison. As he waited for his troop to harness their seahorses, he looked out toward the winding road leading from the kingdom. *Where is Neo?* He gripped tightly on the reins of his chariot while grabbing the horn lying on the seat behind. *He's probably just chasing some poor uninterested mermaids with his buddies.* Well, if that was the case, it was an advantage to him and his soldiers—if his brother had cried off the hunt, then he would have a better chance himself. *Today will be the day I bring my father the head of the beast.*

He lifted the golden horn to his lips and blew. His army followed behind his chariot in sets of twos, each saddled on their large black seahorses. They were a well-trained army, every one as fit as a fiddle. Often, the mermen of Atlantis joined the King's Army at a very young age, leaving their homes as pre-teens to live in a select branch of the palace specifically for new recruits. Occasionally, some older mermen from poor families would volunteer and in return, the kingdom would provide for their relatives.

Kaleb glanced behind him at their stern faces, each one potentially riding to their doom. A knot twisted in his stomach. He already felt that they had lost so much. After all, they had never been allowed to see their families after joining the King's Army, and those who had trouble coping were cast out of Atlantis to live in the wild over the border.

Kaleb whipped at his reins. "Forward!" he shouted. His seahorse growled as it pulled Kaleb's golden chariot forward, its body cutting through the water as it blew bubbles from its huge nostrils.

He had an idea of the direction the beast had gone

in from his last hunt. For one thing, a trail of bloody carcasses had been left in the wake.

"Whoa," he said, pulling back on the reins. His seahorse threw back its enormous, spiked head, causing Kaleb's chariot to stop abruptly. As he stopped, so did the troops behind him. There on the ground, sticking out of the seafloor, were the pointed remains of a sharp white serrated tooth, its jagged edges made for grinding its prey down into neat little chunks. *A very unpleasant death.*

Kaleb swam down off his chariot and lifted the tooth into the palm of his hand, twisting it around. Its white surface was stained at the tips with blood. *It's fresh.* "We are close," he shouted to his troops, letting the beast's tooth roll out of his palm as he headed back to his chariot. Up ahead was a patch of mossy green vines that dangled into the depths of the sea like long locks of thick, wet hair reaching down to the seafloor.

Kaleb paused at its maze-like entrance, putting his hand up to halt the troops behind him. He pushed his head forward into the thick, wet, tangled moss which consumed him into darkness, not a hint of any sign he had ever been there. Here, the thick and lush plant life blocked out any light from the surface, the same effect as an eclipse. He pulled his head back out of the entrance of the mossy maze and dug his hand into the small brown satchel tied to his chariot. "Here we go." He spoke to himself, lifting out a small glass jar filled with a purple jelly-like substance.

He turned to face his soldiers, holding the jar up in his hand. "We need to go through this mossy jungle. I won't pretend it will be easy to see, as most of the surface light will be blocked out by the plants. In my hand is a small supply of ground-up bioluminescent jellyfish guts. It won't be pleasant, but it will help us see each other once we're fully emerged. Everyone, scoop a small amount and apply it to your face. It should be just enough for everyone."

He took a small amount with his index finger, smearing it over his cheeks. The goopy guts dripped down Kaleb's face as the smell of rotten fish filled his nostrils. He gagged, fighting vomit building in his throat as he passed the container to his troop, each soldier's face illuminated through dripping guts smeared across their cheeks like war paint.

"Forward," Kaleb shouted, leading his troops into the unknown darkness of the mossy thicket of this godforsaken place.

Kaleb turned to see one of the illuminated faces disappearing as if consumed by a black hole. *Nineteen glowing faces instead of twenty.* He gripped his trident tightly as an eerie silence washed over the halted crew. The taste of iron loomed in the water around him as he inhaled the metallic scent. One of his men had just died. There was no mistaking the tang on his taste buds, and also no way to deny how much blood had filled the water.

"Stay alert," Kaleb shouted. "The beast is here!"

The clattering of raised swords and axes echoed, resounding in a vile clanking and clashing of sharpened blades and heavy swings, each louder, more vicious, and evil than the last. Kaleb shut his eyes, forcing his focus on the sounds around him. They would have to heighten their other senses if they wanted to survive the beast.

A whoosh came, a sudden gush of rippling water

rushing up, causing Kaleb's chariot to sway.

"It's right under us!" Kaleb heard one of his soldiers shout.

He gripped tightly to the side of his chariot with his free hand, pointing his trident down into the water below like a pitchfork. *Come on, you bastard, come on!* "Keep alert, gentlemen," Kaleb said, peering into the darkness. Not that there was any point in doing so—the only thing that stared back was the darkness itself, the inky void, nothing visible.

The vines around them had become eerily still as if they too were petrified—in both senses of the meaning. Out of the darkness below, something was making its way up toward Kaleb, bubbling up to the surface. His chariot rocked back and forth as his palms grasped tightly to his weapon, its golden prongs sharp and ready to pierce. *Any second now.*

Another whooshing sound and then—

Kaleb stabbed his trident downward as a large mass pushed his chariot sideways, almost knocking him flying. He felt his pronged trident dig into flesh and lifted its sharpened fork-like edges to his face. There, on the middle prong, flailed the skewered body of a silver fish.

Herring. The large mass had been a school of fish passing by, and not the beast. He turned to face his troops, peeling the dead fish from his trident. "It was just a school of…" The sea rocked, a great noise akin to an explosion sent the beast slamming hard into Kaleb's chariot, causing it to shatter as Kaleb tumbled down toward the seabed. His trident glowed as it spiraled down next to him, landing a few feet away in the sand. The cries of his men echoed through the deep waters as his body crashed and plummeted. He yelped an involuntary sound of pain, rubbing at the back of his head and then wincing as he tried to lift himself from the sharp jagged rock which had pierced through part of his left shoulder. He inhaled deeply, cringing through the pain as he lifted himself slowly, maneuvering the deep shard out of his body. His left arm was numb and unsteady as he attempted to swim toward his trident lying on the floor. And as he did so, blood came pouring out of his wound, pooling into the water around. He grasped at his shoulder, applying pressure with his palm. It was all he could do for himself—but no way would it be enough. *Damn.*

The beast's long, pointed nose spiraled down toward Kaleb, its gaping mouth exposing a deep, dark gullet. Kaleb rolled his body to the side as the beast came crashing down beside him, face-first into the sand. Its massive head shook back and forth as it chomped, causing silty sand to cloud the water. And Kaleb's trident was mere inches away.

He reached his arm out, his teeth clenched as the tips of his fingers pulled the shining metal weapon toward him. His fingers fastened around its long golden handle as he jabbed its prongs through the beast's beady eyes. Even then, even when simply piercing an eye, it took such enormous force to penetrate the eyeball. Its skin must have been tougher than hide if this was the pressure required to break through a mere eye.

The beast let out a piercing, seemingly never-ending scream, enough to curdle the blood as it arched its massive head back before collapsing. Its once thrashing—but now so pitiful and writhing—body lay motionless on the seabed next to Kaleb, who leaned upright next to its silent carcass. His heart pounded against his chest, threatening to break loose from his ribs. *I did it. I killed that hideous beast. Kaleb, Kaleb—you did it!*

Kaleb placed two fingers just inside his mouth and let out a high-pitched whistle. If any of his troops were left, they would come to find him. There was no way they could miss a sound like that. And besides, they would already be wondering how he had fared and if he'd made it through. They would be looking for him. At least, they would be if any could still swim.

He lifted his upper torso from the ground, pulling his trident out of the beast's bloodied eye. It parted with a squelch and a soft slurping sound, releasing a flood of accompanying liquid. *Yuck. That is revolting.*

In the distance, he could see the glowing faces of two of his soldiers. *The only two who have survived?* His heart thudded. *Please, let it not be so. They cannot nearly all have perished.*

"Over here," Kaleb shouted, waving his uninjured arm and attempting to plaster a smile across his lips. The dreaded beast had died after all, giving plenty to smile about. But not if the men died.

"Sir," one of the soldiers said, shocked as they approached closer. "You killed it yourself?"

Kaleb smirked. "Well, I guess I did. One thing left to do. Do you have a knife?"

Both soldiers wore a look of bewilderment, glancing at each other and then back at Kaleb.

"Uh, yes sir," one of the soldiers said hesitantly, pulling a long, jagged tooth blade out of his sheath and handing it to their prince.

"Thank you," Kaleb said as he cut into the beast's flesh.

Father will be so proud. See, Father. I became the one you hoped I could.

Chapter 8

Neo got up long before Kaleb, hastily hurrying to the stables in the middle of the night to prepare three seahorses for travel. He had a plan, one that would require some assistance. Although having said that, it really wasn't too hard to convince two of his closest friends, Baric and Casco, to come along with him to meet *that disgusting Inked girl.* They had all been firm friends since childhood, a trio. Like good loyal lackeys, the two followed Neo around like a pack of hounds following behind their Alpha. However, Neo wasn't so naïve that he couldn't see their friendship with him was solely based on status. They would benefit significantly from him becoming King.

That same morning, Britt had gotten up early, rattled as she was out of a horrifying nightmare. She gasped as her eyes flew open, turning her head toward her two sisters' hammocks. *They're both still there,* she thought as she sighed with relief.

She'd dreamt that she and her sisters were trapped in a large metal tank, and every time the lid opened, one of her sisters was duly tugged out into the bright white light of the unknown. It continued until eventually, it was just her all alone in there with four walls around her and no exit.

Britt shook her head as she watched Yuri's tentacles dangling off the edge of her hammock—like hanging veins. Her chest felt heavy as she inhaled one deep breath through her expanded gills. She worried about her sister's growing attachment to a merman. Something had seemed off during his surprise visit. The issue was hard to identify, but they did not want their sister hanging around with someone like that. Whatever *someone like that* was, anyway. They only knew he had left a bad impression. He did not feel right. They were naturally wary of him, and now he had swayed Yuri.

Tanis was snoring in the hammock next to Yuri, her arms and tentacles spread out like a spider in its web, bulbous bubbles of mucus pooling out of her nostrils.

"Psst," Britt whispered, crouching down next to Tanis. "Wake up."

Tanis' eyes blinked open slowly as she let out one large snort. She glared at Britt from half-drawn eyelids. "What time is it?" She yawned, rubbing her eyes while lifting herself to a seated position.

Britt pressed her index finger to her lips. "Shh, follow me," she said, moving toward the veiny entrance of their home.

Tanis rolled her eyes, begrudgingly dragging herself off her hammock, slothful. The ocean current blew across her face, waking her up from her drowsy state as she followed Britt outside their home. "What is it, Britt?" Tanis asked. She crossed her arms over her chest, miffed that her sister had awoken her.

Britt plopped herself down onto a large gray rock and patted her hand down next to her, gesturing Tanis to join her. "Ugh," Tanis said, unmoving. "Just tell me what's up."

"Okay." Britt looked up at her sister with furrowed

brows. "I think we need to follow Yuri today when she leaves to meet that merman again. I don't trust him, Tanis. I got a horrible feeling when he came to our home. We can't just let her go and meet him."

Tanis uncrossed her arms, plopping herself down next to her sister. She reached her hand across Britt's back and squeezed her into a tight hug. "I understand, but wouldn't he have hurt her already if he wanted to? Plus, if we followed her and she found out, she would never trust us again."

Britt leaned into her sister, resting her pink-haired head onto her shoulder. "She wouldn't even know we are there. We wouldn't interfere unless we had to. Really, Tanis. We have to do it." She leaned back, twisting her head to face her sister.

Tanis was still expressionless, unconvinced. She shook her head side to side, surely about to decline the absurd suggestion. She knitted her brows, looking again at Britt. Well, maybe there was something in what Britt said. It just wasn't like Britt to worry about anyone else more than she worried for herself. This time, all focus was on her big sister. That factor alone had to mean something, surely. Tanis couldn't remember the last time Britt had been so concerned for one of them.

"Please, Tanis, I'm very worried about her."

Tanis' eyes darted back and forth between her sister's wide-eyed gaze and everything else—looking at any place she could focus on to avoid the topic at hand.

Britt gazed back, pleading, carefully avoiding her eyes pausing at the ugly scar on Tanis' face.

"Okay," Tanis said softly, nodding. "I'll come with you. But we only get involved if she is in danger. We don't just burst in and interrupt because we don't like the boy."

Britt leaned her head back down onto her sister's shoulder. "Thank you," she softly said. "I mean if something were to happen to her—"

She never completed her sentence, but Tanis wondered if Britt meant she would blame herself for it or whether Britt was even too selfish to ever think like that—even when she *was* at fault.

There was no more time to ponder on it all.

There was a rustling behind them, and Yuri appeared at the entrance of the cave, planted with her hips cocked to one side and her hands poised on her curves. "Why are you both up so early?" she said, tilting her head as she called out to her two sisters.

Tanis and Britt whipped their heads around faster than a tornado.

"Damn Yuri, you scared us." Tanis' voice cracked, threatening to expose her plans with Britt.

Britt chimed in quickly, rising from the rock. "Tanis couldn't sleep. She woke me up, so I came outside to keep her company."

Tanis nodded in agreement. "Yeah, just a bad dream."

Yuri swam down from the entrance, plopping herself down next to Tanis and placing her hand on her back. It wasn't hard to believe that she'd had another nightmare. She had been having terrible dreams since their mother had passed away. They all had.

"Dreams aren't real," she said, rubbing her youngest sister's back, "but I dreamt it was your turn to get breakfast." She smiled, tickling Tanis on her sides where she was most ticklish.

"Stop it! I'm going! I'm going!" Tanis squealed

with laughter as she pushed away from her sister's torturous tickling fingers and retreated to a safe distance.

"I'll try to avoid bringing back mackerel," she said, sticking her tongue out at Yuri and Britt.

"Brat," Britt huffed under her breath, plopping herself down next to Yuri.

Tanis swam past the kelp hammock swings their mother had once built for them, causing them to sway as she faded into the distance.

"Remember how much fun we had on those swings," Yuri said, smiling as she playfully nudged Britt with her elbow.

Britt watched as a blowfish swam through each of the swings behind Tanis as if a circus performer jumping through hoops. Most of the kelp had become tattered with holes, and she had avoided looking at its dilapidated remains. It only made her sad, reminding her of how their mother had also deteriorated, especially right near the end.

"Yeah," Britt said, looking down at the seabed before hastily changing the subject. "Are you sure you should go today to meet that merman? Sister, please don't. Reconsider, for us…"

"Ugh," Yuri's brows furrowed over her icy eyes, looking annoyed. "Why do you keep on insinuating that I shouldn't go? Don't you think this will be good for us? It's a chance to create a bond between them and us. He's a prince, Britt. Maybe we'll be able to come out of hiding, finally. Maybe he can help us—possibly, even more than we think! Don't *you* think so?"

Britt shook her head side to side. "Yeah, and I'm sure that's the ONLY reason you want to see that merman again," she scoffed.

"What's that supposed to mean?" Yuri hissed, jumping up from the rock, her body towering over her seated sister. "I only said I would meet him because we took supplies from him. Supplies, sister! *Medical* supplies. For you, remember? Or have you quite conveniently shelved this fact?"

Britt sprang up, puffing her chest out like a blowfish defending its territory, her scowling face inches away from her sister's grimace. "You think I can't see behind this façade," Britt said, throwing her hands up. "You swim around with this love-struck attitude all the time, just so willing to abandon your sisters for some merman you hardly know!"

Yuri clenched her jaw as her face flushed red. "Don't be so ridiculous," she retorted. "You talk garbage sometimes!" She pushed her sister as hard as she could, sending her tumbling back. She watched Britt's head hit hard against the rock behind them and instantly regretted her actions. Something like this, a little spat between sisters, could so easily end in a serious injury. She already had one beloved sister with a scar that had barely healed. She didn't crave a second.

"Britt, I'm so sorry," Yuri said, reaching her arm down to grab her sister. "I really am sorry."

Britt pushed Yuri's arm away with force, timidity in her voice—unusual for Britt who was all bravado. "Get away from me," she said, lifting herself up and storming back into the cave, holding her hand to her aching head.

Minutes later, Tanis approached, holding up three large fish. "Breakfast is here," she chimed happily. But the atmosphere felt thick with discord.

Yuri sat with her head tucked into her hands, alone on the rock.

"What happened to Britt?" Tanis asked, her mood taking a drastic dive. She felt concerned; couldn't any of them get along together for more than a few hours these days? It seemed there was always some sort of a disagreement brewing among them all. And the stupid thing was that they each hated it, hated being at odds with a sister. They were all each other had after Mother had died, and they were supposed to stick together, not fight. Their mother would have hated all this bickering and arguing. And nobody enjoyed being like this. It had grown into a habit they could not shake.

"It's nothing," Yuri said, looking up from her hands to grab one of the fish from Tanis.

"All right," Tanis replied, shaking her head, leaving Yuri to sit alone on the rock as she went inside to find Britt. She soon discovered her.

Britt was on her hammock, sulking. Her puffy red eyes looked up at Tanis who loitered at the entrance holding two fish in her right hand.

"You okay, Britt?" Tanis swam over, holding up the fish. "All cod today."

Britt forced a smile as she sat up and grabbed one of the fish out of Tanis' hands. "Of course, thanks. Cod's my favorite," she replied, gulping down the fish.

Tanis nodded, pausing in front of her sister. Her lips parted for a moment, tempting her to ask once again if Britt was okay. *No, it will only make her mad.* "No problem," she said, resting down into her hammock. She swung the last fish up into the air and caught it in her mouth, sucking it down. "Britt," she said, peeking at her sullen sister. "Are we still going to follow Yuri?"

"Of course," Britt replied. "Why wouldn't we?"

Chapter 9

Britt was huddled on her hammock in a fetal position, her back facing the entrance of the cave as Yuri swam through its vined curtains and let all the icy current rush in with her. *She'll get over it,* Yuri thought as she brushed through her tangled hair with her hands, plaiting it off into a long fishtail braid. She had to leave soon to meet Prince Kaleb, or so she thought. His name rattled through her head like a cobra sending warm venom rushing through her body; her heart fluttered. Embarrassingly, her sister was right—she had been love-struck. *Poisoned by his venomous charm.*

Tanis was fiddling with the remains of her fishbones, picking in between her sharp teeth as Yuri watched light peeking from the vines and beaming onto her scar as if it were a shameful spotlight. She had to believe that she was not only meeting the prince for her own selfish motives. After all, a prince would have a great deal of influence over his people, especially if he became King. *It's in my sister's best interests,* she thought.

"All right, I'm leaving now," Yuri announced, giving one last polished tug to her braid.

Tanis looked up, rushing from her hammock, barreling toward Yuri as she simultaneously threw her fish bones to the floor. "Be careful," she said, throwing her arms around her sister.

"I will," Yuri said, embracing her youngest sister as she peered over her shoulder at Britt. But Britt remained unmoving. "Goodbye to you too, Britt," she said sarcastically, unlatching herself from Tanis' strong grip. "I see you are keen to give me a warm goodbye."

Britt shuffled in her hammock uncomfortably, positioning her arm over her eyes as she huffed under her breath.

"All right then," Yuri said, casting Tanis a fake salute. "You'll hold down the fort, won't you?"

Tanis nodded back. "You got it, captain," she said as Yuri exited their home.

A few moments passed before Britt sprang from her hammock, causing it to sway behind her. "You ready to go?" Britt asked, swimming past Tanis. "We have to catch up to her." She peeked her head out through the vines, letting them brush through her short pink hair. Yuri was still only just visible in the distance. *Perfect.*

Tanis shrugged. "I guess so."

"Great, we need to hurry," she said, grabbing Tanis by the arm. "We can't let her get too far ahead, or we'll lose her." Britt raced down from their cave, pulling Tanis with her.

Tanis' heart raced as she fought to keep pace with her sister. Her tentacles spun behind her, twisting as she floundered. "Britt, slow down!" she screamed, pulling her arm loose. "You are basically dragging me! I didn't say we should go that fast! I'd never have agreed if I'd known you'd behave like this."

Britt paused, shaking her head at her little sister. "Look, you don't have to come if you don't want to, but something's wrong. I can feel it. And if we don't hurry, she'll get too far ahead. And then we'll blame ourselves if anything—"

She wouldn't say the rest of the sentence. Tanis hurried up.

Britt now gestured toward Yuri, whose body looked like a tiny figurine in the distance.

Tanis rubbed at her arm. "I'm obviously going to come with you, but you have to slow down just a bit, right?" She paused to inspect her tentacles.

"Right," said Britt, sounding peeved.

"And I don't want to be dragged across the seafloor!"

"Fine, slowpoke," Britt teased. "But let's not go at snail speed."

They swam for about an hour, tailing Yuri until Britt finally began to recognize their surroundings like an old picture hashing up a memory. Their sister was headed to their mother's favorite place, a large boulder that plateaued at its peak and overlooked a tall lighthouse nestled on a sandy pink beach.

Britt stopped abruptly, causing Tanis to bump into her from behind.

"What's wrong?" Tanis asked, rubbing her head. "Why did you stop short?"

Britt motioned her hand in a circle. "This," she said angrily. "Do you not recognize where we are right now?"

Tanis spun around until her eyes landed on the pink sand beach.

"Yuri brought us here once, didn't she?" Tanis asked, reading the letters painted on a white rowboat docked on its shore. *L-i-b-e-r-t-y.*

"Yes," Britt said, bobbing in the water as she

watched Yuri in the distance through furrowed brows. "This was our mother's favorite spot." Jealousy bubbled in her chest like a witch's cauldron. Yuri was always able to come here with their mother as she was the eldest. Britt wished she too had a special place that she shared with her departed mom. She inhaled deeply, looking at the lighthouse, remembering the orange sun setting behind its tall peak. *Why would she bring him here to our special place? I am so angry!* And just like the sea, her stomach roiled and heaved.

Chapter 10

Yuri's hair blew in the wind as she leaned her back against the large gray boulder.

Guess I got here first. She looked up at the clouds that were tinted in gray, darkly overcast as if a storm would soon approach. Her eyes shut as she let the cool breeze blow across her face, imagining what the rain would feel like dripping down her cheeks. Yuri loved the rainstorms, always had.

Her eyes had only been shut for a moment when she heard *his* voice.

"There she is," Neo smiled. "You find my cuffs?"

Yuri's eyes flew open as her heart fluttered in her chest.

Neo moved slowly toward her, a panther stalking its prey. Every muscle flexed as he glided through the water from his chest up to his arms. Those chiseled arms that had pushed her against this very boulder.

Yuri froze in place as she bit her bottom lip to stop its quivering.

"You must not have heard me," Neo said cynically, his dimpled smirk turning into a dark sneer. "Did you find my cuffs! How many times do I have to ask?"

The tight grip of hands wrapped around Yuri, pulling back on her arms as the cold metal of chained cuffs slapped on her wrists. She thrashed frantically, throwing her head back as big, curly-haired arms engulfed her, coiling around her limbs to hold her in place.

"What the hell, Kaleb!" Yuri screamed.

Neo laughed. "Oh, I'm sorry sweetheart, but I'm not Kaleb. Did he forget to tell you that he had a twin?" His face twisted into a fake pout.

Yuri contorted underneath the stranger's grip. A rope was tied around her lower body, its harsh and prickly twine digging into her tentacles like the tiny pricks of a needle. If she wriggled and writhed, this twine could even cut her tentacles in two or at the very least, embed itself.

Neo squeezed her pale cheeks, making mocking kissy noises. "Sorry to disappoint, love. I know you were looking forward to wrapping your disgusting tentacles over my brother." He sneered at her, his hot breath inches away from her face.

Yuri slammed her head forward, smacking her forehead into Neo's glowering mug. Blood gushed from his lip as he pulled back, wiping his mouth with his hand.

"I wouldn't piss me off if I were you," he said through gritted teeth.

"Or what?" Yuri responded, her plump lips pulled up over her teeth.

Neo let out a diabolical laugh, his mouth twisting into a dark widened crescent as his eyes popped beneath furrowed brows, a deranged warped face taking over his demeanor. "Well," he said. "Should we teach her a lesson?"

Yuri head twisted from side to side. *Who's behind me?* She felt the warm breath of her captor against her spine as his large hands moved to her neck, choking her like a rattlesnake. His fat fingers blocked the gills on her throat, causing her to gasp. Her body felt numb as her eyes dimmed. The slow loss of consciousness set in, a murky fog blocking out the light.

Neo held up his hands, still sneering as if the expression had been painted on his face. "I think that's enough, Baric."

The hands of Yuri's strangler loosened as she gasped in a breath, her body falling limp against the boulder. Tears streamed down her face as she thought of her sisters and of how she might never see them again. *They were right. I was stupid.*

The sole consolation was that she might get to see her mother again, wherever she had gone to, presumably away in the next realm. Losing sisters was unbearable. Gaining a meeting with her mother—that would be heaven itself.

"Let me introduce you to my friends," Neo said, calling her captors forward. "Baric…Casco." Two mermen swam out from behind Yuri, positioning themselves on each side of Neo like bodyguards.

Neo gestured to his left. "Casco," he said, using words in a way that suggested they were rationed. He pointed to a pompous-looking mermaid with light-blond hair and a snotty upturned nose like that of a pig. "…and you are well acquainted with Baric?" he continued, pointing to his right.

Yuri's mouth gaped open. She had to confess to herself, she had never seen a larger or uglier merman than Baric, a full seven feet of solid bulk, the visible veins in his arms leading down to his curly hair-covered knuckles that had been wrapped around her neck just moments ago. His pea-sized head was tiny in comparison to his body, and Yuri shuddered as she looked into his blackened eyes sunken into his skull. He reminded her of an oversized anglerfish.

"What is it you want?" she asked weakly, her head resting on the side of the boulder. Her wrists throbbed behind her in their restraints. "I am here to meet someone. He'll be here anytime soon."

Neo laughed, jabbing playfully at his two friends. "Well, will you listen to that! She wants to know what I want!" he joked. Then he added, "And as for who it is you plan to meet, you made that very apparent when you said my brother's name."

Baric and Casco laughed along on cue as if Neo pulled strings on their backs like puppets. He held up his hand, and they fell silent.

His grimace faded into a frighteningly stern expression, his lips pulling into a flat line as he inched in closer to Yuri, whispering in her ear, "I want the throne." His hot breath lingered on her skin as she tried to pull away. "And you are going to help ensure that I get it," Neo said, pulling back, holding his arms up in a celebratory manner.

His dimpled grin reappeared on his face, looking so similar to Kaleb's that Yuri momentarily shut her eyes. Yes, their faces were similar, but their expressions were not. There was a meanness and coldness in Neo, something she had not yet seen in Kaleb. *How could I have been so easily fooled?*

Neo turned to face Baric and Casco. "One on each side," he said, pointing to Yuri. "We are taking her back with us."

Yuri's body slumped to the side as they lifted her over their shoulders and tied her down to the back of a seahorse like a wrangled hog.

"Let's go home, boys!" Neo chimed, slapping the back of the seahorse. Its back arched as it moved forward, carrying Yuri's dangling body across its frame.

Casco and Baric sneered at her from the right, saddled on a shared seahorse as Neo led them forward with a wide grin.

Father will have to give me the throne now. I have made a pretty catch tonight. Such a beautiful and delicious "fish".

Chapter 11

Britt and Tanis watched their sister helplessly in the distance.

Tanis' mouth dropped open as if she was going to scream, but only silence came out of her unhinged jaw. She was too scared to scream, also too scared not to. But her own body did what it wanted anyway. She was terrified and couldn't believe what she saw—there was her sister being roped and tied.

Britt coiled her fists into a tight ball. "I knew it," she said, furiously charging forward like a bull.

Tanis extended her arm, grabbing her sister by the shoulder and pulling her back. "We can't just storm toward them unarmed! It could get us both killed." She pointed toward Neo in the distance. "Look, they have weapons."

Neo's sharp blade glimmered from its brown sheath at his side, as if sadistically winking, taunting them like a bully begging for a fight. All three mermen were adorned with a weapon. Casco carried a knife similar to Neo's blade, its silver handle engraved in gold with his name, while Baric sported a large black mallet in a self-made sash across his ginormous frame.

Britt's eyes darted back and forth between all three of them. "No, it's going to be fine," she said, trying to convince herself as she rubbed at her temples.

Tanis squeezed tightly at her arm. "Britt?" Her

eyes filled with tears that streamed across her face and down her scar.

"It's going to be fine," Britt said again more sternly. "We are going to follow them and get her back. No one will ever take one of us away, do you hear? We are three. Not two."

A fear crept into the corners of Tanis' eyes like the reaper of impending doom. She knew her sister was just as scared as she was. She also knew they were both thinking the same thing.

Will we ever see our sister again?

Tanis nodded, pulling her sister into a tight hug. "We have to."

Chapter 12

Kaleb swam into the throne room, dragging the beast's severed head in his left hand. Blood dripped from its gutted neck down the long red carpet that led to his father's golden throne. Even despite the color of the carpet, the bright red stood out. Then—*boom.*

The brown double doors slammed behind him, sealing him in.

His father had always been very strict about who was allowed in this room. However, Ella would let him and Neo play there as children when no one was around. It was their little secret.

Not much had changed from when he was a kid. The walls of the room were still a deep burgundy decorated with golden picture frames. Above hung the same crystal chandelier that he and his brother had used to swing from. Its hanging crystal reminded Kaleb of raindrops, immediately able to send him into a fantasy land when he was small. Alongside raindrops went so many other weird and magical things—snow and huge castles, hairy monsters and goblins.

He swam over to his father's golden throne and ran his right hand across its decorated arms and up the pointed back shaped like the prongs of a trident. Behind it was a dark green tapestry with his father's emblem and the quote, *He darkens the sky for all to see, to protect and provide for his Kingdom to be.*

"Kaleb," his father's deep voice echoed behind him, bouncing off the burgundy walls of the throne room.

Kaleb sprung, dropping the beast's severed head to the floor.

"Hello, Father," he said formally, spinning around.

King Oasis gripped his trident firmly as he swam past Kaleb toward his throne. It was true his hair had become gray with age, but he still moved swiftly in the manner of a confident and agile warrior. His blood-red cape flowed behind him as if a servant to the mighty King, fluttering along in servitude wherever the King went.

Two guards followed behind his red cape, themselves also adorned in golden armor with red emblems of a trident engraved on their chests. As his father took his seat, they positioned themselves on each side like stiff and unmoving statues.

Kaleb pointed to the beast's head which had dropped next to the decorative leg of his father's throne. Its tongue had flopped out of its mouth, and its fleshy gray skin was beginning to deteriorate. The thing stank already, a mix of slaughtered meat at the market—and excrement. "I have brought you the beast's head, Father," Kaleb said proudly.

King Oasis waved his hand, and one of the guards swam forward, lifting the decapitated head from its resting place. Brain matter dripped from the back of its neck as he carried it away.

"I see," the King said in a flat tone, his face stern and unmoving.

Kaleb tilted his head to the side as he watched his father whisper something to the guard on his left, who disappeared behind the green tapestry. "Is that it, then?" Kaleb huffed, throwing his hands up.

King Oasis rose from his throne with his trident in hand. "Well, not according to your brother, it is not." He waved his trident at the brown double doors, and they flew open, smacking against the sides of the walls with force. The guard who had left earlier dragged Yuri into the room. Her tentacles and arms were roped down, and the skin around the knotted twine had become purple and bruised.

Neo swam in behind them with a sneer across his face. "Hello, brother," Neo said, grinning at Kaleb.

The guard threw Yuri forward, and she fell onto the red carpet, letting out a whimpered cry.

"What have you done?" Kaleb screamed. His eyes glared at Neo as he swam to Yuri's side, placing his hand on her shoulder. "I'm sorry this happened to you," he whispered in her ear. "I'm going to get you out of here, I promise. If it's the very last thing I do."

She looked up at him with her piercing blue eyes that had become stained red with exhaustion. A piece of cloth had been tied across her lips like a gag and as Kaleb went to reach for it, a guard pulled him back toward the wall.

"So, it is true then," the King said. His voice was loud with judgment and echoed through the chamber, thunderous.

"Please," Kaleb said, his arms clasped as he knelt. "She did nothing. Let her go."

King Oasis slammed the handle of his trident to the floor. "I will do no such thing! I am still King, and no son of mine will be associated with THESE creatures!" His voice bellowed as the room shook with every word.

Kaleb bowed his head, trembling as his eyes flicked up to see Neo still grinning. *That spiteful bastard.* He charged toward his brother with full force, laying a knuckled punch across his smug face. Despite smearing on medicine, his left shoulder hadn't fully healed since his skirmish with the beast, and he winced as he lifted his right arm to take another punch.

Neo fell back against the wall, catching himself with his palms before springing up and tackling Kaleb to the ground. "I couldn't let you have the throne. Look at the filth you brought in!" He twisted Kaleb's head to force him to look at Yuri, who lay motionless on the floor, her silver hair pooled around her, bloodlike.

"Get off me!" Kaleb shouted, jabbing his elbow into Neo's stomach.

"Enough!" King Oasis roared, slamming his trident to the floor again. His guards moved forward, pulling each of the brothers in separate directions. Neo huffed, crossing his arms as he leaned against the far-left wall, annoyed that Kaleb had gotten the last hit.

"Father," Kaleb said, catching his breath, his left arm propped on the right wall. "I'd like to propose a duel. The winner gets the throne and the right to do with the prisoner as they see fit."

Neo snickered from the corner, pointing to Kaleb and then himself. "YOU want to duel ME? Well, that's an easy win for me…"

King Oasis sat back down on his throne, scratching at his short gray beard as the room became uncomfortably silent around him. "Since you did bring me the vile beast's head, I will grant you this chance but under my conditions, not your own. So listen, and listen well. If you truly both want the throne, you must prove it in a battle to the death. And there will be no need for a judge as Heaven will claim the loser, of course. Say your goodbyes to one another before you fight."

The King's words spun out like a web meant to strangle his sons in some twisted punishment. The brothers glanced at each other for a long silent moment. It was horrid, unthinkable. Kaleb shook his head in a show of pique as he clenched his jaw tightly. His brother's smile had also faded clean off his face now, replaced by a hard scowled frown. Kaleb balled his fists, feeling the roughened fingernails digging into his own palm.

He wanted to hurt Neo, for sure—but certainly didn't want to kill him. Anyway, had there not been enough savagery with the slaying of the monster? What kind of brothers took death to one another?

Yuri's whimpering had faded as she lay passed out on the floor in front of Kaleb. His heart sank as he looked at her helpless body sprawled across the ground.

His father tapped his fingers against the arms of his throne. He was impatient, eager, always keen and excited to see a fight to the death—even when it was between his own twin sons. His cold blue eyes awaited Kaleb's response. Anyone would have thought this as why he had twins, so he could see one die and not know the difference with the one remaining.

"I agree to the challenge," Kaleb said flatly, meeting his father's frigid gaze.

"Perfect!" His father's stiff mouth curved into a piercing smile. "And do you accept this challenge, Neo?" He said, nodding to his other son.

Neo's stomach twisted into knots, and he folded his

arms across his waist, puffing out his chest. "I agree," Neo responded, taking a deep gulp of water into his gills. He had no other choice. His father wasn't asking him but confirming that he would do as he was told.

"Wonderful!" the King exclaimed, raising his hands. "You will both battle in the arena in two days' time. I will get the word out to the kingdom that there will be a grand battle between my two sons for the throne! Everyone will turn out to witness it, knowing that the taking of the throne was fair." He flagged his guards over to Yuri. "In the meantime, the prisoner will be held in the lower chamber cell."

Kaleb watched painfully as the guard dragged Yuri away. How could a woman be thus treated? His fists tightly gripped at his sides again as Yuri's body slid across the red carpet. *It's my fault. It's all my fault.* Thankfully, she was not aware of any of it.

"You are both dismissed," the King said, waving his hands.

Kaleb grimaced as he shoved Neo and then stormed out the brown double doors.

Chapter 13

It was nightfall by the time Britt and Tanis entered the Kingdom of Atlantis. They swam through the outskirts leading to the castle where the non-royals and peasants all lay fast asleep in their beds. Their shutters were drawn on their tiny homes built of discarded human trash.

One thing could be said for these wasted and pointless materials—they were warm and insulating. Use of a large plastic bottle to encase a home or a room could increase the temperature of the sea by a couple of degrees Celsius on a cold night, the minute trapped air particles and seabed mud creating a buffer. Polystyrene, too, was an incredible help. But despite these benefits, they would sooner have been freezing cold and had a clean sea.

In the distance, the golden castle glowed, perched as it was, high upon a raised mound. Surrounding it was a long, guarded gate.

The whistling rush of the ocean's current whispered in their ears as they crept behind each home, carefully avoiding any patrolling guards. The sisters could not see any right now, but they were there. They were always there, ready to spring out on the unsuspecting.

"It won't be this easy once we get closer to the castle," Britt whispered to Tanis, as they peeked out from behind one of the dilapidated homes. Its metal roof hung over them like a melting icicle; at any moment, the whole thing could come crashing down.

"It almost feels like no one lives here," Tanis whispered, looking up at the decrepit roof. "Or should I say, no one should."

She had spoken too soon. The brown wooden back door of the shambolic house creaked open with an elongated moan. Tanis froze with fear, her eyes glued to the opening. Her fingers clenched at her sides.

"Over here," Britt whispered, waving her hands from an adjacent house to the right, which had also been built out of scrap metal. Its roof stuck out unevenly on all sides, leaving the home looking like a deformed starfish.

Tanis shook her head, freeing herself from her paralyzed state as she darted toward Britt as quickly as she could.

A mergirl emerged from behind a rickety wooden doorway. She looked around carefully, twisting her head left and right. Her long green hair flowed down to her hips, emphasizing her petite stature. Her beautiful pink and green sequined tail swayed rhythmically as she spun in a circle.

"Did she see me?" Tanis whispered to Britt, gripping her sister's shoulders from behind.

"I don't think so," Britt whispered back, turning around to see her sister's panicked expression. "But you can't freeze up like that. It could be really dangerous."

Tanis parted her lips to speak, but no words came forth. Her eyes had gone wide with fear.

"Tanis?" Britt said, tilting her head in confusion.

"Uh," Tanis said, pointing behind Britt with a

trembling hand. "Where did the girl go?"

The mergirl had vanished from her doorway as if a magic trick had been pulled across their eyes. *Abracadabra.* All that was left was an empty splintered wooden stoop and a half-open door.

"She, uh, probably just went back inside her home," Britt quickly blurted out, scratching at the back of her head.

Tanis crossed her arms over her chest, rubbing at her sides. "Oh, yes. You're probably right," she answered her sister.

"We should keep moving," Britt said, tapping Tanis on the shoulder for her to follow. There was no way that the two should stay in proximity when there might be sea specters about.

The houses became nicer as the sisters swam behind each of them, inching their way closer to the castle gates. Scrap metal had been replaced by painted white shells with decorative gold trim. It became apparent that there was a significant divide between the wealthy and the poor.

"I guess the merfolk here are more important," Britt scoffed.

Four houses stood between them and the guarded gate, where three soldiers were posted in their turtle-shell armor, each one wielding a long sword and very much trained to use it.

"How are we supposed to get past the guards?" Tanis whispered, peering out behind the golden trim of a large painted house. Its foundation was solid and unmoving unlike the dilapidated scraps of the earlier homes.

Britt peeked over Tanis' shoulder, watching the

guards pace side to side. "I'm not sure."

"Maybe I can help you?" a voice peeped from behind the two sisters.

Tanis and Britt startled, spinning around, only to bump into one another. There, in front of them, was the petite mergirl with the long green hair. Her large brown eyes stared up at them like a lost doe.

Tanis' eyes widened. "Yeah…I don't think she went back inside," she whispered sarcastically under her breath.

"Damn," Britt replied, squinting at the mergirl who brushed her long green hair behind her ears with her hand.

"I'm Sadie," she said, extending her arm out to shake.

Britt examined her stretched-out arm and long bare nails and worked her way up to her youthful face with cute freckles. She was slightly younger than them, probably about fifteen. "We don't want any trouble. Just go back home," Britt said, glaring at her.

Sadie's arm dropped, but still she didn't budge. Instead, she crossed her arms over her chest, cocking her hip to the side with attitude.

Tanis nudged at Britt with her elbow. "Excuse us," she said to Sadie, pulling Britt over to the corner of the house out of earshot of the petite mermaid. "What do we do?"

Britt looked down at the ocean floor, shaking her head back and forth. "I don't know! Is she still looking at us? Can you check?"

Tanis glanced up at Sadie whose arms were still crossed over her chest, and brown doe eyes peered at the sisters inquisitively, interrogation-style. "Yup,"

Tanis said sarcastically. "Definitely looking."

"Damn. Damn. Damn," Britt said, running her fingers nervously through her short pink hair. "What could she possibly want with us?"

Tanis placed her hand onto Britt's shoulder, forcing her to look up. "Maybe she does actually want to help us? We should hear her out."

Britt nudged her body back, causing Tanis' hand to fall from her shoulder. "Or she could be leading us into some trap. It's not like that hasn't happened once or twice before," Britt scoffed, throwing her hands up.

"Look at her," Tanis said, pointing to Sadie. "If that's the case, we could take her down. She's so tiny. And fragile."

Big things come in small packages, passed through both Britt's and Tanis' minds.

Sadie swam in agitated circles now, digging her tail into the seabed, drawing loop after loop in the sand. Britt narrowed her eyes as she looked up at the diminutive mergirl probably weighing in at no more than 100 pounds. Her ribcage poked out of her skin as though belonging to a starving sea lion.

"Well, what is she doing up so late? Doesn't that seem odd to you?" Britt sneered.

"Only one way to find out," Tanis replied as she swam back over to Sadie.

Sadie's tail was covered with sand, and she brushed some of it off with her hand as Britt followed behind her sister, a scowl smeared across her face.

"What are you doing up this hour?" Tanis asked as she folded her arms over her chest.

Sadie's big doe eyes glossed over with tears.

"I haven't been able to sleep since my father left,"

she said, averting her gaze to the ground.

Britt and Tanis ought to have empathized since they knew how it felt to lose their mother. Did the mergirl mean her father had *left* as in being dead, or *left* as in gone out and never come back again? Either way, empathy would've been appropriate. But instead, Britt noisily huffed from behind Tanis, rolling her eyes skyward. "Oh yeah, where did he go?" she asked coldly. "He didn't have a map?"

Tanis stared at her, her upper lip raised in disgust.

Sadie slumped forward, placing her head in her hands, letting out a low whimper. As she sobbed, Britt's face grew pale, and her eyes darted to the floor. Guilt—such a heavy burden for those who bore it.

"My father joined the army so that my mother and I would be provided for. Recently, he left to help the King's son on his quest to kill the beast. We haven't heard any news since he left, and I haven't been able to sleep one bit. I saw you both from my window, and knew you were probably headed to the castle from the way you were creeping around. I just want to find my dad," Sadie sobbed between words, her long fingers extended over her eyes.

"I'm sorry to hear that," Britt murmured, looking up at Sadie's sullen face. "But aren't you scared of our kind?"

Sadie rubbed at her eyes, shaking her head. "Most of us on the outskirts of the castle disagree with the way the ocean has been segregated. It's only the royals that want to keep the divide. It gives them power over the ocean. They aren't nice to my mother and me either."

Tanis' lips curved into a half-smile. It was hard not to like Sadie, who seemed so bright and filled with understanding instead of hate.

Sadie returned Tanis' smile with her own half-grin, out of place next to her red and puffy eyes. "What happened to you?" Sadie asked, pointing at Tanis' scar. Then she recoiled. Asking such a thing was impertinent. "I mean, you don't have to tell me if you'd rather not."

"You don't even need to say that," retorted Tanis. "Because if I didn't want to tell you, I wouldn't anyway." She was unusually brusque and dismissive. Tanis brushed her hair over her blemished eye as if she was burying a dirty secret. "Some of your people hurt me when I was younger," she muttered. She spat out the words, *your people.* Poison-laced words. Venomous.

Sadie visibly flinched and then shuffled uncomfortably, rubbing the back of her neck. "Oh, sorry. I…I mean—" What could she say?

Britt cleared her throat, cutting through the uncomfortable moment. "Anyway, can we get to the point? How do you think you can help us? We need to move quickly. We can't dillydally here all night."

"Well," Sadie said, still scratching at the back of her neck. "You can't just waltz up there. They would just kill you on the spot. I can help cause a distraction, but…"

"But what?" Britt asked, leaning forward, her eyes piercing through Sadie like hot daggers.

Sadie squirmed uncomfortably under Britt's gaze, swaying side to side.

"But," Sadie continued, "one of you would have to stay behind for my plan to work, and I would go with the other into the castle."

Britt glanced at Tanis with a pained gaze. *I have to stay behind.* Her tongue felt like sandpaper against her lips as she went to speak.

"*I'll* stay behind," Tanis chimed in before Britt could get the words out past parted lips.

Britt gripped Tanis by the shoulders with unsteady hands.

"Are you sure?" she asked, clinging to her sister.

"Yes." Tanis nodded before averting her eyes toward Sadie. "What's *your* plan?"

Britt let her shaking hands drop off her sister and tap along her sides.

"Okay, well…" Sadie paused, gritting her teeth. "You are going to need to be bait."

Britt's brows furrowed with anger as the vein popped from her temples. She threw her hands up. "Absolutely not! We need a new plan. I'm not letting my younger sister be bait for some dumb guards!"

"Shh," Tanis said, holding her finger close to her lips. "Don't shout." She peeked her head out from the corner of the house, half expecting the guards to come charging toward them.

She grabbed Britt's hand and squeezed tightly. "This might be the only way. Let me help. We need to get Yuri. It will be okay."

"Fine." Britt sighed heavily, squeezing her sister's hand in return. "But be careful. Extra careful. No risks, you know?"

Tanis forced a smile across her worried face. "You know I will not take any."

Chapter 14

Britt and Tanis crept behind a towering gray home built directly next to the castle's golden gates. A large white overhanging roof with gold trim shadowed them as the great white pillars on each side masked them from the guards. They waited for Sadie's signal.

Sadie was perched behind an adjacent neighboring house, farther back. It was a lovely home, with solid brick walls that kelp had grown up, twisting like vines, and a steady white roof. While it wasn't as nice as the house Britt and Tanis crouched behind, it was more than Sadie was used to.

She leaned her back against the cold bricks, peering out toward the guards who paced back and forth along the edge of the gate. All three were stern-faced, stiff, and wielding a sword in a sheath across their gold-plated armor.

She took a deep gulp of water into her gills before swimming out into the street.

"Help!" Sadie shouted, waving her arms frantically.

Her petite frame soared like a bird, barreling toward the guards who reached at their sides, removing their swords from their sheaths.

"What's the problem?" One of the guards swam forward, his long, pointed sword outstretched.

Sadie's big brown eyes looked up at him. He was a

tall fellow with a long face and beaky nose. His light-gray hair matched his tail that had wide scars riddled across it.

He was a seasoned soldier. His counterparts wore similar scars, and all three glared with their swords pointed at Sadie's thin neck.

"Over there! Over there!" she shouted, dramatically pointing behind her.

That was Tanis' cue.

Britt wrapped her arms around her sister. "Good luck, and be safe."

"I will," Tanis said, pulling away.

Tanis swam in the opposite direction of the gate, counting as she got behind each home.

One, two, three. Her arms felt frozen against her sides as her heartbeat thundered in her chest. *I can do this. I can do this.* She focused on slowing her breathing as she swam into the view of the street, pausing for a moment for good measure.

She couldn't afford to let the guards not see her.

"It's *the Inked*!" screamed the beaky guard, motioning his counterparts to go after her.

They sprang into action, sprinting toward her with their wielded swords. Tanis swam as fast she could, barreling down the street in the opposite direction of her sister.

Britt watched Tanis zoom past her like lightning as the two guards followed her as if a roll of thunder chasing a storm. Her stomach twisted as she peered out to see Sadie fidgeting uncomfortably. The beaky guard had stayed behind, blocking their way in. His arms folded over his chest as he peered down at the young mergirl with squinted eyes.

Sadie cleared her throat loudly.

"Well," she said, turning her previous frantic attitude into one of privilege. "Aren't you going to alert my parents of my safety?"

She spun around, pointing to a random house on the left with a pointed roof that reminded her of a tower where a princess might have been stowed away waiting for her prince.

The guard tilted his head, staring at her with a look of confusion.

"You're the blacksmith's daughter?"

Sadie placed her hands on her slanted hips.

"Yes, I am," she answered smugly back. "Shouldn't you be escorting me home? Anything can happen to someone like me, out after hours."

The guard's eyes narrowed as he uncrossed his arms.

"I didn't know that the blacksmith had a daughter."

Sadie took a deep sarcastic bow.

"Well, here I am, and I believe it's your duty to take me home, especially after I alerted you about a potential danger. What if there are more around? Do you really want to be the coward who didn't take the blacksmith's daughter home? Everyone will talk."

The guard rubbed at the back of his neck nervously, his beaky nose pointing down at Sadie.

"Well, let's go then," he replied sternly, escorting Sadie to the blacksmith's home as she tailed behind him as if marching to her doom.

She glanced over at Britt still perched behind an adjacent house, her head poking out from the large white pillars. *Go,* she mouthed, pointing to the gate.

Britt made a quick beeline, sprinting for the

unguarded entrance. The gate was locked, but she was thin enough to squeeze her body through the narrow golden bars which scraped against her shoulders as she pushed through, leaving pink marks against her skin.

She looked back through the shining golden gate at Sadie being led away by the guards. *I can't leave her,* she thought, crouching down by the gate. *Sadie, why did you have to get yourself into trouble? We could be away now if not for you.*

Britt admonished herself for her earlier comments about Sadie's lost father. Now was not the time to be abandoning her too. The guilt could not be assuaged a second time.

Sadie had positioned herself directly behind the tall guard, who came swimming up to the fortified steel door of the blacksmith's home. It was decorated with faux shields and swords intricately sculpted into its thick metal. He turned to see Sadie still poised behind him, and she smiled, innocently tilting her head to the side.

Three loud knocks came, his fists rapping hard against the metal door.

The door creaked as it opened, sending out the eerie moans of a ghoul.

Pudgy fingers wrapped around the edge of the door as the bald head of a short merman poked out from the opening. He rubbed his eyes with his free hand.

"What's the meaning of this?" he said in between yawns.

The beaky guard nodded.

"I'm sorry to bother you, sir, but I wanted to return your daughter safely to you."

The blacksmith paused, taken aback. His head

tilted as a puzzled expression crossed his face.

"I think you have the wrong house. I don't even have a daughter."

The guard twisted his neck, fully expecting to see Sadie hovering behind him, but she was gone. He balled his fists as panic set in. He had been duped.

"I'm so sorry to bother you, sir. Have a good night," he said nervously as he sprang from the house, racing toward his abandoned post.

Sadie spiraled through the water, swimming as fast as she could toward the gates. Her arms pumped by her sides, as her long sequined tail thrashed behind her, shimmering like the shattered pieces of a broken mirror.

Britt was waiting for her by the gate, her body crouched behind some kelp shrubbery that blended well with her long black tentacles. She grabbed at Sadie's thin arm pulling her through the gate and behind the dark green hedging.

Sadie jolted, throwing her fists up as Britt raised her hands to block her face.

"Easy there," Britt hissed.

"Oh," Sadie sighed a breath of relief, lowering her cocked arms to her sides. "It's just you. What are you still doing here? I figured you'd be halfway to your sister already."

Britt crossed her arms over her chest and looked down toward the seabed. "Yeah, well, I wasn't going to leave you behind after you helped us." She ran her hands through her short pink hair, nervously looking up at Sadie and muttering, "So uh, I guess…thanks."

Sadie rolled her eyes as the corners of her mouth pinched into a half-smirk. "Don't mention it."

In front of them stood a long yellow cobblestone

winding road that wrapped around a tall mound where the golden castle of Atlantis sat at its peak. Just as in the Wizard of Oz, they would have to follow the yellow "brick" road if they wanted to see their loved ones again.

"We should probably start moving before the guard catches up," Britt said. She stared out past the gate.

"Good idea," Sadie replied.

Chapter 15

Kaleb paced back and forth in his bedroom, a huge knot of angry energy pulsing in his chest as he slammed his fist into his bedroom wall, leaving a crumbling hole and his knuckles bloodied. He shook his throbbing hand and plopped down on his bed to look up at the ceiling, which seemed to twist as if it were going to cave in on him. Anxiety was eating him alive the way a parasite set about devouring its host. He needed to see Yuri. He had to make sure she was okay.

The dungeon was at the very basement of the castle where a narrow and twisting, sloping pathway led to the guarded entrance of Yuri's prison. She sat in the corner of a concrete, windowless cell with her face in her hands as two sentinels kept post on each side, watching her every move. They had provided her with a dead crab to eat, which remained untouched on a silver plate. She shoved at it with her tentacle, sending the dead carcass scurrying across the floor as if the crab had somehow magically reanimated.

A few moments ago, a mermaid named Athena had brought her posse with her to sling venomous words at Yuri as if seasoning her up before her impending execution.

She would have made a most decadent meal.

****

"Look at IT," Athena had said, crinkling her nose

in disgust as her long blonde hair fell forward into her face. Her posse had laughed in unison as she slammed her hands against the bars, making a loud commotion as she attempted to evoke a reaction out of Yuri.

"Eww, even her tentacles look slimy. Look! She's like a sea snail. No, like a land slug. I can't believe Prince Kaleb would kiss that!" one of her friends had chimed.

"Impossible," Athena had sneered. "And you really shouldn't spread rumors about the prince!"

"Sorry, Athena," her friend had murmured in a defeated tone.

A metal canister lay on the floor next to the cell and Athena had grabbed it, throwing it toward Yuri's head with a fit of burning jealousy.

Yuri had risen upon being hit, propelling herself to the bars, and reaching through its thick metal slabs like the rabid animal Athena had surely been expecting to see.

Athena laughed, pulling back from the cage. "Let's go, girls," she had said, satisfied with her victory.

****

Yuri rubbed the back of her head where a small bump was forming. She leaned her head against the cold concrete wall and hummed softly, cradling her arms around herself.

Meanwhile, Kaleb was on his way to her when he bumped into Athena and her posse of three. They giggled like a pack of wild hyenas circling him on the twisting metal ramp.

"Hi, Prince Kaleb. Where are you headed?" Athena asked, running her fingers down his arm flirtatiously as if she was taking the first bite.

Kaleb recoiled.

"Don't worry about it," he said, pushing past her and her friends, whose mouths dropped open as their eyes darted toward Athena, waiting for her to break down so they could claim her role as alpha of the pack.

Athena let out a loud faux laugh, tilting her head back. "You know princes. They are always so busy, aren't they?" She smiled with a little wink to concrete her upbeat façade, and her posse returned her forced smile with their own faux grins. No one would be overthrown tonight. "Let's go, girls," Athena said, flipping her hair and leading the way back to her quarters as her posse followed behind like loyal servants.

Kaleb finally made his way down to the dungeon despite Athena's attempt to sidetrack him. He pulled forcefully at the large black looped handles of the great double mahogany wooden doors successfully separating him from Yuri. They swung open, slamming into the sides of the brick walls as he stormed inside the dungeon, where his love sat trapped in a cage.

The two guards jerked, spinning to pull out their swords as one positioned his body to block Kaleb's path to the cell. He was much taller and broader than Kaleb but had the belly of a pot pig from years of sedentary work in guarding prisoners confined to cages. His armor clung tightly to his skin like a belly shirt as his fat hung down, peeking out from the edges. "You aren't allowed in here, Prince Kaleb. It's the King's orders." He crossed his sword over his shielded chest as he spoke the King's mandate.

Kaleb lifted his face inches away from the guard's double-chinned mug. His sour breath stank from behind cracked yellow teeth, and Kaleb's nose crinkled in disgust. "I'm sure my father wouldn't be too pleased at you inviting the mermaids I just passed on my way down here," Kaleb whispered, winking at the guard.

The pudgy guard pulled his neck back, clearing his throat uncomfortably as he lowered his sword. He motioned to his counterpart who leaned against Yuri's cell with his blade lifted and ready to fight. The sword fell to his side as he begrudgingly swam past Kaleb and out the dungeon's wooden doors. "Five minutes," he sneered, glaring back at Kaleb while shifting off to the side with the scuttling actions of a disgruntled crab.

Kaleb bolted to the metal cell where Yuri lay curled into a ball in the far-right back corner. "Yuri!" he cried out, gripping the cold metal bars.

Yuri remained slumped over and unmoving; her face was turned to the wall, and the back of her neck appeared riddled with bruises.

"I'm so sorry," Kaleb croaked. He slid his body down to the floor as his hands glided down the metal bars. "I'm going to get you out of here. I promise."

"You didn't tell me you had a twin," Yuri muttered, still facing the wall. Her voice was hoarse from crying and cracked as she spoke, catching uncomfortably in her throat.

"I know," he responded dejectedly. "I honestly didn't think it was important. I also didn't know my brother could do such a thing. Please, believe me when I say that. I would never—" His voice cracked, and he halted his speech. It was not manly to cry so. His eyes filled up with tears regardless, and if it weren't for the salty ocean in which they lived, they would have come streaming down his face in an unstoppable waterfall.

Yuri twisted her head to see Kaleb's eyes red and bloodshot.

They stared intently at her from beneath his tangled hair that sat atop his head, perched there in a way to rival any disheveled bird's nest. She grabbed at the bars of the cage that divided them. His bruised hands were still tightly nestled around the cold metal, and she reached out to touch them. As her fingers caressed his hands, he grabbed at her arms, pulling her into a deep but very awkward embrace. The caged bars dug into their skin, leaving indents that neither seemed to mind.

"That's enough," the plump guard shouted, pulling Kaleb back by the shoulders. "Time's up! And I shall have to check the girl for concealed objects." The way he called her *the girl* was so dispassionate, writing her off as anyone of importance.

Kaleb's fingers reached out to grab Yuri one last time as the two rough guards dragged him out of the dungeon. He watched as Yuri seem to fade like a distant dream. Soon enough, he was back where he started—outside of the big mahogany double doors which had slammed in his face. "When I'm King, both of you are banished!" he shouted to the guards behind the locked doors, slamming his fists into the hardwood.

There was no response.

Chapter 16

The winding cobblestone road leading to the castle was lined with decorative coral and huge sculpted rocks, all made to look like the chiseled physiques of royal figures. As Britt and Sadie navigated their way up the unlit path, they dodged behind each effigy to avoid being seen.

Britt paused in front of one of the sculptures, examining its sharpened jaw and decorative carved armor with the emblem of Atlantis engraved into the marbled rock. It looked precisely like Kaleb. Her lips quivered over her pointed teeth as she grabbed hold of its mottled neck with her tentacles and twisted until she heard it crack beneath her grip. The head rolled to the floor as she sneered under her breath, "Just you wait."

"Wow, Kaleb must have really pissed you off," Sadie said with wide eyes as she glanced down at the ground, looking intently at the decapitated stone head.

Britt nodded, crossing her arms over her chest uncomfortably. "Let's just keep going," she replied, nudging the stone head with her tentacle as she moved farther up the cobblestone path, leaving Sadie chasing behind to catch up to her side.

Sadie seemed so elegant swimming in the water next to her with her long sequined green and pink fishtail glistening as she swam and matching her hair so well. Britt couldn't help but feel a tinge of jealousy as she looked down at her stocky lower half that scurried up the cobbled stone path like a mass of entangled yet still slithering black snakes. She felt in her heart that she was neither elegant nor beautiful. "Have you been to the castle before? We are going to need to find the best entrance in without being seen," Britt asked, refocusing her mind on the task. "Is there any easy way in?"

Sadie let out a low sigh. "I have been once before—long ago." Then she paused before adding, "And there is never an easy way into these things. Castles are, you know…fortified, designed to keep others out."

"Ah," said Britt. "Well anyway. So you've been before, you say?" She propped her hands on her hips, stopping a moment to face Sadie. "Care to elaborate?"

Sadie's eyes glazed over into a blank stare. "Not really," she said softly. Britt tilted her head in confusion as Sadie turned her face away to hide her crumbling plastered grimace. "Anyway," she went on, "I've only been to the castle once, like I said." Her face melted into a deep frown.

"But you still haven't said why and how, and—"

Britt was plainly not intending to give up anytime soon. Sadie took a huge breath. "They let my mother and me say goodbye to my father after his inauguration into the King's Army. It was the last time I saw him. He just…he just disappeared, you know?"

"I'm sorry," Britt said, lowering her hands to her sides. "Oh right. Sorry." It came out in something of an offhand tone. It wasn't meant to but did anyhow. She was just too shocked at the answer Sadie hadn't wanted to say—and which she'd forced out of her. Her words trailed off as she thought about her own mother, and of how devastated she had been when she died. *Not knowing what happened to someone you love must be even worse. You are such an idiot, Britt. It should've been clear she didn't want to talk. You're so stupid.* Empathy and a deep compassion swirled in Britt's mind. It was just a shame she rarely let them out to be appreciated in the world. Even now, she said sorry, but her tone never showed how much her own stupidity bit into her psyche, how she reproached herself so much.

"Don't worry about it," Sadie said, cutting her off as she took a deep gulp of the ocean water in through her mouth, letting it bubble out of her nostrils before continuing. "You know, at first, it really hurts. Over time, it's a bit like something you put away in a box and then push the box under the bed, and then forget what's in the box. You know what I mean?"

"I know what you mean," said Britt. She patted Sadie's shoulder gently. "I'm truly sorry. I acted like an idiot toward you."

This time, it sounded heart felt, and a tear trickled down Sadie's face because of the kindness. Sadie carried on speaking now, a new energy in her voice as she spun back around. "Don't worry, Britt. It was me who pushed that box under the bed. *I* was the one who pushed away the memories. But I can't deny they're always there, no matter what I do with them. So it was my fault, not yours."

A silence of deep sharing and respect fell between them both, just for a few seconds.

"Anyway," said Sadie, "You were right to keep asking because…because I have just thought of something. When my mother and I were there, I noticed a cellar door being put in right by the stables where they were keeping their seahorses. Maybe we can get in that way. Let's hope."

Britt nodded as her mouth pressed into a thin fine line. "Okay, we'll find that door," she said, pausing to tilt her head, looking at Sadie's sullen eyes. "Sadie," Britt continued, gently nudging at her arm. "If your father is as badass as you, we will find him. I mean, the way you played that dumb guard earlier. You're *such* a genius."

Sadie smiled, and a flicker of hope and positivity seemed to light her eyes now too. "Britt…about my father," she said with a serious tone, but this time, she was joking—only Britt didn't know it yet. Britt feared she had said the wrong thing again. Her gut churned.

"What about your father?" she whispered.

"Well actually, he's pretty dumb," Sadie responded as she giggled uncontrollably.

And that way, the hurt that had lingered in the air between them was suddenly lifted. They laughed endlessly, trying to subdue their sounds in case of alerting someone.

When they reached the top of the mound, a vast castle stood before them built out of solid gold. Its large towers and peaks pointed to the surface like flowers reaching for the sun. They crouched behind a giant golden effigy of the mighty King Oasis with his three-pronged trident aimed up toward the sky. It was the perfect hiding place, nestled in front of the castle's enormous double doors which had been embellished with gems, also surrounded by a circular maze of colorful kelp shrubbery. They blended into the plant life as they peeked out through a mess of tangled greenery.

A pair of guards rested on each side of the double doors, with golden turtle-shell armor, metal helmets and matching red emblems stamped across their chests. They were stiff and motionless and if it hadn't been for their blinking eyes, it would have been easy to mistake them for just another statue planted outside the castle doors. After all, there were so many of them.

"We need to get to the back of the castle, but they'll see us if we bolt for it," Sadie whispered.

Britt's face twisted into a dark and devious smile.

"You up for another distraction?" she asked.

Sadie's curved mouth pinched at her cheeks as she returned Britt's grin. "Always. What did you have in mind?"

The golden effigy of the King was circled by a bed of rocks painted blue like the ocean. Britt picked one of them up, and her wrist bent under its weight. It was heavy enough to get the job done. "If you can distract them, I can see if I can knock them out," Britt said, rolling the blue rock around in her palm.

"Okay," Sadie said, inhaling deeply. "Let's do this." She peeked her head out of the colorful shrub maze, and then moved slowly toward the guards, who brandished their swords quickly upon seeing her. The taller of the two moved forward with his bronze-kissed arm outstretched as he held the sharpened blade to the collar of her neck.

"What are you doing here?" He demanded an answer. His voice was deep with authority compared to his softened features, where his button nose sat centered on a clean-shaved face. The other guard was just as young looking but pale, stocky, and much less intimidating. His sword was drawn but held awkwardly in his hands; he had the look of a boy playing make-believe with a stick.

Sadie froze as the tip of the blade poked into her flesh. "The King sent for me," she blurted out. It wasn't that outlandish of a lie. The King often kept the company of young mermaids and would even occasionally scout Atlantis for pretty mergirls whose poor parents would gladly give them up for monetary means.

The taller guard pushed the sword further into Sadie's skin.

She winced as the blade cut into the sensitive skin over her clavicle.

"Is that so? Where are your parents? They don't want gold in exchange for you?" he said, jabbing the tip of the sword a little farther into her skin.

Sadie winced again, fighting back tears as some of her blood pooled into the ocean water.

The stocky guard piped up from behind his counterpart, his hands trembling around his raised sword, causing it to shake in his palms. "Adam, if she's telling the truth, you just damaged the King's property," he said anxiously as his eyes darted between Sadie and the guard.

Adam tilted his head back, letting out a loud laugh.

"I don't know what you're talking about, Sam. She came to us like that," he retorted sarcastically.

Britt sprinted up. A loud *whack* sounded in the dark. Her hand throbbed as she slammed the large blue rock against the back of the tall guard's helmeted head. He swayed for the briefest moment before collapsing to the floor with a loud thump.

"Hey!" the stocky guard shouted, his hand still

trembling around his pointed sword.

Britt spun around, grabbing the sword with her tentacles and pulling it forward along with the stout guard. The guard's eyes widened as he tried to dig his tail into the seafloor. "Stop!" he screamed. With a swooshing sound, her hand moved in one swift motion, slamming the same blue rock into his helmeted head. Then came another loud whack—sending his helmet spinning around as he collapsed unconscious on top of the other guard.

"Did you kill him?" Sadie asked, her wide eyes frozen with shock.

Britt bent down, placing her index fingers on the guards' necks and feeling their slow pulsing heartbeats against her fingertips.

"No, they are just unconscious. For now," she said, lifting herself.

Sadie let out a deep sigh of relief. "I was really growing fond of the shorter one," she joked, jabbing at Britt's side with her elbow.

Britt's lips curved up into a half-smile, and she quickly straightened them out. She twisted her head, peering at their eerily quiet surroundings. They were lucky not to have attracted any unwanted attention. She looked up toward the ocean surface, where the moon and stars reflected down on the dimly lit sea. The inhabitants of the Kingdom of Atlantis were asleep in their beds, but they wouldn't be for long. Very soon, the sun would rise, blocking out the moon. "We need to get moving," Britt said, "but I'm not sure how we are going to get across to where we need to go without being seen. It will be daylight soon, and we still have to reach the back."

Sadie pointed to the guards lying unconscious on the seabed. She grinned. "I have an idea, but you're probably not going to like it," she said, nudging the short guard with her sequined tail.

Britt shook her head disapprovingly as she uttered the word, "Fine."

Sadie pulled the guard's helmet over her head. Its hard steel hung over her nose and shadowed her eyes, only revealing her thin-pressed pink lips. It was the final piece of her new attire. She looked down at the half-naked guard that she had robbed as she fidgeted with placing his armor around her waist. It hung loosely at her hips due to her petite size, and she felt around for a way to potentially tighten it. Her hands traced the outline of a brown satchel that hung at her side. As she reached into it, she felt her fingers glide across jagged metal grooves. She smiled as she pulled out a set of rounded silver handcuffs and held them out toward Britt.

Britt glided back, shaking her head vigorously, holding her hands up. "Absolutely not!" she shouted, swinging her arms.

Sadie inched forward, holding the cuffs out as if she were attempting to make an arrest. "You have to," she whined. "You can't be a believable prisoner if you aren't cuffed!"

Britt rolled her eyes. "Fine," she huffed, holding her arms out behind her back. "But it's not like your stature is exactly believable for a guard either!"

Sadie cuffed her quickly, snapping in the jagged metal grooves until she heard it lock.

Click. Click.

"Did you have to make it so tight?" Britt said,

trying to roll her wrists from under the metal constraints.

Sadie nodded, placing her hand on Britt's shoulder.

"Yes, it has to be credible. I promise as soon as we are completely out of open sight, I'll unlock you," she said reassuringly.

Britt scoffed under her breath, "You better."

Chapter 17

Neo rustled in his bed, twisting from side to side. He hadn't been able to sleep since King Oasis announced he would have to battle his brother. He rose from his bed, pulling a long sword from underneath his mattress. He had grown paranoid of his brother and of how far he would go to protect his *Inked* love. He rubbed at his sunken eyes as he made his way down to the marbled foyer and outside the great jeweled double doors of the castle. It was still nightfall when Neo arrived at the stables to practice his combat skills. As he lifted his steel sword, a small guard swam by with a familiar-looking prisoner. He dug the blade into the sandy seafloor as he called out to the petite-framed watch guard. "Over here," he said, waving one of his hands.

Sadie froze as she gripped tightly onto Britt's cuffed arms. Her face was flush and warm against the steel of her stolen helmet, and her heart banged against her chest, threatening to rip through her ribs. "The prince saw us," she whispered to Britt. "Don't react."

Sadie spun around to face Neo, pushing her shoulders back as she puffed out her chest. "Yes, sir!" she said, deepening her voice. She raised her hand to her forehead in an awkward salute.

Britt glared sharply at Neo from Sadie's side. Her fingers clutched behind her back as she imagined them wrapped around his broad neck, choking the life out of him.

He was smiling politely at Sadie with a pitying smile that the rich often threw to their servants. "You are awfully small for one of my father's guards," he said, tilting his head, "but if you were able to catch one of those foul creatures, you are well-trained and deserving of the cause." He paced around them.

Sadie bowed her head, and Britt's nostrils flared as she traced him with her eyes. "Thank you, sir."

"Where did you find her?" Neo asked, having finished his laps around them. He bent his head to get a closer look at Sadie's masked face as she squirmed uncomfortably under his gaze. The hairs on the back of her neck stood as if she had been electrocuted as she bent further down into a mock bow. "She was trying to break into the castle, sir," Sadie murmured quickly.

"Well," Neo said and smirked. "Chin up then, for a job well done." His sharp green eyes widened, as he tilted his head peering through Sadie's steel helmet as if he had laser vision. She lifted her head and turned her back toward Neo, attempting to avoid his direct stare.

"Thank you, sir. I really must be going." Sadie pulled on the looped chain of Britt's handcuffs.

"Wait a second, soldier," Neo said, grabbing Sadie's right shoulder. "Are you not going to the dungeon?"

"Yes sir," Sadie squeaked out as she froze under his grip.

He tightened his hold around Sadie's shoulder, spinning her around until her shielded face stood eye-level with his. "I only ask because you are going in the opposite direction." A dark and sinister grin washed across his face.

Sadie felt a hard tug at her side as Britt lashed forward with her tentacles, reaching out for Neo's pulsing neck. He sprung back, grabbing his abandoned sword, the steel point of which dug into the sand. As he aimed the sharpened blade at Britt's heart, Sadie pulled hard on the chains of her handcuffs causing both of them to tumble back onto the seafloor.

"Solider, you need to get better control of your prisoner," Neo shouted angrily. He towered over them.

Sadie lifted herself from the seafloor, dusting the sand off her armor. "Yes, sir. My apologies." She bent down to grab Britt by her cuffs. "You are going to get us both killed if you don't keep calm," she whispered in Britt's ear as she tugged her body up by the cuffs' metal chain.

Britt reluctantly let Sadie lift her, inhaling deeply as she straightened herself. Her face was flush and red as if lava rushed through her veins. She looked at the seafloor and counted backward in her head from ten, taking three more deep breaths.

Neo crossed his arms over his chest as Sadie muttered, "I'm very sorry. I'm new to the castle guard. I'll be on my way with the prisoner." She tugged at Britt's cuffs, giving her a side glance as she tried to maneuver past Neo. She reached into her holster where she had tucked the key to Britt's handcuffs.

The grooved metal fell into her palm.

"Halt!" Neo shouted, holding his hand up. "Where exactly is 'on your way?'"

Sadie froze, giving Britt's arm a tight squeeze as she sneakily unlocked her handcuffs. Britt rolled her wrists from behind her back, careful to not let the open metal cuffs drop from her hands. "Sir," Sadie said as her voice shook unsteadily. "Uh…um…the King…uh…asked me to bring the prisoners directly to him before the dungeon. Those are my orders."

Neo's face twisted into a darkened wide grin. "Did he now?" he asked, wrapping his arm around Sadie's trembling shoulders. "I was headed to see the King myself. I'll accompany you, even make sure you're rewarded for your catch." Neo pushed Britt forcefully with his free hand, causing her to stumble forward. "You see," he snickered, gripping Sadie's shoulder tighter. "Sometimes, you have to be rough with the prisoners if you want them to move." He shoved Britt forward again as she whipped her head back, bearing her sharp pointed teeth in a growl.

Sadie ducked down out of Neo's grip, grasping the handle of the sword from the sheath on her side. She tugged at it, and the long reflective blade slid out of the leather casing mirroring her image on its shining surface. As she held it toward Neo's neck, she felt its weighty metal slipping in her tiny hands. It shook unsteadily as she pulled her helmet off with her free hand, letting her long green hair tumble down like a waterfall.

Neo laughed as he moved closer to her outstretched blade. "Little girl, what do you think you are going to do with that?" He ran the tip of his finger on the point of her sword.

Before Sadie could respond, Britt knocked Neo to the ground, pushing him hard with her tentacles. His head hit against the seafloor as she pressed the chain of the cuffs into his neck. Neo flopped on the floor, a fish out of the water as he struggled to breathe until eventually, his eyes rolled into the back of his head. He was out cold, unconscious and still.

Britt rose from the ground and pulled the sword out of Sadie's small shaking hands, nearly ripping Sadie's arm off with her tug. She raised its pointed blade over Neo's unconscious body, ready to plunge the sharpened metal into his heart.

"Stop!" Sadie shrieked, rushing forward as she grabbed at Britt's shoulder, attempting to pull her back.

Britt shoved her advance back with her elbows.

"Why should I? He's the reason why my sister is in danger to begin with!" She gripped tighter on the sword as she lifted it back over Neo's body.

Sadie swam around to face Britt as her large doe eyes traced *the Inked* girl. "You're not a murderer," she said, tilting her head so her eyes were level with Britt's dark scowl.

"How do you know?" Britt hissed back.

"I just do," Sadie said, extending her hand for the sword. "Plus, if you kill the prince now, guards will be swarming every inch of this place, looking for his killer. We need to be able to get to your sister if you are to help her."

Britt huffed under her breath, "Fine." She handed the sword to Sadie who quickly tucked it back into her sheath where it could do no harm.

"Look. It's almost sunrise," Sadie said, pointing up toward the surface where an orange haze began to line the sky. "We need to get moving now, before this place swarms with merfolk."

The cellar door next to the stables was made of lined oak planks that had grown sea moss around its edges. Its curved black painted handles were rusted and stuck out like a bulbous sore. Sadie reached down, wrapping her thin finger around the handles, arms and neck straining as she pulled back. "It's stuck," she whined as she removed her tightened grip. Her arms shook at her sides.

"Let me try," Britt said, rolling her wrists a few times. She planted her tentacles firmly into the ground, feeling the sandy grains against her suckers as she leaned forward, grabbing the rusted handles. *One...two...three...* Britt counted in her head, pulling back as hard as she could. The door came flying off its rusted hinges as Britt tumbled back against Sadie, knocking her down.

"Ow!" Sadie yelped as she landed back on her elbows.

Britt extended her hand out to Sadie, who begrudgingly grabbed it as she lifted herself.

"Sorry about that," Britt said. "But I did get the door open."

Britt and Sadie peered into the open cellar as if gazing into the heart of a black hole. A winding tunnel had been laced with jellyfish guts, illuminating the way down to the vast darkness of the unknown.

"Yes," Sadie responded. "Yes, you did."

Chapter 18

Neo's eyes flickered open slowly and remained half-drawn as he lay on the seafloor. It must be sunrise based on precisely how the rays hit the ocean, pooling light deep down past the rolling surf. He reached for the top of his head, which throbbed as he propped up his body. *What day is it?*

Confused and disoriented, he finally remembered. A rush of anxiety and misery flooded his body as waves of nausea rose in the pit of his stomach like a storm. *It's competition day.* His gut sank, twisting into a tortured knot again. Just like yesterday. Tonight, he and his brother would be expected to enter the dreaded circular arena; his father would sit on a throne in the center of a crowd that would cheer as he killed his brother. *Or as my brother kills me.*

In his semiconscious state, Neo's mind had flashed back to when he and his brother were kids together. It was strange how the years had flown by, leaving but a trail of recollections. In his mind now were tiny snippets like flashbacks, a fragment of his life, then another, and another. They did not all join up and as the fragments reflected the passing years, he saw how he and his brother had gradually grown in different directions. When they were just boys, Ella would prepare them lunch as they play wrestled outside like bear cubs. As they got older, their interests grew farther and farther apart, no longer showing the common ground they had enjoyed earlier.

Kaleb was adventurous and a little crazy at times, but in a good way. He wanted to explore the entire ocean despite being forbidden from certain territories, while Neo enjoyed and reveled in the comforts of the kingdom. In truth, Neo was already looking ahead to when the kingdom would be in his own hands, under his rule. Neo wanted to live the good life and enjoy all its pleasures. After all, he had already made friends with the children of other high societal families, and they looked up to him as he was the King's son, due to become a great ruler, they hoped.

One day, when Kaleb was about twelve, he had come back from one of his explorations carrying a small blue sand crab. Neo was in his room with his two friends, Casco and Baric, when Kaleb swam by, holding the tiny, frail creature proudly in his hands. Baric had demanded to see it, and Kaleb had opened his palms, revealing the minuscule crab. Casco had snatched it out of his hands, dangling it by its claw as it flailed in pain.

Neo's friends could be cruel and brutal at times, no gentleness or refinement about them. Kaleb sometimes wondered aloud why a prince would even want to befriend such rough types. Even if they came from supposed 'good' families with privilege, they had no manners and no civility. In short, they seemed to be spoiled and ungrateful for everything they'd been given in life. But maybe Neo was already becoming more like them than Kaleb even realized. "Why are you bringing this disgusting animal from the outside into our kingdom?" Casco had hissed, swinging it back and forth between his hands. "Look at it! Ugly thing. It's scared, look!" Kaleb had tried to reach around Baric's massive body to rescue the tiny crab from Casco's grip, but the boy's body blocked the entire entrance of the room.

Neo had wanted to help his brother at that time—but there was a fear of rejection and loss of power that came with standing up to Baric and Casco. Neo's self-confidence was weak, and he had lived a life of protection so far, a little coddled, wary of too many things. Neo had already discovered that if he played along with bullies or with boys who were wayward, it somehow gave him reflected power too; he was bathed in whatever power the boys exuded themselves. "Okay, Casco, come on, just give it back to him," Neo had laughed. He was trying to take a middle ground, to please Kaleb and yet keep the boys happy. If he laughed at their cruelty, it would keep them on his side. So he believed.

But Casco shot Neo a dirty look. "You're just going to allow him to bring any old dirty creature into the kingdom?" he said, challenging Neo as he tossed him the tiny crab.

Neo had looked down at the small crab for just a second. Its pincer dangled off its arm. When he looked back up, Casco was still glaring at him, waiting for a response. "No, of course not," Neo had quickly spouted, flinging the crab back to Casco as he forced a grin on his face. "Disgusting thing," Neo spat. "Kaleb, why bring that filthy beast in here to us?"

The crab had eventually died from being tossed back and forth, and Kaleb was devastated. He barely spoke to Neo after that. An animosity had grown between them. Neo was upset Kaleb could never forgive him, and Kaleb was disappointed that Neo would never stand up to his friends.

Neo turned his head to see the blurry outline of three mermaids approaching.

"Prince Neo," Athena called out, swimming over to him with two friends. "What are you doing on the seafloor?" Her blonde hair floated overtop him in curly spirals as she looked down, staring at him with sapphire eyes. Athena's two friends huddled each side of her. Both were stunning, one with auburn red hair and the other with shimmering purple fins, but neither was anything near as striking as Athena. Most of the men in Atlantis would say she had her own gravitational pull.

Neo sprang up, brushing himself off as he puffed out his chest. "Hello ladies," he nodded as he beamed at Athena and her two gorgeous friends. He never quite understood why Athena had a thing for his brother and not for him. They were alike, were they not? So it made no sense at all. Despite sharing his interest in her with his father, the King still insisted that she was to marry Kaleb. Quietly, his father believed that Athena would stifle Kaleb's need for exploration and put him back on the right track.

"No need to worry about anything," Neo said, bending to grab his fallen sword off the floor. He dusted the sand off the blade and shoved it back into his sheath. "I must attend to some things. Have a nice day, ladies," he said, giving Athena and her crew a wink.

Athena smiled politely, nodding her head. Her blonde hair swayed in front of her face, and she pushed it back with slim polished fingers, running her thin hands past her ear and down her neck. "We are looking forward to the competition tonight," Athena blurted out before Neo could leave, "Do you know where your brother is? I have something to give him. Before it begins."

Her left hand clutched a necklace made of pearly white seashells and as Neo looked down, he clenched his teeth with bitter jealousy. He knew she hoped that Kaleb was the winner, and he would only be a consolation prize. He seethed inside, wondering what was so special about Kaleb. "What is it about my brother that you find so appealing?" Neo's nostrils flared as he spoke. He couldn't suppress his question anymore.

The truth was, Athena was used to getting what she wanted. The less interest that Kaleb showed her, the more convinced she felt she needed him. Neo, conversely, never stopped fawning over her and making his jealousy obvious, driving her away.

The whole kingdom fawned over her perfect beauty, except for Kaleb. So, when King Oasis promised her father one of his sons for marriage, she was given a choice and picked Kaleb. She was convinced he would grow to love her. In her mind, she was the best of all the available mermaids, after all. So, of course he would love her—he couldn't avoid it. "Well, if you win tonight's competition, you won't have to worry about that," Athena snarled as she flipped her hair and swam away with her two friends.

Neo balled his hands into a fist as he watched her fade into the distance.

He took a deep gulp of the salty ocean water and stormed off to find Baric and Casco as he usually did when he was upset about something. And boy, was he upset right now!

Chapter 19

Britt and Sadie leaped down through the open cellar door as if being swallowed whole by a whale. The walls glowed around them in florescent blue, just barely illuminating the path in front.

"You should probably get that sword out," Britt whispered to Sadie. She stared forward into the darkness.

Sadie pulled the long reflective sword out of her leather sheath. She hadn't noticed before, but its handle was made out of solid gold and shimmered in the dark, reminiscent of a treasure chest. She gripped it between her trembling hands, holding the unsteady blade out in front of her toward the darkness, using it as a kind of flashlight.

Sadie was used to feigning toughness; growing up, she had been considered a bit of a tomboy and had spent most of her time with young mermen around her age. Because of that choice of companion, she often got in trouble for roughhousing with the boys.

Her limbs stiffened as they traveled farther down into the winding pit of the unknown. She rolled her shoulders back as the hairs on her arms stood like saluting soldiers. The last time she had felt like this, she had followed her friends to the surface to check out a giant fishing boat docked close to Atlantis. A huge black net hung off the side of the boat, trapping small crabs in its overlapped nylon. Her friend Mason dared her to set the little writhing crustaceans all free, and Sadie had picked up a broken seashell to help her. As she cut into the twisted rope, her tail became tangled in its frayed remains. Mason had managed to get her out, but not without deep cuts ensuing to her tail.

She looked down at the scales that had regrown on her hips. The extraordinary healing had fortunately left behind nothing but a distant memory.

"Over there!" Britt said, pointing her finger. They had reached the end of the windy tunnel, where three colorful doors stood in a row, each one painted a different color. *One red. One blue. One yellow.* "Which door do we use?" Britt asked Sadie as if she had some secret map.

Sadie shrugged. "I'm really not sure." She traced each door with her eyes, scanning back and forth between the three. They were identical in size, all built out of wood but painted in these different vibrant hues.

What could the colors mean? Sadie looked down at the dirt ground. Her eyes widened. "What are you looking at?" Britt asked, tilting her head in confusion.

Sadie pointed to the floor below her. "I think it's another door. Look at how the ground is uneven. The edges are sticking up as if someone forgot to properly shut it."

Britt bent down, leveling her face with the ground. Her eyes caught a glimmer of light flickering out of the unsealed edge.

"You're right. It's another door. But why would someone go through all the trouble to hide it?" Britt asked, digging her fingers into the opening.

Sadie swam over to the other side, scraping dirt

away from the edge of the door until she was able to get her pointer finger under. "There must be something important down there," she responded. She tried to peer into the illuminated gap. *They went down this way!*

The voices of mermen echoed down the winding tunnel, bouncing off narrow walls.

"The prince must have alerted them," Sadie squealed as her eyes darted between the dark tunnel through which they had come and the hidden door that was still firmly stuck in place.

"We have to get this door open now!" Britt said, digging her fingers as deep as they would go into the open groove.

Sadie and Britt tugged hard on the door until they heard a click. It sounded as if a chain latch had finally come loose. The door pulled up like a lift, allowing them to slip right in and travel down as it sealed them within its hidden walls. A bright light stood at the end of a long straight tunnel where the lift came to a stop.

"Come on," Britt said, tugging on Sadie's arm as she moved toward the light.

The tunnel opened to a circular white room lined with weapons and armor. In the center was a large translucent box that illuminated the glowing bright white light. It was sealed tightly with a large metal lock. "Something is in there," Britt said, swimming around the large box, circling. She placed her hand on its surface and felt a warm vibration of steady twisting limbs, similar to resting a palm onto the kicking belly of a pregnant mother.

Sadie grabbed a large wooden-handled ax that had been hung up decoratively on the left wall. "Here," she said, handing it to Britt.

Britt grabbed the ax, lifting it high above her head and slamming it down hard against the metal lock. Despite using most of her strength, it barely dented. She sighed heavily as she lifted the ax again, slamming it down with greater force, but the lock still would not crack. "This is impossible!" she shouted, hurling the ax to the ground in frustration.

Sadie bent down, picking the cast-off tool off the floor. "Let me try," she said, motioning for Britt to move out of the way.

"Yeah, okay," Britt responded sarcastically. She crossed her arms over her chest and maneuvered herself away from the metal lock. "Can't wait to see. This should be interesting."

Sadie lifted the large ax up over her head. It was almost as tall as she was and seemed comically large in her tiny hands. She focused her eyes on the lock and propelled herself up as she swung the ax down with great force. The metal lock came flying off the box, flinging toward Britt, who quickly dodged out of the way as it cracked into the wall behind her head. It left a dent.

Sadie turned and gave Britt a cocky little smile and a bow while throwing the ax to the floor.

"Yeah, whatever… I would have gotten it eventually," Britt said, rolling her eyes.

Sadie ran her fingers across the open metal latch, wondering what was so important that it had to be sealed tightly in a box. *Important or dangerous?* She had heard stories of Pandora's Box and certainly didn't want to be responsible for letting all the world's evil run rampant. "Do you think we should really open it?" she asked.

Britt teased as she grabbed one side of the lid. "Guess you're not the super badass you thought you were five minutes ago, huh?...Help me pull it up."

"Ok," Sadie sighed begrudgingly. "But if we open up some portal to the underworld, it's on you."

Britt shrugged as though she didn't much care. The lid was made of solid steel that had been painted black, and the girl's arms strained as she pulled and tugged as if they were trying to get a jar open that had been sealed too tightly. The veins in their arms bulged until eventually, the lid came loose with a pop. They carried the heavy lid to the side, propping it up against the rounded wall as they caught their breath. The contents inside the open box seemed to whisper to them like hushed voices carried by the wind, or perhaps an indiscernible chatter.

"Should we look together?" Sadie asked. Her voice cracked as she grabbed Britt's hand.

The ax that Sadie had thrown to the ground earlier lay in front of Britt's tentacles. She bent down to grab it. "Let's do this," Britt replied, moving forward with the ax tightly gripped in her left palm as Sadie clutched at her right hand and came following behind her.

Sadie and Britt leaned over the edge of the box and peered at the contents inside.

Three gray bottle-nosed dolphins were huddled on top of each other like cuddling seals. Their skin had been cut, bearing small slashes. A bright silver liquid leaking from their wounds.

Sadie's mouth twitched into a disgusted frown as she pushed herself back from the box edge. "This isn't a box. It's a tank...no, a prison. Why even do this?" Sadie asked dejectedly.

Britt dropped her ax to the floor and reached her hand into the tank. The dolphins flattened their bodies to avoid her touch, as the tips of her fingers grazed gently on one of their backs. She pulled her hand back and stared at the silvery liquid that moved down her fingers and into her palm. It danced in the center of her hand as if it had a life of its own, and then disappeared into her skin, a magic trick all of its own.

"Whoa, that was weird," Sadie said, watching as she inched her body back cautiously.

Britt froze as she stared down at her hand, flipping it back and forth.

She remembered her sister telling her a story of their great ancestor, a giant octopus, and the pauper who stole her magic dolphins. Yuri had always believed her stories to be true and told them as if they were relics from history. Britt, however, never believed in magic like Yuri did. To her, it was just another story her sister told to make them feel proud they weren't born mermaids. "We need to get them out," Britt said as her eyes darted between Sadie and the translucent box.

Sadie nodded. "Okay, grab them out and I'll try to keep them together."

Britt extended her arm into the tank, leaning her body over its edge so her tentacles dangled off the ground. As her fingers closed in on one of the dolphins, there flashed a great burst of light. Then came a loud *whoosh!* Britt went flying black, slamming into Sadie who was pinned against the wall.

"Ow," Sadie said as she rubbed the back of her shoulder which had landed on a pointed helmet. It pierced right through the guard's armor she wore. "What was that?"

"I don't know," Britt said as she lifted herself off the floor, inspecting her body for cuts. "It was like some sort of defense mechanism."

Sadie approached the tank slowly and ran her hand across its side. "Maybe they're just not used to the seeing your kind. No offense."

Britt lifted her arm and pointed to the tank. "Well, by all means then…give it a go, mermaid," she said sarcastically.

Sadie reached her hand in hesitantly, her fingers barely making it over the edge. *Whoosh!* A piercing bright light filled the room, temporarily blinding the girls and sending them flying back against the wall once again. Armor, weapons, and shields crashed down around them as they reached out their hands in a pointless attempt to grab one another. When their vision finally returned, Sadie pointed to the sword that had landed with its sharp pointed blade impaled into the ground right next to her tailfin. It was just millimeters away from having caused a terrible injury.

"Damn, that was close. Could've been—" She was going to say *fatal*. But what would have been the point in that? It was done now. And thankfully, they were both still in one piece.

Britt planted her tentacles into the floor decisively. Her suckers gripped tightly as she pulled the sword out of the ground. "Well, that wasn't so good—I don't think we should try that again," she said, tossing the sword to the other end of the room. The heavy weapon clanged loudly as it hit the wall.

Sadie nodded, biting her lip at the thought of how that could have ended up. She examined Britt's long black tentacles that moved like wild vines around her.

A wide grin crossed over her face. She'd just had an idea.

Britt crossed her arms over her chest, her brows furrowing. "Why are you looking at me like that?"

Sadie sprang up from the ground and swam circles around Britt.

"Okay, hear me out on this. Maybe, I was wrong before and those dolphins don't want to be picked up by any hands. Maybe they need to be picked up by something more closely related to the sea," Sadie said, pausing to point at her tentacles. "You should try again, don't you think?"

Britt huffed under her breath. She almost rolled her eyes, but there was no point in that either.

"You've got to be kidding! We'll probably just get thrown back against the wall again, and this time, you'll actually get speared," Britt said, pointing to the long blade pulled free of the ground.

Sadie crossed her arm over her chest as she leaned her hips to one side. "Okay, you know what? Why don't we just leave them here then? Do you want to just abandon them here to die?" Sadie asked sarcastically as she freed one crossed arm to point at the tank before continuing, "I've gotten you this far, and without me, we wouldn't even be in the kingdom."

"But you… You keep fighting every idea I have. Let's just cut to the chase here. Is it because I'm younger or because I'm a mermaid and it kills you that you actually might get to like me?"

Britt's heart panged in her chest as if Sadie's words had stung her. She looked down at the ground, ashamed as she rubbed at the back of her neck nervously. Perhaps Sadie was right, and she was unknowingly skeptical of her. Sadie was everything Britt wished she could have been growing up. Even with her lower-class status, she was still part of Atlantis. She was still part of a community that didn't see her as a creature who needed to be destroyed.

"I'm sorry; you are right," Britt said, looking up at Sadie. "I really wouldn't have gotten this far without your help. I'm not used to mermaids being nice to my sisters or me. But you are right, I do like you, and I owe you an apology and a thank you."

Sadie held her crossed-arm stance as she tilted her head. "Does that mean you'll try my idea?"

Britt nodded as she grinned. "Yes, but if we get burnt to a crisp by this light blast, I'm blaming you."

Sadie laughed, lowering her crossed arms as if dropping a protective shield. "That's fair," she responded, smiling.

Britt approached the tank. She shuffled slowly and hesitantly forward. The blowback the second time had been a lot worse than the first, and she was afraid another blast might kill them. Only a cat had nine lives. It seemed they were getting into too many scrapes, and too frequently to come out of it well another time. She paused in front of the tank and leaned her body over to peer into the square opening. The dolphins seemed very small and frightened as the three huddled up together in the right corner. It reminded her of herself and her two sisters. When they were little, they used to cuddle up together in the same hammock before bed. They had always protected each other.

She lifted up two of her front tentacles, displaying the lime green suckers that she used to catch her family breakfast most mornings. "Do you really have a good feeling about this?" Britt said, twisting her neck around so her head faced Sadie.

"Just try. What other option do we have? I'm right here with you," Sadie said, placing her hand on Britt's back.

Britt cautiously dipped her tentacles into the tank, letting them sway gently above the dolphins before plunging forward. She shut her eyes, waiting for a sharp zap to jolt up her tentacles and electrocute Sadie and herself with a blast of light, but it didn't happen. She cracked her eyes open to find the three small dolphins swimming laps around her tentacles as if she were their mother.

Before Britt could truly process what was happening, Sadie squealed in a high-pitched voice, "Aw, they love you!" She followed up with, "I was only about eighty-five percent on that working!"

Britt sighed as she shook her head disapprovingly. "Glad you find this so amusing." Each dolphin Britt pulled out of the tank did laps around the circular room, carefully zigging and zagging to avoid going anywhere near Sadie.

"Why don't they like me?" Sadie asked woefully as she watched them zip around, avoiding her the same way they would a predator.

"Well that's a change," Britt said. *For once, I'm liked more than the mermaid.*

The dolphins' bodies were riddled with tiny slashes and cuts. Most had healed but some were still fresh. Britt swam over to one, lifting it with her tentacles. "I think their abuser is probably someone like you," she said, examining the dolphin's tiny body.

It was only four or five feet long as if its growth

had been stunted at an early age. The open cuts on its body leaked the familiar silver substance that had disappeared into her palms earlier. She was careful not to touch any open wounds with her tentacles.

She ever so gently placed the dolphin back down.

"I would never hurt a dolphin," Sadie said sadly as she looked down at the floor, her shoulders drooping like a wilted flower. "Why would anyone do this?"

"I'm not sure," Britt replied. "But I think I might have an…"

A creak sounded.

"What was that?!" Sadie said, cutting Britt off, as her eyes darted toward the tunnel from which they had come.

Britt froze, listening to the faint sound of murmured talking that seemed to get louder every second she stilled. She looked around at the scattered armor and weapons that had fallen on the floor, and at the loose dolphins that zipped around them free from the binds of the square tank. "Someone's coming. Help me hang this stuff back on the walls," she whispered as she grabbed one of the fallen shields behind her, hanging it back up on an open golden hook on the wall.

They both spun quickly around each other like spiders trying to rebuild a web exactly the same way it had been before a storm. Both were hoping not to make any mistakes because the voices that seemed to get closer every moment would not be forgiving if they knew intruders were touching their precious hidden gems.

When everything was back on the wall in its proper place, Britt coiled her tentacles around the three dolphins blanket-style, pulling them close to her side.

"We need to hide," she said, looking around the circular room for any nook or cranny they would be able to crawl into. Their options were limited. The circular room had no other entrance or exit aside from the dark hall via which they had entered. It had become the only pathway for the muffled voices echoing down into the chamber where Sadie and Britt were trapped. There were no windows in the circular white room, just walls decorated with armor, weapons, shields, and a square translucent tank that sat in the middle.

"I'm sorry," Britt whispered, looking down at the dolphins that clung to her sides as she lifted herself into the tank, squeezing the creatures tightly in her tentacles. They thrashed beneath her suckers like toddlers throwing a tantrum as they let out a loud screeching cry that sent a pang running through Britt's heart.

She reached her arm out to Sadie. "Come on, hurry up!"

"Wait, the lid!" Sadie said. She went swimming over to the wall where they had leaned the painted black steel top. Sadie tugged as she swam backwards, dragging the lid across the ground. The muscles in her thin arms twitched as she stopped in front of the square translucent box.

Britt leaned her body forward, throwing two of her free tentacles over the edge of the container. She suctioned them tightly to the sides of the steel top, helping Sadie lift it up over her head. "Get in," Britt whispered as the heavy lid maneuvered over her head, sliding down as her green suckers began to lose their grip on the steel top.

Sadie gripped at the sides of the tank, pushing herself up and over the ledge. The guard's armor she was wearing scratched against the sides of the tank and as she moved, it sounded like nails on a chalkboard. *Scrrrrrrrkkkkk.* She had barely gotten her body halfway into the tank when the dolphins screeched, sending small sparks of hot white light flying off their bodies.

"Ow," Britt shouted, unraveling her tentacles that had been coiled around the dolphins. She quickly smacked her hand over her mouth, hoping that her scream hadn't given them away.

Sadie panicked, pushing herself away from the tank so hard that she toppled onto the ground, landing on her elbows with a loud clank. She looked up at Britt with woeful eyes. "What do I do? They won't let me in."

Britt gazed down at Sadie who was still wearing the guard's armor, minus a helmet. Her eyes darted toward the entrance as the faint voices had become words traveling in a steady stream toward them. "Competition…Arena…My sons…"

"Quick, grab the helmet off the wall," Britt said, pointing to a sizable, spiked metal helmet with small eye slits. The helmet would cover her whole face, making her look like a porcupine.

Sadie did as she was told, wrapping her long green hair into a bun at the top of her head and pulling the spiked metal helmet down over her face.

"Now…what?" she asked. Her breathing had become rapid, and she spoke as if choking on marbles as her body trembled with fear.

Britt scanned the room. "There," she said, pointing to the wall. "See that giant metal shield? Grab it and go lean against the wall as still as you can, with the shield blocking your tailfin."

Sadie pulled the circular metal shield off the wall. It had been painted in blue and red spirals with a large black stamp of a trident in the center as a reminder of the King. She pushed herself up against the wall, holding the shield out in front of her shimmering tailfin, blocking her colorful scales from sight.

"Don't move. I'll be right here if you need me. Hopefully, they won't notice the lock is broken on this tank," Britt said as she sank into the square box, pulling the large black cover down with her.

We must prepare the arena for battle.

King Oasis swam into the circular room, scratching at his beard as though a touch confused. His red cape danced behind him as his advisor swayed by his side with a clipboard. He was a plump, short merman with a receding hairline and bucktoothed overbite. "I want all these weapons moved into the arena for tonight," the King said, spinning around as he gestured to the walls.

His advisor followed him closely, scribbling notes onto the clipboard. "Yes, of course, sir," he sniveled back as he ran his tongue over large protruding teeth.

The King's fingers dragged across the tank in the center of the room as his eyes focused on a piercing-looking helmet. The dolphins shrieked from inside the illuminating box as he tap-tapped his fingers along the glass, swimming toward the odd-looking metal helmet.

He stopped in front of Sadie, examining its sharp spikes.

Sadie froze with fear, shutting her eyes as the King reached out with his pointer finger, touching one of the spikes on her helmet and accidentally pricking himself.

"Sharp," he said, looking down at his freshly cut

index finger that now matched his cape. His eyes darted up toward Sadie's shield, then back to the helmet. "When did we get this mannequin?" he asked, turning to his advisor.

"I'm…I'm not sure, sir." His advisor's voice shuddered as he spoke. "Should…should…I have it removed?" His advisor held his breath as his hands clutched in front of him nervously. He looked as though he was praying for a swift end.

The King ran his hand across the blue and red painted metal shield as Sadie stiffened her body like a statue trying not to move an inch. "No, no, I rather like it. But this shield, have some solider bring it up later along with the spiked helmet," the King said, examining his reflection in its shining metal.

His advisor let out a deep sigh of relief as he jotted more notes onto his board. "Of course, sir, right away," he said, bowing his balding head.

The King looked down at the ratty-looking merman. "You're excused," he said, flicking his hand in a shooing motion.

Without looking up, the advisor scattered quickly to the darkened hall via which they'd come, like cockroaches running from the light. He didn't need to be asked twice.

When he was finally gone, the King looked over at the translucent tank in which Britt sat huddled, grasping tightly to the dolphins, her teeth clenched. "How are my babies doing?" he said menacingly as he leaned over, pressing his ear against the tank.

The loud screeching of the dolphins echoed through the chamber as Britt held her hands to her pounding eardrums.

"Hush now," the King said. "I'll be back soon." He tapped the translucent glass one last time with his hand before straightening himself up and swimming to exit, leaving Britt and Sadie trembling in their hiding spaces.

Chapter 20

Tanis had been swimming as fast as she could as her blue hair chased behind her, blending into the sea like liquid. It had now been over an hour with one of the two guards directly behind her. She had managed to shake off the younger, slightly less fit guard somewhere along the border of the kingdom. He huffed and puffed until he could no longer keep up the chase.

Clearly, he needs more training. She thought once she had crossed back into her territory that the second guard would have given up, but that wasn't the case. Unfortunately, she had underestimated how well-trained an older guard of Atlantis would be.

Tanis turned her head to see his beaky-nosed face propelling himself toward her like a bird diving for prey. *Damn, he's still behind me!* His golden armor shimmered in the water as his gray tail made swift, powerful waves. *I'm not going to make it,* she thought as she gulped in water frantically through her gills. Her vision started to blur around her, making everything seem hazy. She couldn't catch her breath fast enough to make it stop. Her tunnel vision eyes peered forward as she gulped short breaths.

She had made it all the way back to the large boulder overlooking the statuesque lighthouse, to the rock where this had all started. The guard was now gaining on her as her pace unintentionally slowed as if she were a motorboat that had run out of gas. He was now just an arm's length away and reached forward, trying to grab one of her long tentacles that swayed behind her. His callused fingertips scraped against her inky skin like sandpaper as she pushed herself forward. A puff of murky black released from her suckers, causing the water to become clouded behind her. The guard cried out profanities, coughing in between each venomous word, inhaling the hazy water as he swam through.

She paused at the large boulder to briefly catch her breath, leaning some of her weight on its cool gray stone. *If I can get close enough to the humans' shore, maybe he won't follow me.* Tanis turned her head to see her black ink cloud getting lighter and lighter as it dispersed into the water. Soon, the guard would be able to see again, and it would be another hour before she regenerated enough ink for another blast. She would have to take her chance with the humans. She swam quickly toward the shore. Her eyes focused on the sandy pink beach, careful not to turn her head and lose her speed. When she was a few meters away from land, she stopped and turned her head as she lifted her hand over her eyes to block out the sun.

The guard swayed by the boulder, gripping his fists tightly at his side as he stared down Tanis. She returned his harsh gaze with her own furrowed glower. She had gone too far. Even he as a trained Atlantis soldier knew how dangerous humans could be. As they continued their staring contest, he calculated the risk in his head and decided it wasn't worth potentially being seen by them. He huffed under his breath as he spun around, leaving Tanis swaying by the beach.

Two little children were playing on the sandy shore, building sandcastles out of colorful plastic buckets. Tanis watched as the little girl in the pink polka-dot swimsuit slammed her hand down on the freshly made dune, causing it to topple. Her brother sat next to her, neatly piling his mounds with his blue bucket. His eyes squinted as he caught a glimpse of Tanis in the water. He stood up and waved.

His small stature—only about three feet tall—looked like that of a tiny doll in green swim trunks. The little girl followed his lead and stood on her tippy toes, staring out toward the ocean.

"Look, it's a lady in water," the little boy said, pointing to Tanis as his light-blond hair blew in the ocean breeze.

Tanis froze as she sank her body deeper into the ocean, so only her head was visible.

The little girl squinted. The sunlight beamed down onto her long golden wavy hair that hung down to her waist. "Her hair is blue," she squeaked out in awe as she stepped forward in her bright pink polka-dot swimsuit. Her foot knocked into the purple bucket that lay in front of her, and it rolled down the embankment toward the sea. Tanis watched in horror as the little girl sprinted toward the ocean waves. *Where are her parents?* Her chubby legs wobbled unsteadily in the sand.

"Lea!" the little boy cried out, chasing after his sister as the bucket rolled into the water.

The tide was strong, and crashing waves hit hard against the sand with a roar, pulling the bucket deeper into the ocean. Lea jumped in after it and the ocean engulfed her, pulling her out to sea. She let out a blood-curdling scream as her brother stood motionless on the beach. His eyes were wide and he wanted to yell for help but was petrified to move or form words.

Lea's arms flailed in the water as Tanis rushed to her side, reaching out her tentacles. The little girl clung to her as Tanis lifted her out of the water and dropped her tired and limp body onto the sandy beach.

The boy's eyes widened farther as he watched Tanis hovering over his sister's body with her eight long protruding tentacles moving like charmed snakes. "Mom…mom…*Mom!*" he screamed, still frozen in place.

Tanis' eyes welled up with tears as she retreated into the ocean. Her heart throbbed as she looked back safely from the boulder. The little boy had screamed as if she were a monster ready to gobble up his little sister. She sighed as she leaned her head against the hard rock, watching the beach as though this was her job.

A tall woman with long blonde hair and wearing a bright daisy sundress and big sun hat ran down toward the beach from the lighthouse. She scooped the little girl up into her arms, cradling her up against her chest. The little boy pointed to the water, and the woman lifted one of her hands up over her eyes.

Tanis quickly ducked behind the boulder and out of sight. When she peeked her head back out again, the woman was walking up the beach toward the lighthouse with her daughter flung over her shoulder and her son holding her hand.

A shiver ran down Tanis' body, and she rubbed at the sides of her arms with her hands. She had never been alone like this. Seeing a family together had made her realize just how much she missed her own. She took a few deep breaths as she rubbed at her teary eyes. *I have to go back and help them.* She dove face down into the water, letting the cold sea hit up against her face as she swam deeper down.

Chapter 21

Tanis had no plan as she swam aimlessly toward the kingdom. By now, she was certain that the community was bustling with mermaids and mermen going about their day, not to mention all the soldiers guarding the castle. It was about an hour's trip before the castle finally came into sight again. It looked so different to her in the daylight than it had yesterday. Now, she could see the way its pointed towers shimmered in the ocean light as they shot up to the sky like golden missiles, each one ready to blast off and steal her sisters away forever.

She watched from a safe distance, perched upon a mound that lay on the outskirts of Atlantis as merfolk left their homes to go about their duties. They looked tiny in her view, similar to the small wooden characters that popped out of cuckoo clocks and did a little dance before twisting back into their homes. Only here, most of their homes were made out of dilapidated scrap metal and not designed with intricate wood carvings. A nausea rose in the back of her throat as she thought about how different the houses looked closer to the gate. Shambles of junk morphed into well-crafted, white-pillared beauties, a home that she had never known.

She made her way down, slinking furtively behind each scrap metal house, careful to not be seen as a group of boisterous teens passed by. Her back pressed hard against the dented steel of one of the homes as she inhaled deeply, holding in her breath, filled with fear. Most fortunately for her, they were way too distracted in their tomfoolery to notice her. She let out a great sigh of relief and craned her neck to look over at the golden castle gate.

Tanis watched silently, acting as a scouting spy as a merman pushed a black cart of freshly made shields up to the gate. His lips moved in an unreadable motion, and the guards opened the gateway as if he had said some magical password. *Abracadabra.*

Fifteen minutes later, he came back out with an empty cart. *This is my way in,* she thought.

She made her first move, hastily whirling her body toward the back of another shack-like home. As she crouched down in the shadows of its slanted roof, she took a moment to watch the street and observe all the merfolk going about their day. The majority wore no jewels or gems, and their tops were made of woven kelp. But, sprinkled into the mix were smaller groups of the wealthy who traveled together in a tight pack, noses held high as they left their white-pillared homes closer to the gate, wearing colorful silk woven fabric brought down from the castle.

Tanis waited for a clearing in the street before scuttling across to the other side. She had made her way farther down toward the gate, ducking behind a white painted home. Across the street was a trading booth made of mahogany and garnished with all sorts of goods. She could smell the fresh slaughtered fish that sat next to a bin of clothing and jewels. *This must be how Sadie's family afforded food before her father left.*

Her mouth salivated as her stomach grumbled loudly. She hadn't eaten since yesterday morning, but the thought of stealing food was futile; there was just no way. The booth was heavily guarded and run by soldiers of the kingdom. Around the booth was a crowd of chattering merfolk, seemingly all willing to exchange whatever precious goods they owned for a small bite to eat.

Unfortunately for Tanis, this booth sat next to the blacksmith's shop where the black cart she had seen earlier was parked and waiting to be refilled. Tanis' eyes darted between the bustling booth and the black cart she needed to get to. Every few minutes, a portly older merman would come out and throw some shields and swords into it. *That must be the blacksmith.* She bent down to the ground, digging her fingers into the sand for something she could throw. The tiny grains worked their way under her fingernails, digging into the skin and chafing her raw.

A distraction.

The remaining loose sand ran through her fingers, unblemished by any rocks or shells. *Damn.* Tanis looked back up and noticed the house behind which she was veiled had some old shingles made from brick. She dug one of her tentacles into the small cracks and pulled. A piece of the shingle popped off with ease, and she placed it in her palm. *Easy enough.*

She tossed the piece of shingle in her hand a few times, feeling its weight as she set her eyes on one of the soldiers working the booth. *One chance.*

Tanis pulled her arm back toward her ears and pushed the heavy brick forward. It spiraled through the water like a torpedo, hitting the soldier on the left side of his head with a loud thud.

"Who did that?" he screamed, knocking the table in front of him, sending an assortment of fish, woven knitted tops, and jewels tumbling to the seabed. He gripped at his sword tightly holstered at his side as the surrounding merfolk let out a few gasps, backing away from the toppled booth.

"Who did what, sir? Who has created this mess?"

Out of the mass, a red-haired merboy swam forward, scratching at his bright fiery head. His youthful face was sun-kissed with freckles and as he moved like a wind-up doll, the wide eyes of the rest of the crowd followed him silently like an ominous warning.

The soldier's face turned red upon seeing the boy, and he reached out his clenched hands to grab the merboy by his collar, throwing him into the dilapidated remains of the booth. The boy's body slammed to the floor. "You want to be smart with me?" the soldier said, giving him a hard whack with his thick gray and black shimmering tail.

Tanis winced from her hiding spot, feeling nausea building back up in the pit of her stomach. She couldn't help but feel guilt for what she had done. She shook her head, taking a deep breath of water in. Now was her time to move. A circle had formed around the merboy and the soldier, and this mob wouldn't stay occupied for too much longer.

"I'm sorry," Tanis whispered under her breath.

Vibrant blood pooled out from behind the mobbed circle.

She quickly diverted her attention to the blacksmith's unattended cart and counted to three before hurdling her body forward like a stealthy cat leaping off a steep edge. Her body landed into the cart, and she froze there completely still for a moment, waiting to be caught as her heart banged against her chest.

"I guess you'll think twice before talking back!" The soldier's voice echoed through the water.

The public beating must be over, Tanis thought as she pushed some of the armor and shields already in the cart over her body. She lay still for another moment before she heard the youthful voice of a young merman.

"These too, Dad?"

His lanky boyish frame hung over the cart as his thin arms held up two massive helmets embedded with spikes.

"Yes, the King ordered more of those," a deeper voice responded.

Must be the blacksmith.

The blacksmith's son tossed them into the cart, carelessly. They tumbled down, clattering against the swords and shields as one of the spikes pierced the skin on Tanis' ribs. She bit her lips hard between her teeth to avoid making a sound as her eyes flooded.

"That should be everything," Tanis heard the blacksmith say, followed by three taps on the side of the cart. The cart shuffled under her, and soon she was moving.

My plan is working.

Suddenly, the cart came to a jolting stop, and Tanis braced her hand against the sides, trying to hold her body still. *Have we reached the gate?*

"What's this?" she heard the deep raspy voice of a man say. "More armor, swords, and helmets as requested by the King." The blacksmith's son's voice shook as he spoke.

"Is that so?" the guard said, reaching his hand down into the cart.

His pudgy fingers grazed over Tanis' face. She flattened her body as far as she could to avoid his touch. The guard's fingers wrapped around a spiked helmet next to her face and lifted it up. He spun the helmet in his hand, examining the short, sharpened spears that protruded out of its metal frame. "Look at this," the guard said with amusement. "I think I'll keep this one."

The blacksmith's son looked down at the ground as his shaggy blond bangs fell forward into his eyes. "But sir," he said meekly. "Those are supposed to be for the King."

The guard reached out his pudgy fingers and grabbed the blacksmith's son's face, pinching at his cheeks. "Are you going to tell him?" the guard said, tilting his eyes to darkly gaze upon the boy.

"N…n…n…no," the blacksmith's son stuttered back nervously as his hands tapped at his sides.

The guard dropped his grip on the boy's face, leaving red welts where his fingers had dug.

Tanis heard the squeaking of the rusty hinge as the gate cracked open. She held her breath deeply, careful not to let out a peep. *I'm almost through.*

"Proceed forward."

Without another word, the cart was on the move again, and Tanis smirked triumphantly to herself, letting out a quiet sigh of relief.

Chapter 22

Kaleb sat in the center of the sandy circular battle arena with his face buried in his hands. His bloodshot eyes peered up at the empty stadium chairs which sat on an incline around the arena. Soon, these chairs would be filled with cheering merfolk hungry for blood. His father would sit directly in the center of the stadium on his golden throne. And it was from this throne that his father would soon condemn one of his sons to death.

Pfft. Father. Kaleb had never even seen King Oasis as a father.

He and his brother had been fully raised by their caretaker, Ella, who acted as a mother to both of them and was with them every step of the way. She taught them how to swim, pack their lunches, and even yelled at them when they misbehaved. Their father treated them more like a prized medal that he had won, a way to keep his bloodline healthy.

Ella had caused a scene when she found out about the competition. Her fragile eighty-year-old body stormed into the King's chamber, bursting into tears and demanding that he cancelled this "debauchery of a competition." She didn't want her "sons" hurt. King Oasis had found her outburst to be quite amusing until she collapsed from the stress, and he had to get his guards to remove her body from his chambers, a most uncomfortable event indeed.

When Kaleb had heard what happened, he had gone to her room to check on her. He was too late, though; by now, her heart had given out. She was lying like a withered mummy on her bed, stiff and clammy with rigor mortis and mottled bluish skin and lips. Her hand was stuck, reaching toward the sky as if she had been trying to pull herself up again with one last ounce of fight. Kaleb cried out for help, but it was no use. The only parent he had ever known was dead. Ella was gone.

Kaleb drew her name into the sand below him with his fingers. *E-L-L-A. Well, maybe it is better you aren't around to watch the two boys you raised kill each other.*

"What are you doing here?" Neo's voice bellowed from the tunneled entrance. He leaned against its narrow opening, the only way in and out of the arena's center, aside from a small shaft-like elevator in the center of the stadium. This was nestled deep in the ground and required the King's permission to access it. That would be the way they would enter the fight.

Kaleb leaped up startled as he spun to face Neo with a scowl. "It's your fault! She is dead!" he screamed, charging at Neo and pushing him up against the curved cement wall next to the narrow entrance.

Neo grabbed Kaleb's arms, pushing him back into the sand. "I loved Ella too! Maybe it's your fault for mingling with that creature! We wouldn't even be here if you'd just settled down with a mermaid like any sensible person would've done. You have an entire kingdom swooning over you, and you chose *that*. Was I just supposed to let my brother be taken advantage of by one of *the Inked?"* Neo shouted angrily as the veins bulged in his neck.

Kaleb sprang from the sandy arena ground, dusting the sand off his body. "Tonight!" he sneered as he poked Neo in the chest and swam out the tunneled exit.

Chapter 23

Britt pushed the large black painted lid off the tank, and it fell to the floor with a loud *thunk*. She emerged from the top, gasping as Sadie ripped off her spiked helmet and swam toward her, extending her arm.

"That was terrifying," Sadie said, pulling Britt up and out of the tank.

Britt nodded in agreement as her unsteady arms shook with the residue of fear. "Thanks," she said, grounding her tentacles into the solid floor as she looked back down into the tank at each of the tiny gray dolphins.

They were now busy swimming laps around the perimeter, clockwise and then counter-clockwise, then back again, the jolting movements of a broken clock.

Britt lifted her two front tentacles and reached into the tank, grabbing each dolphin out. The moment she lifted them and uncoiled them from her suckers, they let out a tiny squeak of joy, as if thankful to be freed from the walled constraints.

Sadie's mouth dropped open. "Uhhh, Britt!" She pointed to Britt's long black tentacles, shining with an almost radioactive glow.

Britt looked down at them, seeing them all now surrounded by a purple pulsing light. She lifted them up, spinning around in a circle to check all eight. She even counted them systematically in case any had become somehow badly injured or detached. But no—just glowing.

"You are glowing," Sadie said, stating the obvious.

"I can see that," Britt snapped back sarcastically as she flared her arms out. Sparks flew from her fingertips, heated fireworks burning the wall next to Sadie's head. Britt let out a gasp and curled her fingers into her palm, horrified. "Oh! Are you okay?" Britt's eyes darted between Sadie and the wall, and she tilted her head to look at the blackened mark that could well have been Sadie's face. Nobody wanted to see someone's face get injured again—certainly not after Tanis and her poor devastated skin.

"What the hell was that?" Sadie said, gripping at her chest.

Britt looked down at the palms of her hands.

"I'm not sure, but whatever it was…I couldn't control it. It just…well, sparked. As you saw." She pressed her arms against her body again, balling her fists at her side, as if scared of her own hands and the strange power she apparently possessed within them. She didn't want to accidentally hurt Sadie or worse. She shook her head, thrusting the dark thoughts out of her mind.

"We need to get out of this room," Britt said. Now, her gaze focused on the entrance from which they had come.

Sadie nodded. "We could go back up and take one of the three doors, but we won't know where they lead us. It's surely daytime by now, and if anyone sees you with your tentacles, especially since they are glowing now, they will definitely call for the guards."

Britt threw her hands into the air. "These friggin'

tentacles! This would be so much so much easier if I just looked like you."

The three dolphins circled Britt, swimming around her lower body in a crazed whirlpool.

"What's happening?" Sadie asked, pinning her body to the wall.

The dolphins spun faster and faster around Britt, gaining speed on each rotation. The water rushed against her tentacles in waves of fury as the dolphins reeled around her.

"I don't know!" Britt shouted back, unable to move.

A burst of light exploded from the circle, filling the room.

"I can't see anything! I think I'm blind!" Sadie screamed, rubbing her eyes. "It blinded me!"

Britt blinked her eyes rapidly. The bright white light had temporarily blinded her too. She fumbled forward, feeling, inching ahead little by little, trying to find the wall with her hands to steady herself. She blinked again.

A hazy gray outline came back to her vision. She kept close to the wall, sure she would fall if she left its support. There was nothing to hold onto. Her eyelids fluttered. "Everything is coming back," Britt said in a huge sigh of evident relief.

The room looked just as it had, with weapons lining the walls, and Sadie leaning against the opposite side. She was persistently rubbing at her eyes. "My eyes still feel weird," she said.

"Why didn't anything get blasted off the walls this time?" Britt asked, spinning around to make sure her assessment was correct.

Sadie's jaw dropped as she stared at Britt.

"Oh, my God!" Sadie cried. "Have you seen yourself?" She stared as though she had never seen anything like this before. Britt seemed to have become some kind of unpaid sideshow. Sadie's eyes were transfixed.

"What are you looking at?" Britt said, cocking her head to the side.

Sadie lifted her arm and pointed to Britt's lower half. Her eyebrows arched up over her wide doe eyes like mountain peaks.

Britt looked down. Her heart thumped once, loud and fast. This…this was *not her.* This was not her body! Not her form. *Not Britt!* What the hell? "Sadie!" she cried. "Sadie, I…" She couldn't finish. "Sadie, this isn't…it isn't me, is it?" She gasped for breath, frightened, insecure, uncertain. Her eyes darted back up at Sadie and then back down at her lower half. *This can't be. This is not possible!* In place of her eight inky black tentacles was one long purple sequined tail. Each scale shimmered like an amethyst in the light. Britt moved her new tail back and forth awkwardly, trying to swim across the room. She had wanted this her whole life, and now that she had it, it didn't feel like her. It didn't feel right.

Sadie let out a giggle and held her hands up over her mouth. "I'm sorry, but you look like a worm trying to wriggle through dirt!"

Britt rolled her eyes, shaking her head back and forth. "Well, I'm not exactly use to three *magical* dolphins transforming me into a…" She paused before the last word, "mermaid."

Sadie reached out her hand. "Here, let me help

you," she said, grabbing the end of Britt's new tail and moving it up and down in the correct motion. Then she turned her head toward the dolphins who were now fast asleep against the wall, curled into each other the way cubs would. "You know they did you a favor, right? Now we can blend in better."

Britt glanced down at them. They were so small and looked far too tiny to harvest such strong powers. Her bottom lip quivered and she bit down hard with her teeth, fighting every urge to give in to her sadness. Britt would do everything she could to get them to safety, along with her sisters. Her two *missing* sisters.

"Okay, okay! I think I got it!" Britt said, pushing Sadie's hand off her tail. She moved her new sequined one up and down, each scale sparkling as light ran from her hips down to the tip of her new fin.

Sadie smiled, crossing her arms over her chest and nodding encouragingly at Britt. "Better! Not perfect, but much better." She laughed. "You upgraded from worm to snake, for sure."

Britt rolled her eyes as the corners of her mouth pulled into a half-smirk. "Yeah, whatever," she replied, fighting back her smile.

Chapter 24

Tanis' rib cage throbbed from unintentionally being stabbed with one of the spiked helmets. She gritted her teeth, holding her hand pressed against her wound as the blacksmith's son unknowingly pushed her through the gate. The wound was only an inch into her skin, but a black and purple outline had formed around its shallow opening and with every bump of the cart, Tanis winced. However, even more bothersome was that she was unsure where her final destination would be.

As the cart came to an abrupt stop, she listened silently for any chatter that would give her an indication of where she might be located right now.

"These are to be brought to the arena and displayed for the battle tonight," a deep, manly voice bellowed, filled with authority. "Be careful how you handle them."

A battle? Tanis turned her head so her ear could tune into the conversation.

"Yes, of course, sir, right away," the blacksmith's son replied.

And then the cart moved a few inches forward.

"Wait a second!" The voice was back. *It's a guard.*

The cart rocked unsteadily before freezing in place as Tanis' heartbeat sped in her chest like an overused metronome.

Damn. Tanis thought. *He's going to check the cart! No, no, no!* Her hands gripped at the sides of the cart as she prepared herself to swing up like a catapult.

"Yes sir." She heard the blacksmith's son's voice crack.

A loud boisterous laugh followed from the guard.

"Don't be so serious, kid," he said. "I just want to know which of the twins you think will win tonight. My buddies and I have bets on Neo. Where would you put your money?"

Twins? Tanis thought, relaxing her hands that had been gripped so tightly. There was an unnerving pause as she pressed her ear tight against the cart. Her hair fell forward into her face as she listened intently. But even now, she could only catch parts of every sentence, sometimes just the odd word here and there. But there was one sentence she heard in entirety. The blacksmith's son took a deep breath before giving a flat answer. "I agree. Neo will beat his brother, Kaleb."

Tanis' eyes went wide as she covered her gaping mouth with her palm so she wouldn't make a peep. *Wait, Kaleb has a twin brother. Neo? What the…!* She pushed her hair back and felt her head spin, piecing the information together. *It wasn't Kaleb who took Yuri!*

The cart shuffled forward once again as the guard shouted in the distance, "Got another one for Neo! He's really going to love this one! Let him know."

A few minutes had gone by before the cart came to a complete and juddering stop in the center of the battle arena. It had seemed like an eternity to Tanis who had spent the last several minutes counting backward in her head to calm herself, while tapping simultaneously against her sides like an anxious child. Her fingers froze.

Now, there came the shuffling and squeaking of rusted metal chains. The blacksmith's son had grabbed a small metal handle embedded firmly into the ground on the left side of the arena. He pulled up on it, and the rack slid up, displaying a fine but atrocious row of hanging hooks for weaponry. They swung and clanged together as he lifted the metal frame out of the ground.

Tanis' body shook like an earthquake as the blacksmith's son swam over to the cart, reaching his hand in to grab at one of the metal swords adjacent to her head. *Am I going to have to fight him? Please, please, no!*

He swam over to the rack, hanging the swords onto one of the hooks before returning to the cart for another. His hand reached down again, grazing Tanis' blue hair as she gripped tightly to a nearby sword. She clung onto it so firmly—and for everything her life was worth—that her knuckles went white, starved of circulation. *You can defend yourself, you can defend yourself,* she repeated in her head. It was a mantra but not one she was sure she believed in.

"A battle" sounded terrible. She did not wish to be involved in one in any way at all. And she wouldn't be. She'd make sure of it. She sprang up, busting her upper body out of the cart in an explosion of blue hair and flesh, the steel sword wielded in her grip. "Aaaaagh!" she yelled, just as the blacksmith's son also let out a blood-curdling scream as he tumbled back, falling onto the sandy arena. He lifted his hands in the air, inching himself over to the arena wall, his face pallid and his hair bristled on end.

"Please don't hurt me," he cried out. "I'm just the

blacksmith's son! Don't do anything to me, please! I won't hurt you if you—"

"Shh," Tanis said, not at all relishing seeing a male youth so scared of her.

The boy looked about fifteen years old, which was only the same age as Sadie. He was tall and lanky with shaggy light-blond hair that had fallen into his eyes when he took the tumble. His red sequined tail was covered in the dusty sand.

Tanis crawled her way out of the deep black cart, and the blacksmith's son's amber eyes widened as he glanced upon her lower half.

"Are you afraid of me?" she said, approaching him with her black tentacles flared out like live wires and the sword in her hand. The boy's eyes showed immense fear. But still, she couldn't be sure he was harmless, and she had to be ready to protect herself.

The blacksmith's son nodded, pulling his head down into his chest as he pushed himself farther into the wall. If he'd pushed himself any more, he'd have had to disappear through it.

Tanis tossed the sword to the side, lowering her tentacles and extending her arm toward him. Her fingers wiggled freely. "Well, you shouldn't be. I'm not what they say I am. I'm not a monster. Believe me, I'm not." That only made matters worse. Tanis was sure that when someone said *believe me,* they were definitely not to be trusted. Otherwise, why say it?

The boy looked up at her extended hand, and his eyebrows rose. He cautiously extended his own hand to meet hers. An alien race meeting humans for the first time couldn't manage to look more awkward and ill at ease than these two.

She was intent on pulling him up, but his face told a different tale. It said, *I'd really rather not touch you. But I suppose I will.* "What's your name?" Tanis asked. Making polite chat could cover up the fact she was going to grab hold of this boy—the boy who was terrified of her anyway. She pulled him up with ease.

The boy's eyes darted toward the exit as he then tried to swim as fast as he could, bolting toward the open tunnel.

Tanis extended one of her tentacles with a cat-like reflex. She coiled her suckers around him, pulling him back like a spinning dreidel until he faced her. "Look, I'm not going to hurt you, but I also can't have you telling the merfolk that I'm here. So, it looks like you are stuck with me until I accomplish what I came here to do."

The blacksmith's son wriggled under her grip, trying to squeeze out of her coiled tentacles. "I'm Oliver," he said, relaxing his body in defeat. He barely managed a whisper.

Tanis grinned. She had always liked the name Oliver, and it matched the boy's rounded face well. "Well, Oliver…I'm Tanis. Do you think if I let you go, that you will jolt away again? Or can I release you so we can have a conversation properly? I really do only wish to talk." She cringed at her own statement. *I really only wish to talk* sounded just as unbelievable as *please believe me.* It seemed she was just as bad as the boy at offering reassurances.

"I won't jolt away," Oliver responded, realizing that it would be much more comfortable for him not to have the weight of her coiled tentacles pressing on his chest.

Tanis loosened her grip and winced as he dropped to the ground and landed heavily. "Sorry about that," she said. "I didn't mean to."

Oliver pushed himself back up off the floor, dusting more sand off his red tailfin. "Yeah, thank you," Oliver said sarcastically.

There was an awkward moment of silence as they stared at each other. Oliver scratched at the back of his head before asking a follow-up question.

"So, what are you doing on our territory? It's dangerous for your kind here."

"Ha!" Tanis' head tilted back with a sarcastic laugh. "You don't think I know that?" she shouted, raising her hands in the air. *"Your* people took one of my sisters as a *prisoner!* Then, my other sister went looking for her, and the same happened, and now *I'm here."*

Oliver inched back slowly, timidly and just out of striking reach. "Okay," he said, raising his palms in the air in retreat. "I'm not sure how I can help you. I'm just the blacksmith's son. I don't live in the castle."

Tanis' head drooped as she looked at the ground. "So, then you haven't seen my sister Britt, or the mermaid she's with—named Sadie?" She glanced back up at Oliver hopefully.

His head tilted forward as his eyes went wide, and Tanis realized that she had struck a chord. He knew exactly who Sadie was and if Tanis could read his mind, it would whisper that Sadie was Oliver's first and only crush and betray a deep secret. She would know how he had watched Sadie and her father leave their impoverished home so that her father could be fitted for armor in his own father's tiny blacksmith shop. His mind would divulge how he remembered Sadie's beautiful long green hair and how her lovely big brown eyes had looked so sad upon seeing her father in the King's armor. Yes, he had imagined that this had been the only way left for her family to get the food and resources they needed. But his greatest secret was how he wanted to reach out that day and comfort her, and he almost did, but his father had called him away to load up another cart for the kingdom. He had plans to speak to her eventually but felt a deep sense of guilt. His father aided the King, and the armor he made suited her dad, who was taken away from her. She probably would never want to speak to him. In a way, he and his father were also indebted to the King, but they had been much more fortunate than Sadie's family. His family's skill set ensured that they would never have to trade a family member for food.

"Sadie?" Oliver asked, following up skeptically as his blond eyebrows raised into two peaked arches. "The *mermaid* Sadie? My age? Long green hair?"

Wow! He had seen her! I knew it! Tanis moved forward, nodding with excitement. "Yes! That's Sadie! Have you seen her?" she asked hopefully, grinning as she grabbed Oliver's shoulders. It surely constituted just another awkward and superfluous question. Clearly, he had seen her as he'd just described her. No one else was likely to fit that exact description, would they?

Oliver pulled back, slipping right out of Tanis' grip. "Personal space!" Oliver said, holding his hand up as a stop sign.

"I'm sorry, I'm sorry!" Tanis said, blushing as she backed away. She balled her hands at her sides as the grin on her face faded. "I just got a little excited that maybe you could help me find my sisters if you knew Sadie."

Oliver glanced at the exit. There was enough room for him to try to make another dash for it. "I haven't seen Sadie," he responded. "But…" He paused. "I'll get you where you need to go if you think we will find her."

Tanis clasped her hands in front of her in a prayerful posture. "Oh, thank you, Oliver," she said, smiling. Her eyes drifted to the rack behind him on which hung two swords, a silver shield, and a few spiked helmets. "Can I ask you something?" Tanis said, the corners of her mouth pulled into a taut line.

"I guess," Oliver said, shrugging.

Tanis spun around. Her eyes traced from the arena seats to the dusty sand below them and then back to the weapons rack. "This battle tonight," she said, pointing behind Oliver to the weapons. "Does it have to do with my sisters?"

"I'm not sure," Oliver said, turning to look at his reflection in one of his father's shining metal shields. It looked back at him, skewed as if mocking. *The blacksmith's son, held captive by one of the Inked.* He pushed the shield to the side with his hands, causing the rack to shake as he turned back around to face Tanis. She was staring at him intently.

"I overheard a rumor," he continued begrudgingly, "that Prince Kaleb has been secretly seeing one of your kind, and that his brother Neo captured her. The battle is for the throne. However, everyone knows that Neo is the better fighter. Kaleb has no chance of winning. So, there have been whispers of it being an execution.

There cannot be two winners in a fight like this. Blood will run."

"Wait!" Tanis said, gripping her hand to her chest. "They battle to the death?"

Oliver silently nodded, confirming her current discovery. He recognized her curled upper lip and narrowed eyes to be an expression of disgust. It was the same way he felt about these things.

It was barbaric, but the King was both vengeful and a showman. There hadn't been a competition like this since last year, so the kingdom was overdue for a show. The King would revel in it and enjoy every second even when it wound up with the slaughter of one of his own lineage. And of course, as King no one would challenge him or tell him what they really thought. People would still fawn over him, still bow and curtsey, still tell him what he wanted to hear because when they did that, they were praised and would receive better benefits. Or fewer punishments— whichever applied.

Oliver remembered watching last year's debacle. Two seasoned guards had both wanted the Army General position and had approached the King about their desires. King Oasis, of course, had told them they would have to prove their strength in the arena. It was a firm favorite test of his, something he instigated at every opportunity. Any small contest or challenge between two or more citizens had to be fought out in the arena. Everyone in the kingdom would watch. However, on that occasion, he had failed to tell them that this battle would be to the death. So, when one of the guards overpowered the other, he rose tall in victory, having knocked his competition to the ground.

He raised a fist to the crowd, a message that conveyed, *see me, I am the victor! I win this fight and the prize!*

But King Oasis had gotten up from his throne as the crowd cheered. He held up his hand and the crowd fell silent. "Any general of mine knows there are no survivors when it comes to our enemies," he had said, pausing before following up with, "but they also know never to turn their back on their enemy."

The guard had jolted his body around at that very second, but it was too late. The other had risen during his faux win and crept up on him from behind, stabbing through his back with a long sword, pushing it right in. It managed to pierce his heart and cleave the organ in half. The blood pooled out of the gaping wound and came gushing from his lips as the guard's eyes rolled into the back of his head.

At least this year, both parties know it's a battle to the death, Oliver thought. *That's something.*

"Hey," Tanis said, snapping her fingers in front of Oliver's eyes which had gazed off into an empty stare. "Do you know where they would keep the prisoners?"

Oliver's eyes snapped back into focus, meeting Tanis' eager gaze. "Probably the dungeons," he said nervously, looking down at the ground as he shrugged.

Tanis shuffled to the black weapon cart from which she had emerged. There were still some weapons left languishing in its depths. She roughly pushed them aside with one of her extended tentacles. Her hands gripped along the edges of the cart as she then reeled herself back in.

"I need you to take me there," she said, upright in the cart, both hands on her hips.

Oliver took a deep gulp in. "Yeah, that's what I was afraid you'd say," he responded.

Chapter 25

Yuri was curled on the cement floor of her cell. Her head pressed firmly into her chest as she rocked herself back and forth. A rotten fish lay inches away from her head, and the smell of decaying fleshed filled her nostrils. She hadn't had an appetite since being taken captive. She listened as the two guards pacing outside her cell bickered about the upcoming battle between Neo and Kaleb. They seemed certain that Neo would win but were still caught up in debating on how he would do so. Yuri lingered on some of their words.

Bludgeoned. Speared. Axed to bits. Beheaded.

Ugh. She especially shuddered at the word *beheaded.* The vicious spurting of bright red arterial blood into the water and the way a head rolled from the shoulders before the body slumped—it was too much to contemplate, let alone to be forced to see. Her chest felt heavy and sharp as if she had swallowed glass, so she shut her eyes and hummed to herself, attempting to block out the overheard conversation.

But a familiar voice sent a jolt through her body like lightning, a sudden spasm of electrifying pain and reflex causing her to spring up from her fetal position like the petrified victim of Medusa, the monstrous Gorgon. *The King! The King!* Her heart was in her mouth. The King had come to visit her.

"Is the food not to your liking?" he asked, pointing

to the rotten corpse of the fish. "You have to eat—keep your strength up for the battle." He said it as though she was to be one of the fighters. What he meant was that as one of the spectacles the fight's crowd would get to behold, she needed to be in fine form. Or as fine as one could be who had been thus incarcerated. A dark sneer was plastered on his face like a porcelain-painted clown. It curved at the edges a little too high, pinching at his cheeks.

She grimaced, not willing to make a peculiar small talk in silence with facial expressions. Yuri scowled at him anyway before she was able to stop herself. She pushed herself against the cell wall once more. Then she extended out her tentacles, seemingly displaying them the same way a peacock showed off its bright plumage to show that it could not be bettered by anyone around.

King Oasis dismissed his guards as he grabbed a wooden chair that had stood propped against the dungeon wall and dragged it across the cement floor, placing it in front of Yuri's cell. He sat down calmly as if he had been invited to a tea party. The King was always on the lookout for entertainment. But none was to be had here unless he would be amused by the strained and fear-filled face of *the Inked girl*. That was doubtful. He was used to far more interesting sights.

"Have you heard about tonight's battle?" he asked as if talking to a friend about their upcoming weekend plans. He was so casual about it, knowing that would add to the insult and offense.

Yuri let out a low growl from under her breath. Her lip quivered over her pointed teeth which were ready to strike. *The Inked girl's* eyes flashed, ready to take a leap in his direction.

The King continued unamused as he scratched his beard. "I have wonderful news for you. You will be getting a front row seat next to me in tonight's battle!"

The news made Yuri almost topple over as if she had been punched in the gut. She said nothing and made no other sound, just slumped down against the wall. She was still baring her teeth as the King continued.

"I do have a little confession to make. You see, I wasn't the one to come up with this battle. I was just going to execute Kaleb for his traitorous behavior, but then he brought up the fine notion of a duel between him and his brother Neo, and I thought that sounded like a fun event. "Plus, my son Neo is the best fighter in the kingdom—indeed, even way beyond the kingdom—so why not provide a little entertainment for my people? Once Neo kills Kaleb, they will fear him, just like they fear me. He will be the perfect successor for my throne."

Yuri's eyes darkened as they filled with tears that burned as she held them back. She couldn't believe what she heard. The King himself knew this was an unfair battle. Some had labeled it a public execution of his son. He was pleased to agree that it was.

"How can you sentence your own son to death?" Her voice cracked as she spoke.

King Oasis rose from his seat and approached Yuri's cell slowly. He gripped his hands around the metal bars, pushing his deranged face through the gap. His nose and eyes fitted through, leering. "He stopped being my son when he chose to associate with filth like you!" he said through gritted teeth and crazed eyes. The metal bars dented in his grip, and he let his hands drop to his sides as the dark clownish grin reappeared across his face.

"Guards!" he shouted. The dungeon keepers rushed back in without any hesitation, bowing their heads to await orders. "Make sure to have her ready for tonight's battle. I want her roped up and seated next to me," he instructed the guards before storming out of the room as his red cape dragged behind him.

The two guards glared at Yuri, one approaching her cell. He pushed his long, greasy, black hair back with his hand and gave Yuri a dark grin. His teeth were sharp and malformed like jagged-edged rocks. "Any last meal requests?" he inquired nonchalantly, sticking the back of his sword into her cage and poking her on the shoulder.

Yuri leaped forward, grabbing the blade and pulling it back with all her might, but she was too slow and too weak. The guard's reflexes were quick, and he pulled his sword back, causing Yuri to fall forward onto her face.

"Feisty one," he said, laughing.

"Yeah, she almost had you," the other guard laughed along.

Yuri cleared her throat loudly, cutting through their jokes. "Swordfish," she said to be ironic. "I would like to request swordfish."

The dark-haired guard's nostrils flared, and he elbowed his partner. "Go get it for her." His murky slanted eyes refocused on Yuri. "I hope you enjoy your meal; you do know it will be your last?"

Chapter 26

The three small gray dolphins followed Britt around the room, darting wherever she went. Sadie watched with raised brows as they huddled close to Britt, bumping into her new sequin tail every time she paused her restless pacing. "How are we going to get the dolphins out of here?" she asked, gesturing to the tiny creatures.

Britt continued pacing, back and forth, and around in loops. Her new tailfin followed behind her like an extra limb that had grown overnight or a large tumor that wasn't supposed to be there. "I have no clue. I think they think I'm their mom or leader, or something." She paused again to look down at the small gray dolphins huddled around her tail. They squeaked, chattering with each other between clicking tongues. She leaned her hand against the tank and sighed.

"We might have to come back for them," Britt continued, her curved lips pointing into a frown.

"We can't just leave them here!" Sadie said, shaking her head back and forth. "Absolutely not. I won't have it. Just won't entertain it. We'll free them somehow."

"And did I say we wouldn't?" Britt challenged. "I said we might come back for—"

"No!" Sadie's shout was deafening. "They're babies, look at them! They need freeing *now.*"

Britt bent down, picking up one of the small gray dolphins and scooping it into her arms. It nestled into her chest, nudging its head into her soft skin. "I wish we had a choice," she said, turning to the tank. She leaned her body forward, hovering over the opening and readying herself to let her grip loosen on the snuggled dolphin in her arms. It purred and trilled, cat-like, shutting its eyes as it started to vibrate, shaking in her arms.

"What's happening now?" Sadie asked in horror as the dolphin slowly faded from sight.

Its gray skin became pale and transparent, then vanished from Britt's arms. It was as if it had never existed. "Where did it go?" she said, looking down at her empty hands. Her face was a picture of bemusement. She looked all over, seeing no sign of it, not a trace.

Sadie pointed to Britt's collar bone, her mouth ajar.

"What are you looking at now?" Britt asked, looking down at her tail and hoping that it hadn't turned into a lobster claw.

"Your new tattoo," Sadie remarked as she wiggled her pointed finger once again at Britt's collarbone. "Have you seen it? Go look!"

Britt rushed over to the wall and peered into a large metal shield hanging in its center. Sadie was right. There on her left collar bone was a small black tattoo of a dolphin engraved into her skin. She ran her fingertips over it, seeing how it glowed with a sparkling gold.

"Can I touch it?" Sadie asked, approaching Britt hesitantly with her arm outstretched.

"Okay…" Britt responded.

Sadie reached her outstretched hand forward. Her

fingertips drifted over Britt's collarbone before touching down onto her warm skin. She felt the beating of Britt's pulse under her fingertips as the tattoo glowed under her touch, heating up like a hot iron.

Whoosh!

A blast of light extended from Britt's skin, a giant bolt of illumination resembling an atomic bomb. Sadie flew back, slamming against the wall behind her, a resounding thud as she hit. She slid down to the floor, rubbing the back of her head with one hand. She appeared to scream silently, probably in way too great an agony to make a sound. The tips of her fingers had been scorched, and she looked down at her burnt, bubbled skin.

"Sadie!" Britt shouted, swimming over to her and extending her hand. "Are you okay?" Stupid question under the circumstances.

"What the hell?" Sadie said, wiggling her burnt fingers. "I won't do that again. And you know? I'm starting to feel less empathy toward them." She glared over at the remaining two dolphins doing laps behind Britt's back. She hissed.

"Okay, okay. Calm down," Britt said, grabbing Sadie's arm and lifting her back up.

Sadie scowled. "If I get blasted one more time, I swear I'm going to eat them!"

The two remaining gray dolphins froze behind Britt, letting out a few high-pitched angry squeals. Britt turned her head and looked down at them. "I think they can understand us," she said. "That reaction—it can't have been just coincidence."

"Oh yeah," Sadie responded as she pointed her finger toward them. "You little sea slugs better not blast me again. I'm on your side!" She flashed her pointed teeth at them, and they chirped, huddling at Britt's side for protection.

"Stop it," Britt shouted as she caressed the dolphins with her hands. "You're scaring them!"

Sadie rolled her eyes. "Whatever."

The skin of the dolphins was soft against Britt's palms like wet silk despite their scars and blemishes. She lifted the remaining two, cradling them in her arms as she had done previously. Just like the first, they blended into her skin. Britt examined her new tattoo in the reflective surface of a shield, seeing how the three dolphins had formed a glowing triangle on her collar bone. She ran her fingers across her new tattoo, and the glow faded into a solid black.

Sadie's head tilted to the side in amusement. "Whoa, that's crazy."

"Yeah, tell me about it," Britt responded, still staring wide-eyed into the shield. She had never believed in magic or the stories her mother or Yuri would tell her growing up. Now, in just one day, everything had changed. Her new fin swayed behind her in one steady unified movement, rather than the wild flaring of several extended tentacles. And now, in that one day, it had changed from being a case of either believing or not believing. This was not about belief at all. Belief was reserved for fairy tales and myths. This, though, was real. Her own eyes saw what they saw, her body felt what it had felt. Where was belief in all this? There was no place for it. It simply *was* as things appeared—even as strange as they were now.

Her chest tightened as she crossed her arms over her ribs. A hurricane of intrusive thoughts flooded her mind. *Will my sisters accept me if I can't change back?* She ran her fingers one more time over the tattoo. Nothing seemed that remarkable about it now.

"Hey," Sadie said softly, tapping Britt on the shoulder. "We really need to go."

Britt glanced one more time at the reflective shield and then turned to Sadie, nodding. "All right, let's go," she said, puffing out her chest with faux confidence.

The two girls swam out the entrance from which they had come, and up the winding luminescent tunnel to the shaft. It creaked as it lifted them back up to reveal the three colorful doors they had come across earlier.

One red. One blue. One yellow.

Britt pointed to each of the doors. "Where do we go from here?"

Sadie shrugged. "Honestly, I'm not sure. I've never been this far into the castle. What's your favorite color?"

Britt took a deep breath in and exhaled a blast of bubbles out of her nostrils. "Great," she said sarcastically. "I guess we are winging this." The blue reminded her of her sister Tanis' long flowing hair, and she swam forward, grabbing hold of the golden-knobbed handle.

"Blue it is," Sadie said, following behind her.

Britt's hand shook as she twisted the handle of the door. She felt it pop open so easily in her grasp, inviting them into the unknown darkness. She glanced over at Sadie, whose worried gaze mimicked her own.

"New mermaids first," Sadie said, gesturing to the open door.

"Okay," Britt said, puffing out her chest again. *I*

got this. She swam forward through the threshold of the open doorway as Sadie trailed silently behind.

Sadie's long green hair barely made it through the passage as the door slammed shut behind them. *Click. Click. Click.* The sound of locks echoed around them. Sadie shook vigorously at the handle, but the door had locked, sealing them in. "Ittttt's locccked," Sadie said with a stutter, her voice chattering with fear.

The room was pitch black as if they had both been swallowed whole by a whale and become trapped in its belly.

"Why is there no light in here?" Britt said, feeling around with her outstretched palms.

Sadie grasped the back of Britt's shoulders, holding on like a frightened child. "I don't think anyone uses these doors. I think they are only here as an emergency exit if the kingdom is ever attacked," she responded.

Britt's eyes fought to find any glimmer of light, but there was none. There was no crack of sunshine, no slivers of brightness. And without being able to see, it would be impossible to avoid any danger. "There's no way we can move forward without light," Britt said unmoving, with hands still outstretched in front of her. Just then, her fingertips glowed, extending a form of a nightlight across her palm. She wiggled her fingers in disbelief.

"I think your new friends are helping you," Sadie whispered from behind her.

Britt's hands cast a dim light in front. They were in a maze, and three red-bricked walls surrounded them. "We have to turn around," Britt said, spinning at her waist.

The door behind them had vanished.

Sadie moved in closer to Britt. "Wasn't the door just there?"

Britt twisted her glowing palms, peering around her. Every direction she turned was a brick wall, trapping them into a tight cube.

Rrrrrrrrrrkkkkkkkk.

"What's that sound?" Sadie asked, digging her fingers deeper into Britt's shoulders.

"Shh," Britt said, holding up one glowing finger to parted lips.

Rrrrrrkkkkkkkkkk.

"There it is again!" Sadie said, grabbing at Britt's left arm.

Britt spun around, holding up her right glowing palm. The wall behind Sadie had moved backward all of a sudden, allowing them passage through. "I think the walls are moving," she whispered to Sadie as she tugged her along through the open passage.

Rrrrrrrrkkkkkkkkk.

The wall closed behind them again, trapping them into another four-bricked cube.

"What now?" Sadie asked leaning her back against the left wall.

Britt held up her finger. "Wait."

Rrrrrrrrrkkkkkkk.

The wall behind Sadie fell back like a domino, causing her to tumble briefly before catching her balance.

"Hurry," Britt said, grabbing Sadie's arm and pulling her forward. "It's a changing maze. Eventually, we should be able to make it somewhere…I hope."

Rrrrrrrrkkkkkk.

Sadie twisted her neck and watched as the brick wall reemerged behind them, lifting up from the ground, the way a vast gray mountain would come rising from the ocean floor.

The pathway in front was finally cleared of any moving walls. About five meters away was a large double door made of what looked to be solid gold. It glistened in the distance.

"That must lead to the castle," Britt said, nodding toward the door.

Rrrrrrrkkkkk.

The strange shifting noise had not come to cessation quite yet. It continued apace, a kind of sliding sound of something heavy, something cumbersome traveling on rails, perhaps. Or perhaps not. Perhaps it was the transformation of something other-worldly, not material at all. The maze continued to change behind them in any case, twisting and folding. Despite not having anyone to trap, with each change came the familiar-sounding screech, like a painfully starving creature crying out for its next meal.

"I guess we chose the wrong door," Sadie said as the hungry maze continued to growl.

Britt's eyes were fixated on the door, and she froze into a blank stare. She heard the faint whisper of a voice echoing through her head in a low hum, a static or a vibration.

The tiny whisper of a secret.
What?

She jumped out of her own skin. Her eyes snapped back into focus.

"I think those three doors were meant to stop intruders from entering the castle. And I reckon each room was specifically set up to allow passage out of the castle with no difficulty. The walls would have flattened if we were to leave," Britt replied with her newfound knowledge.

Sadie's mouth cranked open in a fishlike maw. "How did you know that?"

A huge whooshing sound came again, and a sliding noise, then a thud. "Watch out!" Sadie screamed. She pinned Britt down to the ground before she could respond. A large blade had fallen from the ceiling of its own accord and now swung like a pendulum over their bodies. Sadie stared into Britt's golden-brown eyes which moved back and forth swiftly and looked desperately frightened. They would not leave the object that had almost claimed her life.

Her eyes traced the shining blade that had just bypassed slicing off her head. Her skin felt soft against Sadie's like fresh silk; she couldn't deny her growing attraction for Britt. Something about her edgy lone-wolf behavior evoked a need for discovery.

"Wow, thanks," Britt said after a few moments. "I was almost decapitated."

The blade's back-and-forth motion slowed, and Sadie smiled.

She rolled her body off Britt's chest. "Don't mention it," she said, barrel-rolling her way to the golden door. Her locks of green hair spiraled around her as she rolled, and Britt tried not to stare, but she made everything look so effortless.

"Come on," Sadie said, waving her hand at Britt.

Britt rolled herself forward, positive that she didn't look as graceful. Her pink hair whacked at her face as she twisted, sticking to her cheeks, itching and tickling.

When she reached the double doors, she lifted herself up, brushing tangled strands of hair from her face. The golden double door's curved handles twisted to a point, trident-shaped.

Sadie reached for Britt's hand while grabbing the left door handle with the other. Britt's fingers intertwined with hers, twisting like the tendrils of kelp sneaking up from the sand as she reached for the other handle. Sadie's mouth arched into a smirk as she whispered under her breath, "This better not lead to killer crabs or something."

Britt exaggeratedly rolled her eyes as she fought back the twisting curve of her mouth. "Don't jinx it," she said, trying to maintain a stern face. Her right hand felt clammy against the pronged handle, and she squeezed Sadie's hand firmly with her other. "We open on the count of three," she said. "One…two…" She inhaled deeply, an unfathomably long breath before uttering an extended, "three!"

They pulled at the handles, and the double doors flew open with the force of a phoenix emerging from flames. The doors shuttered with a loud echoing bang against the walls of the room like the flapping of mighty panicked wings.

Sadie shut her eyes, convinced that something was bound to emerge and attack them.

"Sadie, look!" Britt shouted.

Sadie peeked forward through half-squinted eyes, her arms outstretched and blocking her face.

In front stood rows of seats where merfolk had piled into a packed open arena, every seat taken, and many observers—eager and excited for a good show and a great turnout—drifted in the aisles and filled every tiny gap between the arena seating rows.

They floated in a long corridor leading down to a steep pathway. The golden doors had shut behind them and miraculously disappeared.

Sadie lowered her hands to her side, circling once to take note of the brick wall that had once been two large golden doors. "What in the…." Sadie said, her mouth ajar.

Britt was fixated on the arena. She had never seen so many merfolk in one place before, and none seemed to notice her at all. She glanced at her new purple sequined tail and then at Sadie who effortlessly spun around with her own tail under perfect control, moving as gracefully as a trained dancer. Agile and beautiful mermaids packed this place out. Despite looking like them, she felt as if she were a pigeon in a sky full of doves.

"What's going on?" Britt asked, pointing to the stadium.

"I'm not sure," Sadie responded, tilting her head to stare down the long corridor and into the arena. "It might be a competition between some of the soldiers. Sometimes, the King likes to make them battle for certain positions; maybe my father will even be here."

Britt's eyebrows furrowed over wide eyes. "I have to find the dungeon. It's the most likely place my sister is. God help her if she's there and we miss her."

Sadie nodded, biting at her bottom lip nervously before responding. "I guess this is where we split up then," she replied, glancing down at the ground.

Britt pulled her into a tight embrace, squeezing at her sides. "I guess it is," she answered, softly. Her arms brushed against Sadie's soft green hair as she released her coiled grip.

Sadie looked up at her and smiled. "Since when are you a hugger?"

"I'm not," Britt said, spinning around and swimming away, leaving Sadie dumbfounded. She watched as Britt's pink hair faded out of sight. It felt as if a piece of herself had left with her. *A void. A fathomless chasm.* A lump formed in the back of her throat, and she swallowed hard, forcing it down. She hoped that Britt could find her sisters and be reunited with them, just as she could with her father. She bit at her quivering bottom lip and turned to face the packed arena. *Guess I better find my seat.* Her gut heaved.

Chapter 27

Oliver begrudgingly pushed the cart carrying Tanis forward, his nervous palms shaking unsteadily beneath his grip. He knew precisely where the dungeon was but wasn't sure what excuse he could make to get them there.

"Ow, easy up there. Do you have to hit every bump?" Tanis whispered from below the cluttered weaponry.

Oliver's eyes shot down into the cart where strands of Tanis' blue hair peeked out from under a metal shield. He reached down and moved it slightly to the left, fully covering her head. "Shh, we are almost there," Oliver whispered back.

The entrance around the back of the castle led to a windy pathway that twisted and turned like a corkscrew down to the dungeon. Two tall double mahogany wooden doors stood in front of Oliver and his cart. He twisted his head to the left and then to the right. *Where are the guards?* He reached his hand forward hesitantly for the looped black metal handles of the door. His fingers barely caressed its rusted surface when the doors flew open with a great force. Oliver gasped, jumping back against the wall behind, pulling the cart and Tanis along with him.

Tanis' head banged against the side of the cart, and she covered her mouth with her hands to avoid making a peep. *Ow.*

"Come on now. There's no use in fighting!" A large guard with silver hair appeared from the doorway. Yuri was flung over his shoulder like a skewered pig, chained up and ready to be roasted on an open fire. And her pained, desperate, and pleading eyes looked about the same too, knowing the fate to befall her next.

Her body jolted back and forth on the guard's shoulders, causing him to sway to keep his balance. She wasn't going to make it easy for him. It was about all she could do—just resist, just sway, just keep him off balance. But a large-framed and muscled second guard appeared from behind the other. He scratched at his dark brown beard and then grabbed hold of Yuri's jerking bottom half. From the corner of his eye, he spotted Oliver.

"What are you doing here?" he asked as Yuri wriggled beneath his arms.

Oliver trembled. His hands shook, and he clasped them tightly in front of him. "By the King's orders," he said as his voice cracked with each word. "He, uh, he said to bring these weapons down to the dungeon and to make it quick."

The bearded guard let his hands drop from Yuri's chained bottom half, leaving his silver-haired counterpart to struggle a second time with the recalcitrant and kicking prisoner. He approached Oliver, slowly creeping, stealthy. "Why would he do that?" the guard said, tilting his head and attempting to gaze into Oliver's cart.

Oliver shook his head back and forth. "I'm not sure, sir," he squeaked in between heavy breaths. "I don't question the King! My place is to take the orders, sir!"

Yuri let out a high-pitched scream, and the bearded guard twisted his head.

"Get control of her!" he screamed at his counterpart.

Oliver peered down at Tanis, whose face was twisted into a pained expression.

Her heart pounded in her chest as she fought every urge inside herself to leap out of the weapons cart and rip at the guard's flesh.

Oliver shook his head discouragingly. *No.*

Tanis' nose flared in a small defiant show. She glanced back across red cheeks and sank herself farther down into the cart.

Yuri continued to thrash her body back and forth. Her lungs strained as she screamed, and the silver-haired guard struggled to keep his grip. His balance had become unsteady, and he swayed this way and that, hitting the walls around him.

The bearded guard let out a deep sigh before turning back to face Oliver. "Do what the King said, and leave quickly." He glared at Oliver as he poked at his chest.

"Yes, of course, sir." Oliver stammered back. "What I need to do will be very quick, sir."

The bearded guard grabbed at Yuri's lower half, and the two carried her away.

Tanis pressed her ear against the cart and listened as her sister's screams faded into the distance. There ensued a moment of silence before Oliver tapped three times on the side of the cart. "It's safe to come out now; we're alone," he said, backing away.

Tanis' head popped out. However, her mouth

wasn't twisted into a tight smile. Instead, her expression had been marred by a drooping loose frown. Both her eyes were bloodshot and matched her flushed, blemished face. "My sister," she said, sobbing into her hands. "Britt would have done something. She would have known how to save her, right there and then. She just would!"

Oliver reached his arm forward. His hand extended toward Tanis, and she grabbed it. He pulled her, helping her out of the cart with ease. She was lighter than he imagined she would be. The dark inky tentacles gave her a stocky appearance but really, she was tiny and light—and vulnerable. "There was nothing you could have done," he said, letting her hand drop once she was safely out of the cart. "We wouldn't have been able to take those guards."

Tanis looked past Oliver and through the open mahogany double doors where a tiny cement cell stood with rotten food on its floor. "We need to go after her," she said sharply to Oliver.

Oliver raised his hands in the air. "No, no, no," he said, slowly backing away from Tanis. "I got you where I said I would, but now I need to be going. I can look for Sadie myself."

No way! No way was Tanis about to accept that! Tanis leaped forward pinning Oliver to the left double door. His spine made a cracking sound like a crushed nut. "Listen, you little pipsqueak," she said, flashing her pointed teeth. "You are going to help me save my sister, or I will shred you apart. And I will do it as painfully as possible—right here, right now. So, which is it to be?"

Oliver heaved in a few deep short breaths before his head bobbed forward unconsciously.

"Oh, damn!" Tanis said as Oliver fell forward into her arms. She laid him down onto the floor and bent over him. "Damn, damn, damn!" "Wake up," she said, slapping at his cheeks.

Oliver's eyes blinked rapidly a few times before opening. Tanis hovered over him eagerly, her face inches from his. She looked a bit like a caring nurse awaiting her unconscious patient coming back to life. Only when reality hit him again, she was no nurse. Nor caring. Just waiting. He blocked her with his hands as his face wrinkled into a fearful grimace. "DON'T EAT ME!" he cried out.

Tanis' mouth curved into a sneer, and she tilted her head back, letting out a smug laugh. *He really believed I would eat him. What a prize nincompoop!*

Oliver's wrinkled grimace transformed into one of confusion. His brows arched over his eyes as he tilted his head.

Tanis shook her own head as she looked down at him, expectant but also amused. "My kind doesn't eat your kind. You don't even look remotely tasty to me. I only said that so you would continue to help me. I'm sorry," she said, extending her hand down to Oliver. "Plus, at least one of my sisters is probably with Sadie, and that sister is most definitely looking for Yuri."

Oliver begrudgingly grabbed her hand, letting her tug him back up off the floor. He looked a weakling by comparison to her now—and he felt like one. The roles of a few moments ago—where he had suddenly realized how light she was—had been reversed. Now he was the weaker one among the two and was red-faced.

The sad truth was Oliver knew exactly where they were taking Tanis' sister, but he wasn't up for telling her. In truth, he wasn't even sure he had a heart to tell her either, even if she would wish to know. The facts he would have to impart to her were loathsome and horrific. And if they couldn't save the ones who were taken there, then what point revealing it? He had seen prisoners brought to the arena before and watched as they were ripped apart by half-starved tiger sharks to entertain the castle's privileged members. His family's business as the local blacksmith meant he always had an invitation to these events. *Lucky him.*

However, he had sworn that he would never attend another event after the atrocity he had witnessed at the last one. The images, the memories, still robbed him of sleep every night. The defeated soldier's wife had leaped up in her seat upon seeing her husband slain in the arena. So, naturally, they roped her down and let tiger sharks rip her to shreds while the crowd cheered.

"It's for the best," the King had said. "Now she can be with her departed husband! She did beg us not to take him away from her, after all. You all heard it too, didn't you?"

As Oliver caught his balance, he pulled his hand back from Tanis, brushing it at his side and nodding over at the black cart. "Just get back in," he said with a hint of irritation to his voice.

Tanis didn't question it. She climbed back into the deep black cart, pulling herself down under its weaponry. "I'm sorry to put you in this situation," she said, once fully covered.

"Yeah, whatever," Oliver responded, refusing to look at her. "I'm sure you're *very* sorry."

The arena was packed as they approached the main seating entrance.

Tanis leaned her ear against the walls of the cart and listened to the loud murmurs of merfolk cheerfully talking in excitement about the upcoming battle.

How can they be so cheerful about coming to watch a deathmatch?

The thought caused her stomach to twist into tight knots, and she gripped at her sides, trying to swallow down the nausea rising in her chest. She wanted to stay—because she had to. But she wanted to run— because she *needed* to. In reality, she felt she could not do either. She was caught there, trapped. But even that thought was one she could not allow herself to believe or think about for long. How could she find herself "trapped" when others truly were, literally?

A tall guard kept post at the entrance. His muscular, veiny arms were crossed over his chest in a stiff power stance, and his bald head glimmered. "Please identify yourself," he said, glaring down at Oliver.

Oliver tilted his head back to meet the guard's gaze. "I'm the blacksmith's son," he said, trying not to stare at the guard's burly biceps. "My father and I always get invited by the King since Father and he are friends. Father was, unfortunately, unable to make it." He sounded credible. "It promises to be a great show," he added for good measure.

The guard's arms unfolded at his sides, and Oliver saw they were filled with scars and bruises. *The mark of a seasoned soldier.* He leaned his bald head forward, peering over at Oliver's weapons cart. His eyes scanned everything. Every small detail...

Oliver pressed his body against the front of the cart, blocking the guard's view. "Yeah," he said nervously. "I didn't have time to bring the cart back home before the battle started. Don't want to miss anything, you know? My father, being such a good friend of the King, will expect me to be punctual so I see everything and can report back to him. Of course, the King will also wish to hear how we enjoyed it, so my father needs sufficient detail to say he was here himself. No one wishes to offend the King—do they?"

He said do they in a way that intoned, *and you'd better not harm the friendship between any man and the King—or you may see your head chopped off.* It should make the guard think twice. He flashed the guard a cheesy grin that barely pinched his cheeks, but the guard's eyes were still fixated on his cart, and he continued to move forward.

Without turning, Oliver reached his hand down into the cart, arching his back against its side. His fingertips grazed against cold rigged metal and pulled out the first thing he could grab, a long, thin-bladed sword that his father had welded this morning. Its handle was made from an emerald stone, and it shimmered as he twisted it in front of him.

"Your sword's looking as if it has seen better days," he said, pointing to the guard's side where a dim blade sat tattered against his hip. "How about we trade, and I'll get my father to clean up your old one? Call it a favor from the King's friend for allowing me inside promptly."

The guard's eyes fixated on the emerald-stoned sword.

The temporary distraction had worked. He reached at the sheath on his side and pulled out his rusted sword, handing it over to Oliver with one hand as he simultaneously grabbed at Oliver's shining upgrade with the other.

"There you go," Oliver said as he pushed the cart past the guard who was examining his new weapon. When he made it through the entrance, he looked back to see the guard waving around the emerald sword like a child fighting another with a stick. *Moron.* "We're here," he whispered down into the cart.

Oliver had parked the cart toward the back of the stadium, above all the seats that wrapped around like an O-shaped track. A group of passing mermaids spun their heads around briefly; a slight look of puzzlement masked their faces. Oliver nodded back at them, smiling with a tightly closed-mouthed grin. *They must think I'm talking to myself.* They nodded back politely and continued their way to their seats.

Tanis popped her head up, peering over the edge of the cart. The bottom of the arena was so far away from where they stopped, and a sea of bobbing merfolk heads obstructed her from a clear view. Directly across from them, on the other side of the stadium, stood the King's golden chair in its private booth. Its arms curved down into spiral, but its back was pointed into a trident like much of the décor in the kingdom. Next to it sat a plain wooden chair that seemed unremarkable and sat unoccupied. Her eyes traced the crowd around the King's throne booth and settled onto a child gleefully playing in the audience. The child's chubby face was tilted back into a deep laugh as if his parents had brought him to a circus and not a deathmatch. If only he knew. She gripped at her twisting stomach that felt as if worms were wriggling their way through her intestines. She darted her eyes away from the laughing child and then saw her.

Sadie—sitting a few rows down from the King's booth, looking into the crowd. "Sadie!" Tanis let the words pour out of her mouth before the palm of her hand leaped over her lips. She dove back down into the cart as her chest rose and fell.

Two mermaids twisted their heads around from their seats, darting their eyes for the source of the sound. But they could see none. It must have been their minds playing tricks. They looked at each other with puzzlement as Oliver leaned against his black cart.

He cleared his throat and cried out. "Sadie!" He tried his best to make his voice sound high-pitched. "Sorry," Oliver said, glancing at the bewildered mermaids. "I thought I saw my friend over there." He pointed across the way with his index finger.

The two mermaids shrugged, and then turned back around to face the arena.

Tanis peeked her head out again, peering over the edge. The seats next to Sadie were filled with strangers chattering to each other, and her sister Britt was no place in sight despite how many times she blinked. "We need to get to the other side," Tanis whispered as she looked up at Oliver.

"Shh," Oliver whispered back. "Get back down."

Tanis did as she was told, ducking back down into the dark cart. From inside its depth, she tried to stretch out each of her tentacles that had become cramped in the tight space. She lifted them along the walls, and they made a cracking sound like snapping crab claws. *Ugh.*

Oliver pushed past several crowds as he tried to maneuver himself and the cart to the other end of the stadium. His brows felt heavy and tight over his eyes, and he tried to make a conscious effort to relax his face so as not to give himself away. He pulled his mouth into a tight faux grin as he nodded politely at passing merfolk.

When they had finally made it to the other side of the arena, they were still five rows away from where Sadie was nestled. Oliver tilted his head, examining the pathway leading down to the seating area. It was narrow, and he was certain his cart wouldn't fit.

"I can't fit the cart down the path to Sadie," he whispered down to Tanis. "I'm going to have to leave you here for a moment."

"Wait, what?" Tanis said, popping her head back up.

"Get back down," Oliver said, pushing Tanis' head down with his hand.

Tanis whacked at his hand with her own, and he recoiled his arm. "Okay, jeez, don't mess my hair up," she said, sinking back down into the cart. "And be quick."

Oliver took a deep breath then made his way down the narrow pathway to Sadie.

The crowd around him had become blurred in his vision like a dream, and all he could see was her long green hair that perfectly framed her face. His heartbeat pulsed in his ear as he got closer to the girl he had once let down. *Will she even remember me?* His fingers were balled into tight fists, and he cracked at his knuckles nervously.

"Sadie," Oliver said meekly, scratching at the back of his head.

Sadie was three seats into the row and hadn't heard

him. She continued to stare forward into the crowd, her eyes scanning circles around the stadium. The overweight merman in the aisle seat twisted his jowly double chin to look up at Oliver. His nose pointed up in a haughty manner.

"Can I help you, boy?" he said as his mouth curved into a gregarious smile.

Something about his grin seemed sinister and disingenuous to Oliver. It was as though he wore a mask over his face. None of the high-class mermaids or mermen ever seemed genuine.

"Sorry, didn't mean to bother you," Oliver responded. "I was just trying to get her attention." He pointed at Sadie with his index finger.

"Well, you have to call her name louder than that if you want her attention, boy!" the overweight merman said as he threw his flabby neck back, letting out a boisterous laugh. He reached his pudgy fingers across the two merfolk next to him, who shot him daggered looks as he tapped Sadie on the shoulder. "Miss, Miss!"

Sadie jumped back in her seat as he startled her out of her focused trance. Her head spun to meet his gaze. "Yes," she said, frazzled as she twisted the rest of her body to face the aisle. Her eyes drifted up and over the fat merman's head to where Oliver drifted, nervously fidgeting with his hands. Her eyes traced his face and sunken eyes.

"Sadie, I need to talk to you," Oliver said, looking up from his hands.

Sadie tilted her head as a look of puzzlement arched across her brows.

"I'm sorry, who are you?" she asked politely.

Oliver's heart sank as his lips quivered into a

frown. *She doesn't remember me.* "I'm the blacksmith's son," he said, trying to hide the wounded sadness in his voice. "Oliver."

Sadie's eyebrows arched over widened eyes. "What do you need me for?" she asked as she traced Oliver's body from head to toe.

Oliver's eyes darted between Sadie and the weapons cart he had left unattended, the one that harbored a fugitive of Atlantis. A group of teens were making their way over to it as they pointed their fingers and chatted with each other.

"You need to come with me now," Oliver said with urgency, reaching his hand across the row. The group was getting closer to his cart. He needed to be there to intercept.

"What are you looking at?" Sadie said, tracing his eyes to the weapons cart that stood alone on the pathway behind them.

Oliver's hardened eyes focused on Sadie.

"Trust me," he said as she shook his extended hand at her. "Come on!"

The overweight merman chimed in, pushing Oliver's forearm back with his pudgy fingers. "Listen, kid, if the miss don't want to go with you, let it be."

Oliver lowered his arm. His eyes darted over again to the cart where the young merteens were approaching from inches away. Oliver bit at his bottom lip, hard. He would have to leave, whether Sadie was with him or not.

"Okay," Sadie said, grabbing his fleeting arm. "I'll go with you."

Oliver latched onto Sadie's hand, pulling her up and out of her seat. He had heard her say she was going, so now he would spring into action—and fast. Being pulled so hard, the end of her sequined tail whacked into the overweight merman who let out a grunt as she was pulled into the aisle.

With Sadie's arm clutched beneath his hand, he zipped up toward his cart, dragging her behind him like the long tail of a thresher shark.

When they reached the cart, Sadie pulled her hand back. "What gives?" she said, irritated as she rubbed at her wrists. "I don't understand any of this."

Oliver laid his hands across his cart as he watched the noisy merteens swim by. He cast a glowering look just in case any considered taking away the cart. His head twisted to follow them as they moved past him. "Oh, it's just the blacksmith's cart," he overheard one say. He bent forward, hovering over his cart like an animal guarding fresh meat as Sadie stared at him through a squinted glance. She crossed her arms over her chest and huffed.

"Um, hello?" she snapped. "What the hell do you want from me?"

"Psst," Tanis whispered from inside the cart. "Sadie!"

Sadie swam back hesitantly from the cart as her head tilted in confusion.

"Sadie!" Tanis whispered again.

Sadie propped her hands on her hips.

"Who's in the cart?" she said, grilling Oliver with her eyes, brows knitting.

Oliver lifted his index finger to his lips and beckoned her over with his free hand.

Sadie hesitantly swam forward, crossing her arms over her chest. When she reached the edge of the black cart, she tilted her head forward and peered inside. There she saw a familiar blue like the ocean, electrified.

"Hi," Tanis said, smiling up at Sadie as her blue hair fell from her face.

Sadie's mouth hung ajar as she dropped her arms to her sides.

"Tanis?" she said, trying to whisper as a flood of questions pooled past her open lips. "What are you doing here? How did you even get here? Did anyone see you?"

Tanis shook her head, rubbing at the tip of the scar that ran across her left eyebrow. "No, no one saw me. I've been in this cart the whole time." She shuffled her cramped tentacles around. "Oliver's been helping me. I needed to make sure you and Britt were safe. Where *is* Britt?" Tanis whispered back. She lifted her head slightly, trying to peer out of the cart, looking for Britt.

Sadie looked down at the floor as her face flushed an uncomfortable red. "She went off on her own to find the dungeon," she said, looking back up at Tanis' sinking smile. "She thought she might find your other sister there. I stayed back to see if I could find my father. Usually, most of the soldiers show up to these events in case things don't go as planned."

Tanis felt her bottom lip quiver again, and she bit down hard as she shut her eyes. "Typical of Britt to go off on her own," she said as she shook her head.

Trumpets sounded from the arena, and Tanis' eyes snapped open. "What's that?" she whispered to Oliver and Sadie.

King Oasis appeared with his trident gripped tightly in his left hand. He swam into the King's booth as his red cape chased behind him. He sat down on his golden throne, his presence hastily followed by two familiar guards carrying Tanis' chained sister, gagged with a rope. They threw her body down onto the wooden chair next to him, and it came to rest with a thump, slumping to the side.

"I think the show's about to start," Oliver replied with disdain.

Tanis popped her head up briefly to see her sister tied and gagged next to the King. Her fists balled into her palms as her long nails dug into her skin, causing her to bleed down her wrists.

Sadie laid her hand onto Tanis' shoulder and squeezed. "Soon, but not right now," she whispered to Tanis.

Tanis' nostrils flared as she ground her teeth. "Not soon enough," she replied.

Chapter 28

Britt wrapped her arms around herself as she swam through the kingdom, hoping to find access to the dungeon. She was not a stranger to doing things alone, but the last several hours she had spent with Sadie played on her mind. She rubbed at her arms as if a cold chill ran down her spine. Being alone felt different this time. Britt had gotten a glimpse of what it felt like to truly have a friend outside of her sisters, a friend who was a mermaid. Of course, in her current state, she was a mermaid herself.

She ran the tip of her long fingers over her newly formed tattoo; as they grazed over her skin, the dolphin's own glowed purple beneath her touch. She dropped her hands which swayed at her sides as her eyes darted to left and right.

Try not to draw attention.

It wasn't too hard to blend in. She looked like them too now, from the tip of her bright pink hair to the bottom of her newly purpled sequined tail. Merfolk had been swimming past her freely, barely looking up from their conversations with one another. It was an odd feeling to not be looked at like a circus freak.

"Oh, hey there!"

The words shot from behind her.

Britt jolted her head around to see a young guard swimming up behind her. He circled around, blocking her path as he ran his hands through his black hair. Britt traced his body up and down as his chiseled arms swung at his sides. He tilted his head and gave a little half-cocked smile. *Dimples.*

"I haven't seen you around the castle before. Are you friends with Athena and her group? You sure are pretty enough to be," he said will a full toothy grin.

Smooth.

Britt's mouth curved into a faux polite smile. "Maybe you just haven't looked hard enough," she said, attempting to playfully push past him. Her bare shoulders brushed against his cold metal armor, and he lifted his arms, stretching them out like a barricade.

"Touché," he said, blocking her move.

Britt's nostrils flared as the faux grin faded from her face. She huffed under her breath as she pushed at the guard's left arm. "Move," she hissed, as her eyebrows pinched together at the bridge of her nose.

The guard's smile morphed into a scowl, and he grabbed at her wrist. His fingers dug into her flesh, leaving red marks on her skin as he pulled her forward.

"Where are you taking me!" Britt shouted, thrashing her new mermaid tail back and forth.

He dragged her into the castle's stable, slamming her body into an empty stall. The seahorses screeched next to them, bubbles steaming from their nostrils. They looked upset, frightened too.

"Ow," Britt cried out. "You're hurting me!" She jolted her wrist back to no avail and swung at his sides with her free hand. "Get off me!" she screamed as she leaned into his shoulder and chomped down with her pointed teeth, digging into his flesh.

The guard winced in pain, and his eyes shut briefly,

but it wasn't enough to make his grip loosen. He pinned her arms down to her sides as her new mermaid fin slashed back and forth uselessly.

"Get off!" she screamed again as that tattoo on her collar suddenly glowed purple and spread across her body with a rush of light, bursting outward, a ball of radiating energy.

The guard tumbled backward as his arms flailed behind him in a desperate attempt to brace his fall. He landed back onto the floor as he squinted, lifting his hand over his brows to block out the light. When it subsided, Britt had all eight tentacles back. She lifted them, inspecting each before her eyes darted to the fallen guard. She reached forward with her two front tentacles, coiling him.

"You're one of *the Inked*," the guard said between troubled gasps.

Britt squeezed a little harder.

Pop!

The guard screamed as his left arm snapped. "Get off me!" he cried out.

Britt shook her head as her lips peaked into a devious smirk. "Why?" she said, tilting her head. "Why would I? You didn't get off me when I asked you to."

The guard whimpered in her grasp. "Please, let me go!" he said, sobbing.

Britt uncoiled her tentacles and watched as he dropped forcefully to the ground. He scurried to the corner of the stable as he clutched his injured arm.

"Where are the dungeons?" Britt said, looking down at him, looking ready to lunge for him.

The guard looked back with disgust, the look she was accustomed to. His top lip lifted over his pearly white teeth in disdain. "Why do you want to know?" he asked crudely.

Britt reached one of her long tentacles forward, wrapping green suckers around his remaining undamaged arm. The guard pulled back as hard as he could, slamming his back against the corner wall of the wooden stable as the seahorses in the next stall let out loud, shrieking cries. It was no use, Britt had him cornered.

"Because if you don't help me, I will break your other arm," she said, squeezing him tightly.

The guard's face wrinkled into a tight wince. "Stop," he cried out. "Stop! Why do you want to go to the dungeon? It's empty. There wouldn't be any point in it."

Britt uncoiled her tentacle, pulling it back. She crossed her arms over her chest and stared down at the quivering guard. "What do you mean by empty? My sister is there," she said, tapping her tentacles impatiently on the seafloor. "I know she is. So don't try telling me lies."

The guard's head tilted back against the stable wall as a dark grin appeared across his face, showing all his pearly whites. "Oh dear," he said menacingly. "You don't know that they brought her to the arena? That's a shame. It's probably the last time you'll get to see her."

Britt shook her head. "No, that can't be," she said, attempting to shake the thought of never being able to see her sisters again. Her eyes darted to the left wall where black reins hung on a matching black wall hook. She reached across, grabbing them off the wall.

The guard inched himself back farther, digging his hands into the sandy seafloor. "What are you going to do with those?" he asked as she approached him with the reins.

Britt tied the guard up; he resembled a pig at a roast. His arms were bent behind his back and tied tightly to his tail. "You won't get away with this," he screamed as he writhed on the floor.

One last thing, she thought as she looked down at her tentacles and watched them transform back into a shimmering purple fin.

Chapter 29

Trumpets sounded as the King rose from his throne to address the crowd. His long, woven, red cape adorned his broad shoulders and flared behind him as he rose.

"Merfolk of Atlantis," he said, pausing for a moment as the cheers of the crowd settled. "Today, you are in for a real treat! Today is the day that the successor to my throne makes himself known! Today is the day that one of my sons will prove himself a worthy adversary!"

The crowd cheered as Tanis poked her head up out of the cart. "Someone likes theatrics," she hissed behind her locked jaw as the King continued.

"Now, I know some of you have heard the rumors that my son Kaleb was intermingling with one of *the Inked*," he said, pausing as the crowd booed and hissed.

He held up his hands and the crowd silenced with his motion. "I know how it must look, but that simply isn't true."

What a freakin' liar, Tanis thought as she ground her teeth in anger. Her ears ached as her jaw gnawed back and forth.

King Oasis gestured his hand over toward Yuri.

She slumped, tied up and barely conscious in the seat next to him. Her head drooped forward as her shoulders tilted off to the left, and a guard quickly swam forward to readjust her.

Tanis rubbed at her eyes that began to pool with tears masked by the ocean water. Her big sister looked frail now—as if a shell of her former self. Yuri's face was flat and pulled at colorless, sunken cheeks.

"You see," the King continued. "We found this creature wandering our castle. She was trying to kidnap our children to use as leverage against us!" King Oasis shook his head disapprovingly as the crowd broke out into a sea of worried buzzing. He held his hand up, once again silencing the crowd. "Quiet please," he said as they gradually settled. "The prisoner has been heavily sedated and will be executed by tonight's winner!"

The once worried buzz of the crowd transformed into a wave of clapping and cheers that slapped against Tanis' ears with fury. Her face flushed red, and her eyes sent a daggered stare aimed at The King. Sadie squeezed at her shoulder.

The King once again held up his hand and the cheering quieted to a dim murmur.

"But before tonight's battle, I'd like to make another announcement. My son Kaleb has slain the beast which terrorized our water," he said, snapping his fingers.

A bulky-looking guard with large, tattooed forearms swam forward, holding the beast's severed head in his extended hands. Its mouth was propped open to display its piercing teeth, and its eyes were rolled into the back of its head. Dried and pungent blood had congealed on its mouth and nose, while other fragments of dry blood dropped from the cleaved neck.

Tanis' eyes were glued to the King's booth as she

peered over the edge of the cart. She recognized the monster almost immediately as the creature who had attacked her and her sisters. It felt like a lifetime ago. She swallowed hard, choking down a knot forming in the back of her throat. She would go back to that very moment if it meant seeing both her sisters again.

Oliver peered down at Tanis' red face as he listened to the hushed whisper of the crowd, gossiping amongst each other like schoolgirls. He fidgeted uncomfortably, rubbing at his arms as his eyes dropped to the floor. He had never felt more uncomfortable living in his own skin, as one of the merfolk.

The King continued, "Now while we don't normally recognize our soldiers as individuals, I have granted each of my sons a last request. My son, Kaleb, has stated that he wishes to acknowledge the fallen soldiers. Before our battle commences, we will be reading the names of each one assigned to my son."

A young merman with ginger hair, freckles, and red tail who sat on the left-hand side of the stadium shouted out from his seat, "What was Neo's last request?"

The crowd seemed to let out a unified gasp before falling silent. Everyone's eyes were glued on the King, known to be prone to violence and anger. It was unheard of to interrupt like that.

King Oasis squinted at the young merman and then tilted his head back, letting out a deep belly laugh that shook fear into the crowd. They followed his lead, laughing along uneasily as they gave each other apprehensive glances.

"Oh, my boy Neo," the King said, still chuckling as the crowd's forced laugh died down. "His request was a little more primal. If he wins, he will marry the fair and noble Athena."

Athena had a front-row seat, just below the King's section and next to her noble father, Marcus. She bowed her blonde head in acknowledgment, and the crowd cheered. She would do as she was told if Kaleb were to die.

The King leaned over to the tall, lanky guard on his left who was the complete opposite in stature to the bulky tattooed guard holding the beast's severed head on his right. He whispered something into the guard's ear. He nodded and then quickly vanished from the booth.

I bet we will never see that outspoken merman again, Oliver thought as he faded out of sight.

"Now where was I?" the King said. "Oh yes, the names of the fallen soldiers." He snapped his fingers once more, and the bulky guard to his right placed the beast's head on the floor and pulled a scroll out of his satchel.

He rose upright, decked out in the standard gold tortoiseshell armor with a red emblem of a trident across his chest. His green sequined tail swayed gently back and forth as he cleared his throat.

"Robert Gusto, Maxwell Harris…"

Sadie's eyes widened as she felt her chest tighten, as if the guard's hands gripped around her lungs, squeezing tighter with every name he read off his scroll. She took a deep gulp, crossing her fingers at her sides. *Please, no. Not my father.*

"Toby Dawson, Emanuel Olson, Jacob Glider…"

A terrible sense of dread sank deep into her core, writhing its way through her.

"Lorenzo Fin, Drew Humming, Bradley Reeder, Samuel Ashton…"

"No!" Sadie screamed at the top of her lungs as her eyes pooled with tears. Samuel Ashton was her father, and now she knew for sure that he was gone. Just another soldier who'd been taken as a casualty by a corrupt King.

Tanis ducked her head back down into the cart as the entire crowd spun their heads around to face them. Oliver froze with his arms pinned to his sides as his heart beat against his chest.

"Can I help you, dear?" the King asked forebodingly, shooting daggers with his eyes.

Sadie sprang forward, looking like a slingshot being propelled toward its target.

"Sadie, no!" Oliver shouted as he reached forward to grab her tailfin, which slipped out of his fingers like algae-covered kelp, taken by the ocean current.

Sadie swam as fast as she could toward King Oasis. Her long arms extended out and pushed the water to the side. Sadie's doe eyes narrowed as they fixated on the King's throat. The King's guards leaped up from their posts, but he quickly summoned them back with a small hand gesture and calmly watched as she sprang toward him across the arena, her hair blazing like green flames.

"Enough!" the King shouted as he rose from his throne, holding up his hand with a flattened palm to make them stop.

The whispers and gasps of the audience fell silent as a purple glow emitted from his palms. He threw his pointed fingers forward as lightning sprang from his fingertips.

Oliver looked on in dismay as the bolt struck Sadie through her chest. Her eyes rolled back into her head as she spiraled down into the arena.

Tanis had popped her head back up, peeking over the edge of the cart. "Look," she whispered to Oliver. "She's still breathing." Sadie's chest rose and fell with every shallow breath she took but she was still alive.

Oliver bit down on his lips nervously as he watched her helplessly.

"Guards," King Oasis summoned as he sat on his throne. "Bring the girl to the dungeon, and I will deal with her later."

Two guards swam into the arena on command and carried Sadie's limp body away. Her head lolled to the side as they watched her disappear through the tunneled exit.

"We have to go after her," Oliver whispered to Tanis.

Oliver's face twisted with a pain that Tanis knew all too well. She had felt the same way when her sister was taken; no words would have been able to comfort her. The anger hadn't gone away, especially now as Tanis could see her sister within reach. "I understand how you feel, but we have to be smart about it. We will go after Sadie, I promise, but right now, we must wait. You understand? Everything has a perfect time. And this time is not yet perfect to bring Sadie home. Everyone is on high alert. If we try to leave now, it will look suspicious," she whispered back.

Oliver nodded, crossing his arms over his chest as his nostrils flared.

"Now, where were we?" the King said as he reached for a dark silver flask nestled into the seat cushion of his golden throne. He lifted the flask to his parted lips and took a quick sip of the contents before slipping the flask back under his seat cushion.

Tanis scratched at her chin as she tilted her head quizzically. "What's in the flask?' she whispered to Oliver.

Oliver had heard rumors about a special potion that the King consumed to generate his powers. Then again, they were just rumors; Oliver never believed any of them, and there were enough rumors in every kingdom to fill a sinking ship. And after all, they seemed so far-fetched and ridiculous when he thought about them. Merfolk went around telling stories of magic dolphins whose silver blood was powerful enough to destroy full armies, and anyone who drank the blood would become altered. Rumors even ridiculously stated that drinking the potion would provide anyone who drank it with powers beyond their wildest dreams, slowing the ageing process dramatically. However, Oliver had never seen any magic dolphins in the kingdom. He thought the whole thing to be just a creative tale that the children spread.

"It's rumored that it's a potion for his powers," Oliver whispered back as he shrugged his shoulders. "I never really believed in such thing. It's probably just booze."

King Oasis rose once more from his throne. "Thank you all for coming to tonight's battle," he shouted, boisterously addressing the crowd with flaring spirited hands. "You are all in for a great treat! Today is the day where the fate of your next King is decided!"

The crowd roared and clapped, and King Oasis paused for a moment as they settled down before he spoke again. "Each of my sons will be given an assortment of weapons and armor for your viewing pleasure. They may use whatever is in the arena below. Their own selection is what may ensure their life—or assist to bring about their death."

The King waved his arms, and two guards swam into the arena, lifting the two weapons racks out from the ground. They slid up with the squeaking crank of rusted metal that echoed through the stadium. Oliver felt his stomach twist as he looked down at the two racks that he had stocked earlier with swords, shields, knives, axes, helmets, and other weaponry. Nothing was missing. Every possible weapon was right here.

"They will fight to the death," the King continued. "But to make things even more interesting, I will be adding a third component for your viewing pleasure today."

He raised his hands, and a purple light glowed from them once more, extending out from the tips of his fingers in an aura. The beast's head that lay next to his tailfin rose from the ground and floated into the arena. Its body slowly regenerated before the crowd's eyes, a bloody puzzle being put back together. Merfolk gasped in their seats, sharing glances with one another as they leaned slightly closer to their loved ones. They looked confused, dazed, bewildered.

Tanis peered over the edge of the cart with wide eyes as her heart pounded in her chest, a savage drumbeat. The beast that had attacked her sister blinked its beady eyes open as its tail waved back and forth, causing ripples in the water. Its pointed teeth protruded out of its mouth like daggers ready to pierce as it thrashed its head back and forth, examining the crowd.

A *swoosh* sounded, elongated, seemingly going on forever. The beast twirled its body around, causing sand in the arena to rush upward before jolting its massive head forward toward the audience. Its jaws clamped up and down as it sped ahead, ready to tear flesh from the crowd.

Screams of terror echoed across the stadium as panicked merfolk fled their seats, gripping their loved ones.

Boom. A great impact sounded, ricocheting. *Crack!*

The beast's face had crashed into an invisible force shield around the arena below. Its pointed nosed smashed inward as it let out a loud hiss and circled the arena, repeatedly bashing the side of its body against the unseen wall as if it were trying to break a window.

The King rose from his seat and let out a deep bellowing laugh that shook his core. "Don't be frightened," he said, still chuckling. "The beast can't leave the arena below. Please, please do take your seats. The shield will be up until the battle is over. You are all safe. It is a mere spectacle, a plaything to watch and keep you attentive."

Safe. We are all safe.

The word made Tanis roll her eyes. She and her sisters certainly weren't safe, and she was beginning to recognize that the merfolk of Atlantis knew their King was insane. He had just trapped them in a heavily guarded arena with a flesh-eating monster for a death battle.

She watched as the scattered merfolk were herded back to their seats by the King's guards like escaped cattle. Each one was silently taking their seat as if brought to a slaughterhouse, fear visible in their eyes.

"Why don't they just try to leave?" Tanis whispered to Oliver.

Oliver looked down at Tanis' scalp which peeked out of the top of the cart. The blue hair wasn't exactly the best camouflage color. "Because they are more afraid of the King than of the beast, of course," he whispered back as he placed the palm of his hand on her head and gave her a shove. His voice took on a tone that insinuated she ought to have known already. But it was true; this king was heinous and terrifying. And her head should not have been made visible. "You need to be careful! If you are seen, we both die." He pushed her back down into the cart.

Tanis smacked at his hands as she glared at him. "I know," she whispered back, agitated as she fixed the top of her hair. "And by the way, you don't have to push me like that. No one even saw me. They are too fixated on the monster."

Whether that be the King or the beast.

The King cleared his throat loudly once the crowd was back in their seats. "Without further ado, let the competition begin!" he said cheerfully. He raised his hands in the air, and the crowd cheered on cue like mind-controlled zombies as the sounds of trumpets filled the arena.

Kaleb and Neo waited silently on a platform under the arena. Aside from the tunnel, it was the only way into the fighting area, and their father was the only one with the access code to this platform. He had escorted them there earlier with five colossal guards who kept watch with crossed arms and ensured they didn't escape. The guards had positioned themselves in a circle around the platform to prevent either of them from fleeing. Guards' watch had become mandatory after several mermen scheduled to compete were found hanging in their bedrooms the night before like dangling chandeliers.

Kaleb and Neo's attire sparkled in the reflection of the shiny black platform below, emulating burning stars as they looked down in silence. Both were dressed head to fin in traditional soldier attire, their chests covered with gold-painted tortoiseshells, metal chain links hanging over their tails.

"Brother," Neo said as he tilted his head to face Kaleb.

Kaleb looked up, gazing straight forward past the guards into the darkness of the room, ignoring his brother. It was an empty room painted black with nothing but a red door locked with an access pad and the platform. The room only had one purpose—to get champions into the arena without them escaping or harming themselves or the guards. There was no way in or out once the King had placed them there, and no way to avoid his brother's prying eyes.

Neo stared at his brother's stern face and pressed lips through his own furrowed brows. It was like looking into a shattered mirror, only the image refused to face him, and the pieces seemed to scatter as if part of himself were breaking away. He had never meant for it to come to this. His hunger for the throne had gotten the best of him. Now he was paying the price for that greed. He took a deep gulp of ocean water as he thought back to the moments when they were kids before he had become friends with Casco and Baric. They were almost inseparable back then.

Ella would read them stories before bed, but they

wouldn't go to sleep. Instead, they would stay up and play, and if they were too loud, Ella would come in and yell at them as any mom would.

Neo's heart throbbed in his chest and he pushed his shoulders back, trying to brush off the feeling. "You should know, I didn't mean for it to come to this. I didn't know our father would take things this far. I worried that *that* creature might have cast some spell on you. You're my brother."

Kaleb bit down hard on his tongue but could no longer hold the rage he felt building inside him. He snapped his head toward his brother as his bloodshot eyes threw a flamed daggered gaze. "Yuri isn't a creature! She's just a girl you damned to death! And you lost your position as my brother the moment you chose your need for the throne over me," Kaleb shouted as his heart pounded and his fists coiled into a tight ball. "So all I have to say to you now is, good luck."

Kaleb refocused his burning gaze on the red door as the lingering of his words felt fresh and bitter on his tongue.

Neo shook his head disapprovingly; he had nothing more to say. Soon, they would be in the arena, and he would have to kill his brother or be killed by his brother. There was no other way. He turned to face straight into the darkness.

The platform squeaked beneath them and set off, moving upward toward the stadium. Both brothers stole one last glance at each other as the platform breached the top.

Time's up.

Chapter 30

The large black platform came to a relentlessly squeaky halt. It took only moments for the brothers to realize they weren't alone in the arena. The beast had whacked them down with one swoosh of its mighty tail, causing them to collapse onto one another. Its sharp jaws spiraled down above them like a twisting waterspout. Neo and Kaleb quickly rolled their bodies in the opposite direction as the beast's chomping jaws crashed into the sand.

The crowd cheered wildly as the beast recovered. It was shaking its sand-covered head back and forth furiously.

Kaleb's eyes darted toward one of the weapon racks, and he lunged his body forward, propelling himself across the arena as the beast chased behind him in a deadly game of tag. He reached his hand out, grabbing onto the gem-encrusted handle of the closest sword and tugging it free from the rack. Kaleb lifted its long, pointed blade over his head as the beast came thrusting toward him with his jaws clamping. He slid under the beast's massive body, dodging his clinching jaws as the point of his blade pierced into one of the beast's fins. The beast spun in a circle, tossing Kaleb's body into the side of the arena like a rag doll, the blade still fully submerged in its flesh.

Kaleb's head slammed into his father's force field,

and he slid down the wall, temporarily stunned. He had missed the beast's heart, but with one of its fins damaged, its swimming slowed, and bright gushes of blood pooled out of its wound.

The King shouted from his golden throne, clapping his hands together gleefully, "Well played!"

Neo had gotten up off the sandy seafloor and watched with arms crossed as the beast's tilted and injured body closed in on Kaleb. It would be so easy just to let him get eaten, swallowed whole by the beast. Then he wouldn't have to end his brother, but as he watched the beast's mouth open wide, something in him stirred, and he felt his heart being tugged as if pulled by a puppeteer's strings. He zoomed over to the weapons rack and grabbed at a spiked flail. Neo spun it around and around until the spiked metal ball had gained enough momentum. He let it fly toward the beast's head.

Whack!

The spikes pierced into the beast's beady left eye, and Neo pulled hard on the handle of the flail, ripping the beast's eye out with one swift tug.

The beast's head tilted back as it let out a horrendous scream. It lashed forward toward Neo, frantically chomping its jaws. Neo pulled back quickly, but not quick enough; the beast had managed to clip the edge of his tail, leaving a bloody gash.

The crowd let out a synchronized gasp as Neo sprinted for the other end of the arena. He gazed over his shoulder. The beast was right behind him, following the trail of blood dripping from his tail.

Kaleb's eyes fluttered as he slowly came to his senses. The tip of his tongue tasted bitter and metallic as he blinked his eyes a few times, trying to focus. *Red. Why is there red?* Then he saw it.

The beast was in his focus, and his sword was still jammed into its right fin. But that was not where the blood was coming from. His brother was doing laps around the arena as the beast chased closely behind him. Blood pooled from his brother's tail and into the water, leaving a murky red haze.

Kaleb lifted himself. His shoulders felt stiff and bruised, and he bit down on his bottom lip as he bolted toward the beast, ignoring the pinging pain in his limbs. He dove under its massive body and grabbed hold of the sword still stuck firmly in its fin. With one quick slash forward, he pulled the blade through the beast's flesh, severing the fin.

The beast spiraled down like a corkscrew, slamming down onto the arena floor. Its body thrashed viciously, clouding the arena with billowing sand.

Kaleb held the bloody sword up over the beast's head and plunged it down with all his force. Its body went still as King Oasis rose from his throne, clapping. "Well done, well done!" he shouted as the crowd cheered along.

Kaleb's lips curved into a toothed sneer, and he swam over to the weapons rack, pulling a wooden-handled ax from its inventory. There was a look of fury and determination in Kaleb's eyes. His arms strained with every blow.

"Here's the beast's head again, Father. Hope you are proud," Kaleb said, furiously tossing the massive head toward the King's throne. It hit against the force field with a loud bang as its blood-dripping head bounced back into the arena, nearly knocking Neo down.

The audience gasped in horror and then fell completely silent as if a storm was about to roll in violently.

King Oasis tilted his head back and let out a maniacal laugh, tapping at his sides as he always did when greatly amused. The crowd awkwardly laughed along as they glanced at each other, gripping at their seats. "Oh, my dear boy, once was enough. That was just a warm-up for the real battle," he said, snapping his fingers. The beast's carcass slowly vanished as the King took another swig from his flask. "Although, I was hopeful that your brother would have brought me his head this time."

The King glanced over at Neo, looking him up and down with disappointment. Neo felt himself shrink under his father's stare and diverted his gaze to the floor as his face flushed red. His father knew exactly what to say to pit him and his brother against each other. He had been doing it all their lives, competition after competition.

Neo glanced up at Kaleb through squinted eyes and felt a surge of jealousy pulsing through his veins in a liquid envy. He balled his fists and puffed out his chest, trying to rebuild his wounded ego.

"Neo," the King said, pointing to his tail with an open palm. "It would be an unfair match to let you battle your brother in that condition." A ray of light cast from the King's extended hand and lifted Neo upward into a bursting ball of glowing brightness.

Kaleb covered the top of his eyes with his hands and squinted. He could hardly see his brother, who seemed to have been consumed by the glowing mass.

Moments later, the light expanded like a silent explosion and then disappeared. It was as if it had never existed. Neo was left floating there with a dumbfounded look across his face, and his tail fully intact.

Kaleb looked down at his own injured and scratched-up arms. His shoulders still throbbed between the blades with a dull pulsing ache. His father wouldn't help him, though. He wasn't dumb. He was well aware that his father wanted him dead, and he needed Neo to succeed in killing him. In the King's mind, he had dishonored the family by intermingling with one of *the Inked.* If Neo was injured, it would provide Kaleb with the leverage he needed to win, possibly, and he couldn't allow that.

Yuri began to come to her senses next to the King. She let out a tiny groan as her eyes blinked slowly open and looked down at her frail arms chained to the wooden chair.

"Oh, good! Look who's awake, just in time!" the King spouted gleefully.

Kaleb's top lip retracted over his teeth as he scowled at his father. His face seemed to soften as his gaze drifted to Yuri, sitting next to him, frail and weak. She bobbed in and out of consciousness as if she had been drugged.

Kaleb shook his head impulsively, refocusing on the weapons rack. The sooner he ended this, the sooner he could save her. He swam to the rack and pulled out a long steel sword, a matching shield, and one of the King's favorite spiked helmets. He thrust the helmet over his head and banged the blade against the shield, impatient.

"Well, that certainly got you ready for battle. I see you decided on a traditional weapon," the King said, sneering through a faux smile. He turned his attention to Neo whose arms were still uncomfortably crossed over his chest.

"And what's the choice for my other son?"

The crowd watched silently with anticipation as Neo swam over to the weapons rack. He ran his hands over the ax, then the sword, then the flail.

Which of these could I kill my own brother with? He twisted his head, peering over his shoulder at Kaleb, who stared intently at Yuri and their father. His face was red with anger, and his hands gripped so tightly around his sword that the veins protruded from his fingers. Neo did not doubt in his mind that his brother would kill him to save that girl.

"Well, my son? The audience is waiting. We don't have all day!" King Oasis shouted from his golden throne as he took another sip of his flask.

Neo grabbed a mace from the rack, along with a shield and a spiked helmet. As the better fighter, he knew the mace would be able to damage the tortoiseshell armor they both had donned. He slid the spiked helmet over his head and turned to face his brother.

They were dressed identically, and if it hadn't been for their weapon choice, it would be nearly impossible to distinguish them from one another.

"Excellent choice," the King bellowed out. "Now, please move forward to face each other."

The two brothers swam forward, facing each other.

Kaleb's eyes pierced through his spiked helmet and blazed with rage.

"For the record, I am truly sorry it has to come to this," Neo said, meeting his brother's gaze beneath his spiked helmet. "No man wishes to see his brother die, much less by his own hand."

Kaleb didn't respond. Instead, he lifted his sword and steadied it in his hands, keeping his gaze focused on Neo. Neo nodded silently as he raised his mace, finally understanding that there wasn't enough time for his brother to forgive him. There were only seconds left before one of them lay dead on the arena floor.

The King rose from his throne, addressing the crowd. "Tonight, my sons will battle to the death. The prize will be my throne!" he shouted as he lifted his hands in the air.

The crowd cheered wildly, clapping and shouting from their seats, and the stadium to shook with their excitement. The noise caused Yuri to jolt in her chair as she came to her full senses, pushing the gag away from her mouth with her tongue.

"Kaleb!" she shouted, finally able to piece together what was going on.

Kaleb spun his head briefly to look up at Yuri, awake now but still roped down.

Her silver hair was knotted around her pale face filled with wide-eyed dread. She met his gaze with her deep icy eyes as he silently mouthed, *it will be okay* before turning back to face his brother. The tattooed guard positioned behind the King reached forward, tucking the gag back into Yuri's mouth as she bit down onto his pudgy fingers with her sharp pointed teeth.

He pulled his blood-dripping hand back as he shouted, "Freak!"

The King squinted at Yuri as he excused his guard

who hustled away like a scampering crab to tend to his wounds. He refocused his gaze on the arena as he lifted his mouth back into a sharply pointed grin that wrinkled at deranged eyes. "You will hear three drumbeats. When you hear the final beat, the battle has started. Whoever is left alive will be my heir. May the stronger son win," he said, glancing at Neo. He retook his seat.

A young blond merboy appeared from behind the King's booth with a red sash across his chest that held a small matching red drum. He lifted the drumsticks toward his face and brought them down upon the drum. From now, a single drumbeat interspersed each move of the two sons.

One lift of a weapon—a bang.

Kaleb and Neo steadied their grip on their weapons as the crowd went silent with anticipation.

One stare—a bang. And so it went on.

Neo and Kaleb lifted their shields.

Bang...

Kaleb slashed his sword forward at Neo.

Bang.

Neo arched his back, dodging Kaleb's swing as the end of his blade clinked against his armor. He spun his body around in a backflip, kicking up the seafloor sand into Kaleb's eyes and jabbing his mace forward. It hit him hard against the chest, cracking into his tortoiseshell armor and sending him flying back against the arena wall and onto the floor.

The King clapped wildly from his throne, leading the cheers of the crowd as Yuri squirmed uncomfortably from beneath her chains letting out loud murmurs, which were anything but joyous. She was not dead but might as well have been. She cried and whimpered for herself—but also for all those who were suffering, beaten, defeated, slain, and slaughtered at the King's hands.

Neo lifted the mace high over his head and bolted toward his brother. He swung it down as hard as he could, but Kaleb was too quick. He rolled his body out of the way as the mace came smashing down into the ground by his head and became shrouded into a clouded puff of sand.

Neo grabbed the handle of the mace and tugged. The spikes had become embedded in the sand, and as Neo strained to pull them out, Kaleb saw his chance. He lifted his steel sword up from beneath the clouded puff sand and stabbed through Neo's shoulder with the blade.

Neo let at a wailing cry that echoed through the stadium and seemed to bounce off the walls as if it were mocking him. He pulled back hard, jerking the mace out of the ground with the sword still intact in his shoulder. He bit down on his bottom lip and winced. Now, he pulled the blade slowly out of his wounded flesh. His eyes narrowed on his brother as he sent the bloody sword flying toward him.

Yuri's eyes widened from her seat as she screamed out from beneath her gag, "Kaleb!"

The sword pierced through Kaleb's tailfin, and he fell back down, digging his fingernails into the ground as he crawled toward the weapons rack. His body dragged behind him, heavy and juddering, and as he scudded across the ground, he left a trail in the sand.

Neo, Neo, Neo!

The crowd cheered as Neo swam forward toward his brother. His mace dragged behind him as he paused to look up at his father, who looked back intently as he nodded encouragingly with a wide grin across his bearded face. Neo's focus shifted to Yuri seated next to him, rocking back and forth beneath her chains as her lips moved under her gag, her screams drowned by the arena of merfolk chanting his name.

Neo, Neo, Neo!

As Neo closed in, Kaleb's hands reached for the sword embedded in his tailfin. His eyes flickered as he wrapped his fingers weakly around its handle. He had lost a lot of blood and as he tried to pull the sword out from his tail, his heart pounded in a slow, throbbing beat as if this were death knocking at his door. His head lolled back into the sand beneath his spiked helmet, and he forced his unsteady focus on Yuri's ice-blue gaze as his body went limp.

Neo's hands trembled around his mace as he towered over his brother, whose eyes flickered in and out of an awakened state. He bent down, pulling his brother's spiked helmet off his face and tossing it at the side of the arena where it hit the wall and tumbled to the ground. All the color had drained from Kaleb's face, and he looked like a painted white corpse, a mere zombie of his prior self. Neo raised the mace over his head beneath his shaking hands and steadied himself to take the final blow. He had wanted this moment to prove himself the worthiest for the throne; finally, he would be able to show his father that he was better than Kaleb. But, as he looked down at his brother's face, *his face,* his gut twisted into his chest, knotting into a ball of regret that settled on his heart. Kaleb might never forgive him, but he also wouldn't be able to forgive himself if he ended his own brother's life. He slammed the mace down into the ground next to Kaleb's head with a loud thump. "I won't do it!" he shouted, raising his hands as he spun in a circle, addressing the crowd who whispered, sending a shock wave of gossip across the stadium.

King Oasis rose from his seat with his fists balled at his sides. His face turned as red as a boiling crab. "I did not teach my sons to quit halfway through a battle," he bellowed angrily. "Finish what you started!"

Neo stared down at his unconscious brother whose head tilted toward Yuri. He looked down into his empty palms, free of his brother's spilt blood, and back up at the spiked mace dug into the sand, inches away from Kaleb's cheek. He grabbed its handle, lifting it out of the sandy ground and hurling it across the arena and out of reach.

"I will not, Father!" Neo shouted back through gritted teeth as he met his father's dark scowl.

The crowd let out a unified gasp. No one ever dared to defy the King.

King Oasis grabbed his flask from under his seat, and chugged the remaining contents, throwing the empty container down to the floor. *Clink.* His eyes ignited with bright white light that extended out like lasers, piercing through Neo's entire body and pinning him to the back wall of the arena. He lifted his golden trident and pointed it toward his son as though proffering a condemning finger.

Neo tried to slash his tail back and forth but felt as if several guards were holding his body down, threatening to rip him limb from limb. He was completely immobilized by his father's powers, rendered almost frozen, a mere mannequin of his own self.

"I had high hopes for you, son," the King bellowed, shaking the pointed trident in his hand. "But I cannot have someone so weak leading Atlantis. So you will end this, or you will die!"

Neo's focus shifted to his brother lying on the floor. Kaleb's head lolled to the side, and his green eyes had opened to meet his brother's familiar gaze. *I'm sorry,* Neo mouthed silently. His eyes refocused on the King as he took a deep gulp of salty seawater into his lungs. He felt the words building in his chest, the same way a scuba diver might feel rising too quickly on an empty tank, lungs fit to burst. "I will not do it," Neo said firmly. "I said, I will not do it!"

Kaleb reached his hand out with his last ounce of strength toward his brother as his eyes blinked. His mouth was dry and cracked as he tried to say, *don't...I forgive you...don't,* but it only came out as a low gurgled murmur.

The King's face lit up. A raging fire inside his body scorched him. His tightly gripped hands probed his trident forward. "Then you will die!" he shouted, as a burst of light exploded out of his trident's pronged tips.

Neo's body was instantly torn into pieces as if a bomb had exploded from his chest. He hadn't had the chance to cry out before his head rolled onto the arena floor, his limbs scattered into a dismantled puzzle.

The audience cringed from their seats, gripping their children tightly. They were used to the violence, but like a brainwashed cult, they remained shocked and in disbelief that the King could kill his own blood—and all so violently.

Kaleb let out a loud, wailing cry that broke from his lungs like an orca breaching the surface.

The King's face cracked into a dark smile. "Ah," the King said, throwing his hands up and addressing the crowds. "My other disobedient son is still alive. Perhaps he can redeem himself!"

The King pointed his palms toward Kaleb's limp body, and it floated into the center of the arena as if carried by the ocean waves. A ray of purple light surrounded Kaleb as his wounded fin slowly healed and the blood pooled back into his body.

He gasped as he felt himself come back to life, arching his back as his eyes widened.

The light dimmed around Kaleb's body until it was finally gone, and he was left floating there as if nothing at all had happened. He looked down at his tail and arms. No cuts, no bruising, no blood, but something *did* happen; his brother had been murdered, and the girl he loved still sat before him in chains next to a monster he had once called his father.

The King lifted his other palm, and Yuri was elevated from her seat. The chains she was bound with fell off her. She stretched out her arms and tentacles as the King dropped her freed body into the arena.

"Yuri!" Kaleb cried out, swimming toward her with arms outstretched.

Yuri let herself crash into him in an ungainly manner. It certainly was far from graceful. She gripped tightly at his hips as she pressed her messy-haired head against his chest.

"The rumors are true!" a merman with raven black hair shouted from the audience, pointing his finger into the arena.

Athena sprung up from her seat, seizing the opportunity to be a conquistador. She felt as if venom rose in the back of her throat, and she wanted to take a killing bite. "Traitor!" she screamed as her crew of lackeys followed her lead, echoing her words in a chant.

Traitor! Traitor! Traitor!

Soon, the entire audience was chanting along, except for Tanis and Oliver.

Tanis recognized Athena immediately. She raised her hand to the scar that ran across her eye, where Athena once dragged the sharp edge of a shell. It was her forever reminder, a permanent reminiscence of how much her kind was hated.

"That's enough!" the King shouted, sending the crowd into a halted silence. "My son will have the opportunity to redeem himself. Before him is a creature who threatens our way of life and purity. We cannot allow this!"

As the crowd cheered wildly, Oliver looked down at the floor, embarrassed by his community. His face flushed from the shame that he had once feared their kind too. The lies of the King were the only knowledge he had known about *the Inked*. His father had told him as a child that if he didn't go to sleep, *the Inked* would get him. *They will grind you up into a potion or eat you for supper!* It was small stories like this that were dangerous, tall tales that made an entire community hate what they had been taught to fear. Oliver shook his head disappointedly as the King spoke further.

"To prove his loyalty to the kingdom, my son will slay this disgusting *Inked* creature!"

Kaleb looked down at Yuri curled into his chest.

Her face was adorned with dark rings surrounding her icy blue eyes. She was shattered, and all he wanted to do was escape with her and never look back. He squeezed her tightly in his arms as he looked up at his father through furrowed brows. He would never harm her. His father would have to kill him first.

King Oasis reached his long arm, pointing to one of the weapons racks. "Kaleb, choose your weapon," he said firmly beneath pinched lips.

Kaleb stared back at his father, unmoving. His green eyes burned with rage, hopeful that they would set ablaze his father's golden throne.

Yuri grabbed at Kaleb's forearm, wrapping her hand around it gently to comfort him. His skin felt soft, unlike the callused skin of a warrior. Her eyes darted back and forth between Kaleb and the King, whose lips had curved into a grimacing grin, baring his teeth. It was hard to believe that Kaleb shared any part of himself with such a monster.

"I said, CHOOSE YOUR WEAPON!" the King screamed, causing some of the audience to jolt in their seats.

Kaleb crossed his arms over his chest, refusing to budge as he shook his head.

King Oasis' nostrils flared as he lifted his palms, pointing them toward Kaleb. A ray of light sprang from his hands, hitting his son in the chest. His body froze, seeming like a stiff board in Yuri's arms, as if a single tap would make him crack. "I can't feel my body," Kaleb said as his mouth twitched to get the words out.

The King twisted his fingers as if controlling a puppet, and Kaleb's arms moved in a taut robotic motion as if he truly were connected to strings.

"Yuri, move away," Kaleb shouted through his stiff lips. "I'm not in control of my body. I don't know what he'll make me do!"

Kaleb's body twisted and contorted toward the closest weapons rack. His arms reached out, grabbing a broad metal ax. He bit down on his tongue as his fingers wrapped around its wooden handle. *Please no.*

Yuri bolted to the opposite end of the arena. Her heart pounded in her chest, and the feel of the familiar anchor was back, weighing on her like crippling anxiety. Her eyes scanned the circular arena and its high walls that were surrounded by a magical dome. There was nowhere to escape.

Kaleb swam toward her with the ax swinging in his hands.

Yuri dove under him, dodging the first swing. "Stop, Kaleb!" she screamed as the ax came swinging down at her tentacles. The blade cut through the water as she zoomed out of the way, and its sharp edge crashed against the sandy floor.

Kaleb's face strained as he tried to fight his body. His lips creased at the edges, wrinkling with discontent as his eyes flooded with salty tears. His mind was still his, but his body belonged to the King. He was a puppet with no strings, and his creator controlled him. "I can't, Yuri," he shouted, ripping the ax out of the sand. "You are going to have to kill me. Grab a weapon!"

Yuri dodged another swing of his ax as it chopped through her long silver hair, leaving strands floating in the water, looking like scattered silverfish. She bolted to the other side of the arena, swimming backward, keeping her eyes focused on Kaleb as a moving target. "I can't do that," she cried out, shaking her head. "I can't kill you!"

As Kaleb drew closer to Yuri, he focused his mind on the ax in his hand, staring at it as his fingers tightly wrapped around its wooden handle. *Drop it. Drop it. Drop it.*

Tanis watched in horror from the audience, peeking her head out of Oliver's cart as Kaleb continued to spring on her sister, wielding the ax wildly over his head. Her fists balled tightly in her palms as her lips peeled back over her teeth and she looked at Oliver with fury through her scared-eyed gaze. "We need to get to the King. We have to stop him," she said as her voice shook, and she fought back angry tears, leaving an uncomfortable lump in her throat.

Oliver's eyes shifted from Tanis to the arena, and then back at Tanis. He fidgeted uncomfortably, wrapping his arms around his chest and tapping at his sides. If he didn't help her, her sister would die, and it would eat at him like a parasite, slowly consuming his insides with deep regret. He shut his eyes and opened them slowly to see Tanis still staring at him with her flurried gaze. "Fine," he said, shaking his head disapprovingly. "But this is a suicide mission. I'll see if I can roll you in the cart to the other side, but after that, you are on your own."

Tanis' lips curved into a dark sharp-toothed grin as she redirected her furrowed gaze at the King. "That's all I need," she said, nodding.

Chapter 31

Yuri's heart beat hard in her chest and she felt the heavy burden of fatigue inching up her tentacles, weighing her down. She couldn't keep outswimming Kaleb, whose eyes pleaded with her while his body tried to chop her into pieces. She circled the weapons rack, grabbing a steel shield and sword off its shaking hooks as Kaleb bolted toward her from the other side of the arena with a twisted look of pain across his face.

"Stab me," he cried out, swinging the ax at her head.

Yuri hoisted her body to the ground, barrel rolling to avoid the blow. She lifted her shield as the ax slammed down against the metal. "I can't," she cried back. "I don't want to hurt you!" She dropped the sword and ax on either side of her and spread her body out in the sand in the form of a snow angel, exposing herself to Kaleb. "If this is the end. This is the end," Yuri said, looking up at Kaleb with her deep ice-blue eyes.

Kaleb fought his arms, straining at his temples as they rose over his head with the ax gripped in his palms. "Yuri, please no!" he cried out as he towered over her body, fingers trembling on the wooden-handled ax, ready to strike.

"STOP!" Britt burst into the arena, her hands radiating a purple glow that cut through the King's force field.

The crowd broke into a panic, scattering as they overpowered the guards at the exits.

Britt's body blazed in purple hues, and the tattoo on her collar spun as if the dolphins were swimming circles on her skin. She pushed her palms up toward Kaleb, and a ball of light spiraled from her hands, hitting him in the chest. His body was thrown back against the arena wall, and he tumbled down into the sandy seafloor.

Yuri's neck cocked back and her eyes widened as she traced her sister's new body. It looked like Britt from the waist up. Same short pink hair, honey brown eyes, and angled face. However, she glowed purple like jellyfish in the night and in place of her long black tentacles was one beautiful sequined tail.

Before Yuri could part her lips to speak, Britt propelled herself toward Kaleb, wrapping her hands around his throat.

"Britt, no!" Yuri shouted, chasing after her sister with her arms extended.

King Oasis shot up from his throne, a loaded spring. His fists clenched at his sides as he recognized the familiar glowing purple hue; it was the same bright purple that had originally surrounded him when he began drinking the dolphins' blood for their powers. His lips curved over his teeth as he realized that his source had been compromised.

He had been harnessing the dolphins' silver blood since stealing them from the great ancestor of *the Inked*. Drinking the blood had given the King abilities beyond his wildest dreams and had allowed him to age at a much slower rate. He had created an entire kingdom from their blood, and he would be damned if he let some disgusting octopus-like creature steal it from him. King Oasis reached behind him for his flask and lifted the metal spout to his lips. The contents inside had run dry, and he threw the flask down onto the floor angrily. Soon, his powers would be depleted.

"Guards!" he shouted, beckoning his army through his force field and into the arena.

Twelve guards charged at Britt through the tunneled entrance. Their bodies were covered in thick armor and their swords tilted to a point.

Britt spun her body around, and she pounded her fist into the ground. A blast of light rippled through the sand akin to a pressure wave, knocking all twelve guards to the seafloor and rendering them unconscious. Her eyes blazed as she lifted her palm out toward the weapons rack. It shook with huge force until a sword flew from it, swinging hooks and sending it into Britt's open palm. She pointed the blade at Kaleb who slumped against the side of the arena as Yuri barreled forward, blocking her path.

"No, Britt, stop!" Yuri screamed, holding her hands out in front of her as a barricade.

Britt pushed forward, shoving Yuri with her every move. "Why are you protecting him? I saw him kidnap you! We wouldn't even be here it weren't for this merman!" Britt screamed, jabbing her sword past Yuri at Kaleb.

"It's not what you think!" Yuri screamed, pushing Britt's arm back before the sword could pierce through Kaleb.

Britt coiled her arm back and then jammed her sword forward once more. Yuri leaped up, blocking the blade as it slid through her abdomen. She collapsed to the ground, landing on top of Kaleb as a puff of blood filled the water around them.

Britt gasped as she let her hands loosen from the blade. Her lips parted into a quivering open gape. The glowing purple light around her disappeared as if it had been consumed by a black hole throbbing in her heart. "Yuri!" Britt screamed, reaching her trembling hand forward. Before her fingertips could even graze her sister's body, she was blasted by a ball of light sending her spiraling back. She focused on pushing her body forward, holding her arms out and slowing herself before she could crash into the arena wall.

King Oasis's hands were raised and pushed together, prayerlike. As he pulled them apart, a lightning bolt formed between his palms, reflecting the bright electricity in his darkened eyes. Britt froze. She hadn't seen this before, and while she'd only had her powers for a short while, it was clear that the King had years of experience.

"You don't know how to harness your new powers fully, do you?" he said mockingly as his lips curved into a dark grin. "You just let the anger take control." He flung the lightning bolt at her, and Britt dove into the sand, sliding to avoid the hit that struck down by her head. It was followed by a loud booming that throbbed at her ears, and she gripped at the sides of her head as she tried to get up.

King Oasis was already forming another lightning bolt between his palms, his eyes glowing with rage as he aimed his hands at Britt. He hadn't noticed that Oliver had pushed his large weapons cart next to his throne.

Tanis sprang up, diving at the King with her fingers clawed. She impacted him in a slam.

The King fell back, toppling over his throne as Tanis wrapped her tentacles around his neck. The lightning bolt flew aimlessly out of the King's hand and hit into the sand next to Britt's body, turning to a blackened pile of ash. She looked up at her sister coiled around the King. "Tanis!" Britt shouted, raising her hand toward the King's booth.

Tanis wrestled with the King, her tentacles suctioning around his neck, causing the veins to bulge out and throb under his skin. As she squeezed tighter, his body lit up, burning at her limbs. She let out a yelp, curling back her tentacles instinctively, recoiling.

Oliver swam to her side, reaching for her shoulders to pull her up as the King rose from the ground as though resurrected.

The King reached his palms out and pulled Tanis and Oliver forward with his powers. It was as if they were being gripped, choked by an unseen force. Oliver and Tanis grasped at their necks, struggling to breathe as they dangled like hung ornaments under the King's powers.

Britt's eyes bounced between Tanis and Yuri; both her sisters needed her help. She swam over to Yuri, placing two fingers on her neck and feeling the slowing pulse of her heartbeat on her fingertips. She wasn't conscious but was still breathing and alive. The sword was still sticking out of her abdomen and rose and fell with every shallow breath her sister took. "Hang in there," she whispered in her sister's ear, "I'll be right back. Just keep breathing."

Britt shot up toward the King's throne. She did a

backflip, whacking the King down with her new tail, which shimmered as it slapped against his skin. Tanis and Oliver dropped down to the ground freed from his power as they gasped in water through their gills.

"I've had enough of you!" The King's voice boomed with rage, as he thrust himself back up, grabbing at Britt's throat with his bare hands.

The gills on Britt's neck were blocked by the King's chubby fingers, and she gasped for breath beneath his clutches, thrashing her tail back and forth.

"Let her go!" Tanis cried, springing up from the ground and biting into the King's arm with her sharp pointed teeth, leaving an open bleeding gash across his skin.

The King pushed her body back, elbowing her in the stomach, and she toppled over onto Oliver, who fell back, hitting his head against the arena's metal railing. The King held Britt's throat in one hand as he formed a spear made of light in the other.

Britt's twitching eyes widened. Soon, she would lose consciousness, and both her sisters would die at the hands of this monster. She took one last look at both of her sisters lying unconscious on the floor. Tanis had collapsed over onto Oliver, and Yuri was slumped over Kaleb with a sword sticking out of her chest. Tears pooled in her eyes as she realized she was alone again, and she would face death by herself.

The King's mouth twisted up into a wide, clownish sneer peaking a little too high at his eyes. "As soon as I kill you, the dolphins will be mine again," he whispered in her ear. "And I'll make sure that none of your kind ever swim in this sea again!" King Oasis gripped the light spear in his hands, twisting it around in his fingers.

"This might hurt a little," he said menacingly as he winked.

Britt closed her eyes, readying herself to embrace death.

King Oasis thrust the spear at her heart.

His fist hit against her chest, and she opened her eyes to find his hands barren. The light spear had completely disappeared. He snapped his fingers angrily as small sparks flew from his fingertips, but he was unable to muster another spear. The King's fingers curled into his palm as his darkened eyes glared at Britt under furrowed brows. He was all out of power. "No need for magic," he said, wrapping both hands around her throat.

Britt writhed under his clutches, squirming as he squeezed the life out of her. As she struggled, the tattoo on her collar glowed and the drawn dolphins circled on her skin three times before a burst of light exploded from her chest.

Britt fell to the ground, gasping to catch her breath as the King pulled back, lifting his hands to his eyes and squinting under the luminous glow.

When the light finally dulled, Britt traced her body with her eyes, all her limbs still intact but something had changed. Her tentacles were back. She ran her fingers across her collar bone. No dolphin tattoo.

The scream pierced through her ears, and she held her hands to them as she looked up to see the three dolphins biting into the King's flesh, ripping him apart piece by piece. Each bite they took caused him to shrivel as if he was rapidly aging before Britt's eyes. Soon, he was nothing more than a shriveled bag of flesh piled on the floor in tiny bloody pieces. The dolphins gobbled him up, as if he were a mess of rotting but tasty sardines.

Chapter 32

Tanis' eyes blinked open. Her body was strewn across Oliver's lap. A bloody cut ran across his forehead like a river, dripping down into his brows. "Oliver," she said, slapping his face with the palm of her hand. "Wake up."

Oliver groaned as he opened his eyes. He reached his hand gingerly to his reddened cheek.

"Wake up!" Tanis shouted, giving him another slap on the cheek.

Oliver lifted his hands in retreat as he raised his torso. "Holy hell, I'm awake! Stop hitting me!" he said, his voice agitated.

Tanis wrapped her arms around his neck, pulling him into a tight hug. "I'm glad you're okay!" she squealed happily as she squeezed him.

Oliver's whole body tingled with excitement. He patted her on the back awkwardly as he pulled himself back from her embrace. His eyes darted between Tanis and the seafloor. "Umm, you too," he said uncomfortably, dropping his hands to his sides.

"TANIS!" Britt shouted, waving her hands as she swam to her sister and Oliver. "You okay?"

Tanis lifted herself up from the ground as her sister barreled toward them. She placed her hands on her back and stretched her spine, twisting a few degrees to the left, then the right. "Yeah, I'm fine," she said, wincing as she turned her neck which throbbed from bruising. "Where's Yuri?"

Britt grabbed at Tanis' hand and squeezed. "She's in the arena and she's hurt. Come on!" She pulled at Tanis' arm, dragging her sister with her through the opening she had ripped in the King's force field. Oliver glanced around at the empty stadium seats, took a deep gulp of water through his gills, and followed the sisters down into the arena.

Yuri's body laid sprawled over Kaleb's lap on the arena floor. The large metal sword jammed in her ribs moved ever so slightly with her shallow breathing.

"What happened to her?" Tanis shouted, rushing over to Yuri's side. She knelt beside her sister's body and sobbed.

Oliver followed after her, placing his hand on her shoulder and squeezing gently. He stared down at the ground as his mouth twitched into an uncomfortable, quivering frown.

Britt shook her head, collapsing to the ground as her eyes welled up with tears. "I just wanted to kill her kidnapper," she sobbed, letting tears drip from her eyes and dissolve into the ocean as quickly as they came. "I didn't mean to hurt her."

Tanis shook her head in disbelief. "Kaleb is not her kidnapper," she cried out. "That was Neo, his twin!" She pointed to the sprawled out remains of Neo's limbs in the arena.

Britt glanced over at Neo's head that lay a few feet away. His eyes were still open wide, glassy and white, yet with a pained and bewildered expression as if he had never expected to die. His mouth was ajar as if he wanted to taunt Britt for not being the one to end him.

She had been so distracted by her anger she hadn't even noticed the bloody remains, but her sister was right—he looked precisely like Kaleb. She had made a grave mistake.

Kaleb groaned from underneath Yuri. He was beginning to regain consciousness, his blurry eyes refocusing on the heavy weight in his lap. As the haze cleared from his eyes, he saw Yuri's pale face resting on his chest, her long silver hair draped over his left arm. She looked so beautiful. But she also looked beaten down, abused, tormented, and as though she had entirely given up. There was no color in her. "Yuri," he said weakly. But there was no response. His eyes traced her body, starting from her tentacles to her chest, and freezing at the large sword protruding out of her ribs. "Yuri!" he cried out, feeling a rush of adrenalin pump through his body. His neck flew back as he let out a loud wailing cry that echoed through the arena.

Yuri's two sisters knelt at each side of him, sobbing into their hands. Behind them, Oliver swam back and forth, nervously rubbing at the back of his neck. "Don't die," Kaleb said, running his hands through Yuri's silver hair. "Please don't die."

Britt reached over, grabbing at Tanis' hand which trembled under her shaking palm. "What do we do?"

Kaleb interrupted before Tanis could speak. "You have my father's powers." His voice cracked with every word. "Use them to save her."

Tanis' eyebrows raised into a hopeful peak as she shook at Britt's hand. "That's right! You can bring her back to us just like the King brought back the beast!"

Britt's mouth pressed into a tight puckered frown as she looked down at her tentacle curled into the sand;

it had once been a temporary shimmering fin. She didn't know how to tell them that the dolphins had left her, and she had no clue where they had gone. She ran her fingertips over her bare collar bone as she met her sister's hopeful gaze. "I'm sorry, Tanis," Britt said, shaking her head. "My powers are gone now. The dolphins left me."

Kaleb cocked his head. "Dolphins?"

Britt's lips curled up over her teeth as she shot Kaleb a dirty look. "That's what I said," she hissed as she traced his face with her eyes—the face that looked so similar to the one that stole her sister away.

Oliver cleared his throat, still nervously rubbing at his neck as he paced. "Wait—that would mean…"

Before he could finish, Kaleb cut him off. "That the stories are true, and the dolphins chose her," Kaleb said, nodding as he cradled Yuri in his arms.

"No," Britt said, lifting herself from the ground as she shook her head vigorously back and forth, crossing her arms uncomfortably over her chest. "They didn't choose me. I told you all, they left. They *left* me."

Yuri's lips were turning blue, and her head flopped to the side in Kaleb's arms as he brushed at her hair with his fingers.

Kaleb's forehead wrinkled as his brows furrowed over his piercing green eyes, and his free hand clenched at the sand below him. His temper rose from the pit of his stomach and into his throat like lava pouring from the tip of a volcano. "You have to call them back!" he screamed at Britt. "Your sister is dying!"

Tanis grabbed at Britt's hand, looking up at her from the sandy ground with her large eyes that were bloodshot with exhaustion and grief. "Please try," she said, squeezing at her sister's fingers as she pleaded with her, rocking back and forth in the sand.

Britt looked up at the translucent force field that surrounded the arena, turning it into a prisoned dome. The hole she had cut through with her seemingly lost powers had regenerated, and they were trapped within the King's magical sphere like tiny glass figurines in a snow globe. Only there were no magical dolphins in sight to dance around them as her sister's life rattled in the hands of death.

The arena had gone eerily silent as Kaleb, Oliver, and Tanis stared at her with pleading eyes, as if expecting her to form miracles like a Greek goddess.

She looked down at her bare hands, which no longer radiated a purple glow. She wiggled her fingers hopelessly.

Yuri's skin was turning blue at the tips of fingers and the curve of her lips, slowly spreading across her body like a plague.

Britt sighed heavily as she balled her fingers tight at her sides. "I'll try," she said, breaking the uncomfortable silence. She took another deep gulp of seawater through the open gills in her neck, letting the cold water blow out of her mouth as she swam into the center of the arena. She then lifted her hands over her head as if summoning a storm. "Dolphins…come!" she said, awkwardly pausing.

Nothing.

She swayed her hands back and forth. "Dolphins, I summon you!" she said with agitation still lingering on the tip of her tongue.

Nothing.

Britt let her arms drop to her sides with frustration

and defeat. "This isn't working," she shouted. "I wish they were here, but they aren't and there's nothing I can…" Her words trailed off as the seafloor below her shook, vibrating the grains of sand beneath her and penetrating through her body. She swam over to Tanis, pulling her into a tight embrace as they both trembled in each other's arms. Oliver huddled behind them, crouching next to Kaleb who continued to cradle Yuri in his arms the way one cradled a newborn.

"I'm so sorry, Tanis. I wish none of this had ever happened," Britt cried as she rocked her little sister back and forth and her messy blue hair tumbled down her left shoulder, a waterfall of blue.

"Wait, look!" Oliver shouted, pointing to the center of the arena.

It had cracked open like the jaws of the beast, threatening to pull them all into its jagged gullet. A ray of light beamed out the newly formed crevasse, causing them to squint and turn their faces or be blinded by its glory. The silhouettes of three dolphins shot out of the cleft. Their bodies were translucent, and as they swam, a trail of light followed behind them, a long, hanging veil. They circled the arena, joyous and free.

"They're beautiful," Tanis said, her mouth gaped open with awe.

Kaleb coddled Yuri in his arms, looking back and forth between Britt and dolphins. Britt met his gaze and nodded as she squeezed at Yuri's hand. Her sister's face was sunken like a mummy, and there wasn't much time left to save her, but she would have to try.

Britt lifted herself off the floor, feeling the sandy grains of the arena against her tentacles as she shuffled her way into the center for a second chance. The warm sand stuck to her suckers, and she had forgotten how good it felt to be grounded to the seafloor. Mermaid tails were beautiful but weren't always practical. When she reached the center, she dug her tentacles deep into the sand and raised her arms over her head, reaching her fingers toward the surface. "Please save my sister!" she screamed out as loud as she could.

The three dolphins came to an abrupt halt, freezing in their spots like beautiful sculptures as their translucent bodies glowed like luminous algae in the night's sea.

Britt lowered her arms slowly as one of the dolphins broke from its frozen stance and approached her. The two others followed closely behind, three glowing angels of judgement. Britt collapsed to the floor, squatting with her tentacles tucked under her as her heart pounded in her chest and she looked up at their radiant beauty with tears in her eyes. "Please," she begged, clasping her arms in front of her. "Help my sister."

The first dolphin let out a cry before its translucent body rushed through Britt's chest. She collapsed back into the ground. Britt shook as if possessed by spirits as the two other dolphins dove into her chest, disappearing into her glowing skin.

"Britt!" Tanis screamed, rushing over to her.

Oliver followed behind her, resting his hand on Tanis' shoulder. "Wait," he said, pulling Tanis back.

Tanis froze in her spot as Britt's body began radiating a familiar purple hue and elevated from the ground. Her back arched as her eyes opened to reveal a bright deep violet.

"What's happening to her?" Tanis asked, reaching

for Oliver's hand on her shoulder.

"The stories are true," Kaleb cried out from behind them. "My father stole these creatures from the protector of the sea, Yuri's great ancestor, and Atlantis was built on a lie." He looked down at Yuri's sunken face in his arms and twisted his hands around her silver hair. Unlike Yuri, Britt's floating body was filled with energy, life, and power. His hands trembled around the curve of Yuri's cheeks as he remembered the story that she had told him when they first met at the boulder that overlooked the lighthouse. Her face had been flush with color then, reminding him of the sunset, and he had laughed at the notion that a silly children's tale could be true.

Kaleb cleared his throat which panged with the pain of held back tears. "They choose Britt as the new protector of the sea. They are assimilating with her now. She's the chosen Queen." His voice cracked as he spoke.

Britt's body tingled with energy as if an electric current were pulsing from the tip of her head to the edges of her fingertips. Her vision had become crystal clear, and as she floated in the center of the arena, she saw tiny, microscopic creatures crawling on her skin. She lifted her fingers, wiggling them in front of her eyes as a voice echoed in her head. At first, it was just the sound of crying dolphins, but then there were words. She lifted her hands to her ears, cupping them behind her earlobes. the dolphins were speaking to her, and now she could understand.

"Save. Please save. Save."

Her deep violet eyes shot their intense gaze at Yuri who lay still in Kaleb's arms. She stretched her hand forward, reaching toward her sister as a ray of white light extended from her palm, lifting her sister off Kaleb's lap.

Yuri's body floated to the center of the arena as if being dragged by a current until her tiny frame came to a halt next to Britt.

"Pull the sword."

Britt's floating body slanted upward until she hovered over her sister's corpse. She reached forward, nervously grabbing the handle of the cold, sharpened sword with her trembling hands. She tugged gently and as she did, the blade slid slowly out of her sister's ribcage with ease. Britt's eyes widened as she realized that the more she pulled the sword, the livelier her sister looked. The blue faded from Yuri's face, and her cheeks flushed with rose. As she pulled the final tip of the blade out of her sister's chest, her wound disappeared as if it had never existed.

Yuri let out a gasp as her eyes flickered open. She reached her arms out, rising from the dead. "Britt!" Yuri said, throwing her arms around her sister's neck.

Britt squeezed her back tightly as if she were holding on for dear life. "Never leave us again!" she cried out, rocking her sister back and forth.

Kaleb steadied himself on his elbows as he tried to lift himself. His arms trembled under him, shaking from his elbows to his shoulders. "Yuri!" he called out as he tumbled over into the sand.

Yuri's head spun around to see Kaleb injured against the arena wall. His body was covered in bruises and cuts, his skin spotted with black and red bruises and angry welts. She broke from her sister's arms, extending her hands as she rushed toward him. "Stop,

stop, don't get up," she said as Kaleb tumbled forward again.

His cheeks were covered with wet grains of sand, and Yuri brushed her knuckles against his bruised skin, wiping away the grit caked onto the curved creases of his face. She placed her hand on his back and guided him to the arena wall.

"I'm truly sorry for the mix-up," Britt said as she approached behind them. She placed her hand on Kaleb's shoulder, and a radiating light pulsed from her fingertips and into his skin, causing his veins to glow.

His open wounds closed up gradually, stitched up by an invisible thread. As he regained his strength, he grabbed onto Yuri, pulling her into a tight hug.

"I'm sorry too," he sobbed into the base of her neck. "I never meant to get you or your sisters into any of this. If you never want to see me again, I'll understand."

Yuri pulled back, looking up at Kaleb's deep green eyes that reminded her of the moss that grew outside their home. In a way, he now also felt like her home. His light-brown hair was a frazzled mess at the top of his head, and she lifted her hand to reach his cheek. "I could never do that," she said, brushing her fingertips across his skin.

Her plump lips slightly parted as her words leaked out like honey to Kaleb's ears. He cupped her face with his hands, bending at the waist as he pressed his lips into hers to taste her sweetness.

Yuri lifted her chin forward, returning his kiss until she felt the pitter-pattering of tapping on her shoulder blade.

"Ahem," Tanis said, clearing her throat loudly.

Yuri turned to see Tanis swaying behind her. Her doe-like eyes were wide and creased at the edges as she smiled with a large open grin that showed most of her pearly pointed teeth.

"Tanis!" Yuri shouted, leaping forward as she pulled her little sister into a tight hug.

Tanis wiggled beneath her grip, arms pinned at her sides. "Okay, okay! You're going to squeeze me to death," she giggled.

Oliver glided next to Tanis, his hands uncomfortably stiff at his sides. He looked down at the ground, flicking the sand with his tail.

"Who's this?" Yuri asked, pointing to Oliver.

"Oh, this is my new friend, Oliver, the blacksmith's son," Tanis said, pressing her head against Oliver's shoulder. She tilted her head back to let out a loud snorting laugh. "He helped me because he thought I was going to eat him. No—let me correct that. He *was sure* I was going to eat him!"

Yuri's lips raised into a half-grin. "Ah, nice to meet you, Oliver," she said, nodding.

Oliver's face flushed red as he pushed his shaggy blond hair away from his face. "You too," he muttered, scratching at his head as he mustered up the courage to speak. "We still need to get Sadie," he said firmly. "And I'm worried it won't be easy with the entire kingdom on high alert. We did just kill their King."

Britt's ears perked up the moment she heard Sadie's name. Her head whipped in Oliver's direction, and she rushed over, barreling toward him like a loose cannon. "What happened to Sadie? Did she ever find her father?" she asked, halting inches away from Oliver's face.

Tanis reached for Britt's arm and squeezed it as Oliver looked shamefully down at the ground.

"Her father died in the hunt for the beast," Tanis said, still clutching at Britt's arm. "When Sadie heard this, she got so angry that she tried to go after the King. He nearly killed her, but she was still breathing when they dragged her away. We think she might be in the dungeon."

Britt's mouth unhinged, slanting down into a frown. Her heart panged as if the sharped edge of the blade had pierced through her chest. "No, that can't be right. Sadie would never allow herself to get caught like that. She's too clever," she said, rambling quickly as her eyes darted between Oliver and Tanis.

"I'm afraid it's true," Oliver said, meeting her gaze from beneath his furrowed brows.

Britt lifted her hands into the air, throwing them up, frazzled. "Well, we have to go get her then," she said, letting her hands fall to her sides.

"Who's Sadie?" Yuri asked as she leaned back into Kaleb's arms. He wrapped them neatly around her from behind as she huddled back into his chest.

"Sadie is a young mermaid who helped me get through the castle gate," Britt said, her lips quivering as she spoke. "If it weren't for her, Tanis and I wouldn't be here. We owe her, and we can't leave her there."

Oliver raised his left hand. "I second that," he blurted out quickly.

Yuri's mouth curved into a warm smirk. "Of course, she must be very important to you," she said, twisting her head back to look at Kaleb behind her. "We will do whatever we have to in order to save her."

Kaleb looked down at Yuri's ice-blue eyes and

smiled at her as he squeezed her tightly around the waist. He then cleared his throat and looked up at Oliver, whose distraught face reminded him of his own when he saw Yuri tied and bound by his father. "If there's any way I can persuade some of the merfolk to help us, I will. I just don't think I'm the most favored right now in the kingdom. To be honest, they probably hate me even more than they hate you, but I will help you fight if it comes to that. If it weren't for you and Tanis coming back for your sister, she would be dead. So I owe you both a great debt," he said sternly as he rocked Yuri back and forth in a tight hug.

Oliver nodded. "Thank you," he said as his shaggy hair fell forward over one of his eyes.

Tanis smiled, brushing his hair out of his face with one hand as she playfully punched him on the arm with the other. "And you know I'll help you. You don't even have to threaten to eat me."

Oliver didn't even flinch. His eyes were stern and focused on Kaleb, who had broken from their circle and was swimming toward his brother's decapitated head.

Neo's eyes were still open, glaring back at Kaleb with a familiar-looking green. Kaleb bent down, picking the severed head off the arena floor. He stared at his brother's gaped mouth and hollowed cheeks, shaking his head in disbelief. He looked over at the huddled circle from which he had broken. The three *Inked* sisters and the blacksmith's son all frozen, uncomfortably still, watching him with looks of despair painted across their tired faces.

He raised the head in his hand, holding it up toward the surface. "You're not going to like what I'm going to ask," he said, staring at Britt.

Britt threw her hands up as her head shook furiously. "Absolutely not!" she shouted angrily, crossing her arms over her chest.

Kaleb gestured to the exit, pointing with his index finger. "He could help us get to Sadie. I guarantee that there is a mob waiting for us out there. Neo might be a scoundrel but he's a good fighter and might be able to sway some to let us pass."

Britt's tentacles tapped nervously in the sand. She bit her tongue as her nails dug into the sides of her crossed arms, causing tiny indents in her skin.

Yuri reached forward, placing her hand on her sister's shoulder before she could explode with rage. "Britt," she said, softly squeezing at her skin. "Maybe Kaleb has a point. If we are truly outnumbered, we can use all the help we can get." Yuri moved forward, carefully centering her body between Britt and Kaleb like a shield.

Britt nodded her head at the decapitated remains of Neo. "He kidnapped you, and you want me to bring him back?" she shouted as she shot a harsh, toothed scowl at her sister.

Yuri pulled Britt into a tight hug, gripping at her sides. "It will be okay," she whispered in her ear. "We outnumber him. Plus, you hold all the power now." Yuri let go of her sister's sides and peered into her newly violet eyes. "If he isn't willing to help us, I will personally give you my blessing to disembody him again."

Britt's lips curved into a small smug smile, and she quickly bit at her tongue to stop her mouth from giving her away. She cleared her throat, readjusting her face into a tight scowl. "Fine," Britt said bitterly as she puffed out her chest. "But if he even looks at any of us the wrong way, I will rip him limb from limb slowly. He will wish he had stayed dead!"

Chapter 33

Athena had gathered a mob of merfolk around the tunneled entrance of the arena. Her father, Marcus, second in command to the King, was positioned at the mob's front. He was a large merman with a silver fox appearance. He scratched at his chiseled jaw that was adorned by a dark gray stubble as his piercing blue eyes surveyed the mob. His black tail followed closely behind him like a long cloak, thrashing back and forth as he swayed in front of the outer arena entrance.

At the front of the mob, Baric and Casco were dressed head to fin in steel armor, each bearing a weapon and ready to strike. Baric's fat fingers were wrapped neatly around the handle of a spiked club, and he swung it back and forth through the water while Casco hovered next to him with one hand on his hip and a sword in the other. Both had been shocked at Neo's final moments in the arena. They had expected him to kill his brother and take the throne.

With Neo in power, they would have risen in status themselves, but instead, they had been utterly disappointed. It wasn't that hard for Athena to recruit them into her mob. They wanted revenge on Kaleb and *the Inked,* who had stolen away their dreams of one day ruling alongside the King.

The remaining mob consisted of members of Atlantis's royal families who were both threatened over the potential loss of their status and fearful over *the Inked* infiltrating their kingdom. They had been told their whole life that *the Inked* were enchantresses capable of dark magic, who would steal and eat their children if given the chance. Fear can lead to hatred, and in this circumstance, it was true. They hated what they did not understand and would die to defend their status and kingdom from it.

Athena had been the whispering mastermind, gossiping down the societal chain and helping fuel the hatred with false rumors. She felt bitter that Kaleb had chosen *one of those creatures* instead of her. She was considered the most beautiful mermaid in the kingdom and was certainly not used to being rejected. Her outer beauty was the perfect storybook image of a mermaid, but her insides bubbled. This fight was personal, and she would make sure every one of *the Inked* sisters was sentenced to death, and Kaleb would watch.

Her long blonde hair swayed behind her as she swam to her father. "Any luck getting through the force field?" she asked, running her fingers innocently through her hair.

Her father, Marcus, shook his head no. His jaw was tight and clenched and his mouth pulled into a firm straight line. He bore the face of a seasoned and composed warrior. "They will have to come out eventually," he said sternly. "We will just need to be patient and prepared. They can't stay in there forever."

Athena huffed, blowing bubbles out of her nostrils as she looked over at Casco and Baric. They had gathered large stones and were tossing them at the arena entrance. Each one they tossed was disintegrated into ash the moment it touched the King's powerful force. She crossed her arms over her chest as she stared, tapping her tail against the sandy seafloor. *The only one able to get through the force field was that disgusting Inked girl. If only I could harness her powers.*

Chapter 34

Inside the arena, Britt rapidly swam back and forth, preparing herself for what she was now calling another "magic trick." Kaleb had morbidly gathered the remains of his brother's scattered body parts into the center of the arena, a tower of dismantled flesh.

"That should be it," he said, placing his brother's severed head down, the final piece to a puzzle.

Oliver, Tanis, Yuri, Kaleb, and Britt formed a circle around Neo's remains as they held tightly onto each other's hands, forming a linked chain.

Britt's gills expanded on her neck as she took a deep gulp of water in and blew bubbles out through her mouth. She focused her eyes on the pile of limbs before her, the bloody remains of a monster who had taken her sister from her. Her stomach twisted, and she leaned forward involuntary as the muscles in her abdomen flexed tightly. *How am I supposed to do this?* She was ever hopeful that the voices in her head would respond.

Every cell of Neo's broken body spiraled in her view; her vision had become something extraordinary but also something that frightened her. She shivered as she shut her eyes to concentrate, but then realized even with her eyes sealed like closed blinds, she could still see everything around her. It was a different view, the energy of a life force echoed through her in colorful rainbows. *What's happening to me,* she thought as her ears rang.

Are you sure?... Are you sure?... Are you sure? The voices in her head were back, pulsing in her ears.

She looked down at the ground, shaking her head wildly, trying to pour out the voice of uncertainty that insisted on answering silently in her mind. *No.* The truth was, she didn't know if this was a good idea at all. And she hated Neo for what he had done.

You have to want it... You have to wish for it...

Britt opened her eyes to see her sisters' faces staring back at her, their eyes wide and eager for her to perform another miracle. She bit down tightly on her bottom lip before letting the words regurgitate out of her mouth. "I want it. I wish Neo would return to us," she whispered with disbelief in her own words.

"We hear you."

Britt's hands broke from the chain-linked circle, leaving her sisters' arms swinging at their sides. Her fingertips glowed a familiar radiating purple light, and she lifted them up, redirecting them at Neo's bloody remains. The light radiated from her fingertips like a rainbow and created a glowing bubble around him. She watched in awe as every cell in Neo's body repaired itself one by one, gluing each limb together anew. Her eyes darted between her sisters and Neo's body. Their hands were held over their faces and eyes, blocking out the blinding light. They couldn't see what she could.

Finally, the light dimmed, and Neo let out a loud gasp, rising halfway from the seafloor as if having night terrors. His hands swept down his body as a look of bewilderment crossed over his flushed face. Five familiar faces looked at him, including his brother Kaleb.

"Kaleb?" he asked. "What happened?" He pushed back on his hands, fumbling in the sand to get up.

Tanis held a sword out to his neck. "Don't move too fast," she said, jabbing the pointed blade forward as she glared at him.

Neo raised his hands over his head. "Okay, okay," he said as his eyes darted between Kaleb and Tanis. His head was throbbing at his temples and his mind felt foggy. He shut his eyes, convinced he was dreaming, and then opened them back up to find the same scowling faces glaring down at him. What had happened in the arena after the fight?

"You were dead," Kaleb said, breaking the silence. "Britt brought you back."

Kaleb pointed over at Britt, whose lips receded over her teeth into a tight grimace.

She pushed her short pink hair back and held Neo in a sharp stare as he studied her.

His eyes broke from her glare as he noticed the empty arena chairs behind her. "Where's Father? Where is everyone?" he asked, bewildered as he lowered his hands.

Tanis pushed the sword closer to his neck, and the tip of the blade scratched at his skin, leaving a red indent. "You ask a lot of questions for someone who should be thanking us," she sneered.

Yuri reached her hand over, touching Tanis' arm. "Calm down," she said softly to her sister as she squeezed at her wrist.

Tanis huffed under her breath, "fine," as she lowered the sword from Neo's neck and dragged it across the sand below her in tiny circles.

Kaleb extended his hand for Neo to grab. "Come

on. There isn't enough time to explain everything in detail. Father is dead, and Britt now has his powers. She was able to bring you back because we need your help," he said, wiggling open-palmed fingers in front of Neo's face.

Neo grabbed at Kaleb's hand that so perfectly matched his own except for a few new scars that wrapped around his thumb. "That's a lot to digest," he responded, as Kaleb helped pull him off the sandy seafloor. He brushed the sand off his tail and looked up to find the three *Inked* sisters staring at him, ready to strike. Yuri's tentacles were curled into anxious knots as she leered forward at Neo, as Kaleb placed his hand gently on her back.

Neo fidgeted uncomfortably, scratching at his arms as a circle of those he had wronged formed around him, seemingly a ring of judgement. Every face was easily recognizable except for one, a lanky boy with shaggy blond hair that seemed to fall over his eyes.

Is that the blacksmith's son?

"It is," Britt responded with a hiss.

Yuri tilted her head in confusion, eyebrows raised on her forehead. "What is?" she asked, bewildered.

Britt crossed her arms over her chest. Everyone stared at her. Their heads had tilted, and their wide befuddled eyes lingered on her response. "What is everyone looking at?" Britt snapped. "He asked if Oliver was the blacksmith's son. So I responded."

The hairs on the back of Neo's neck rose like tiny spikes as the color flushed from his face and his eyes darted to the floor. *Can she hear my thoughts?* He looked up from the seafloor to find Britt gawking at him, her jaw wide open. Their eyes locked onto one another's, and in the silence, they exchanged each other's unheard fears.

"What's going on?" Tanis asked, breaking the uncomfortable silence. Her head tilted to the side as she moved closer to her sister, placing a gentle hand on her back.

Britt's lips quivered as she spoke, shaking with every word. "I can hear his thoughts," she said, breaking her gaze away from Neo.

Yuri pulled Britt and Tanis into a tight huddle. Her eyes darted between her two sisters, one who looked the same and the other whose eyes burned with a new violet ember. "It's okay," she said, squeezing at Britt's arm. "Once we are home, you will learn how to control all of these new powers. Maybe we can even figure out how to give them to someone else if you don't want them, but right now, we have to figure out how to get back."

"Yuri's right," Kaleb said from behind them, pointing to the arena entrance. "There is no doubt in my mind that an army or mob is waiting outside that entrance for us." He looked over at his brother Neo, whose arms were folded over his chest. His muddled eyes were drifting over the empty arena seats. "Brother," Kaleb said, jolting Neo out of his trance. "I'm going to need your help."

Neo's head snapped in Kaleb's direction. "With what?"

Kaleb rolled his eyes and sighed heavily, letting a stream of bubbles blow from his flaring nostrils.

"Have you not been listening?" he said agitatedly. "There's a mob probably waiting for us, outside this arena. You can help us sway some to join us, and if not, you can definitely help us fight. There is a mergirl in the dungeon who needs help, and we won't leave without her."

Neo glanced over at the tunneled arena entrance where he and his brother had held their last fight over the death of Ella. His father's force field was still holding strong, an unbreakable globe around the arena, which meant that they could either stay here forever and starve or face whatever waited for them on the other side. His eyes shifted to Britt, who glanced back at him with a dark sneer. She was their only chance of survival now, and the only one who could break through his father's force field.

Kaleb cleared his throat loudly. "So, will you help us?"

Neo huffed as his eyes traced the space between Kaleb and the arena exit. "I guess so." *But I don't really have a choice, do I?*

"So sad for you," Britt responded sarcastically.

Neo's neck snapped forward as his face flushed red. "You can at least try not to read my mind," he hissed.

Britt lunged at Neo, and Yuri quickly grabbed onto two of her tentacles, pulling her back as Neo fell backward, catching his balance before almost tumbling in the sand.

"Calm down!" she screamed as she grappled with Britt's flaring tentacles, pinning them to the ground with the help of Tanis.

Britt's nostrils flared angrily as she took a deep gulp of seawater to calm herself down and shook her sister off her tentacles. She pointed one of her long bony fingers at Neo. "Don't forget, I can incinerate you if I need to!"

Neo smiled back with an unbothered cheeky grin that sucked in at his dimples and before things could get even more heated, Kaleb held his hands in the air, positioning his body between his brother and Britt.

"Enough!" he said patronizingly as he waved his hands. "We are going to need to come together if we are going to make it out of this arena alive. So it's best if you two put your differences aside before we leave! Can you do that?" His gaze said, *well, you'd better!*

Britt huffed, crossing her arms stubbornly over her chest as she tapped her tentacles in the sand. "Fine by me." She shrugged, just to emphasize her point, looking petulant.

"And you?" Kaleb said, turning to his brother whose mouth was still curved into a dark sneer.

Neo nodded his head forward into a faux bow. "Well, I suppose I'll be on my very best behavior then, brother," he said sarcastically.

Chapter 35

During the quarrel, Oliver had swum to the edge of the stadium and was doing laps against its cement walls. He paused in front of the arena entrance and turned his head so that his eardrum faced out into the tunneled darkness.

"What are you doing?" Tanis asked, swimming over to him with her head cocked skeptically.

Oliver raised his left pointer finger to his lips. "Shh."

Tanis' eyes narrowed as she turned her head so that her ear also faced the tunneled entrance. She pushed her blue hair behind her ear and cupped her hand around her lobe. Sure enough, she heard the mutters of voices coming from outside of the arena entrance. It sounded like the inaudible whispers of a seashell.

"I can't make out what they are saying," she whispered to Oliver.

Oliver looked over at Britt in the center of the arena; his arms were folded tightly around her chest. Her violet eyes were bright and aimed at Neo with an intentional, piercing stare.

"I can't either," he said, turning back to Tanis. "But maybe your sister can tell us what they are planning and how many are out there."

Tanis sighed as she nodded in agreement. A lot was about to be expected from her sister, but they would need her powers if they were going to escape. Once they cracked through the protective force field around the arena, there was no turning back. They had to get this right. "Britt!" Tanis shouted, waving her hand at her sister.

Britt's lips curled over her teeth as she gave Neo one last scowl before swimming over to her sister. Kaleb and Yuri tailed behind her, carefully watching her every move. "What is it?" Britt said, brushing her hands through her pink hair.

Tanis pointed inside the dark tunneled entrance. "What can you hear?" she asked.

Britt turned her body so that her left ear faced the dark tunnel. She took a deep inhale of seawater as she shut her eyes.

The rippling sound of waves echoed through her body, and she could not only hear the voices outside of the arena, but she could also see the crowd as if they were gathered right in front of her, readying their weapons. "Athena," she cried out.

Kaleb grabbed Britt by the arms. "What about Athena?" he asked as he stared at her intently, squeezing at her sides. Britt opened her eyes which were glowing in deep purple rays. Was she about to death ray her way through Kaleb's body? He let his hands drop from her sides as he moved back apologetically, his head down.

"She and her father have gathered an angry mob," Britt said as her eyes dulled back to a normal violet. "There's about thirty, all armed with weapons. Including the two mermen who kidnapped Yuri, to begin with. They are trying to figure out a way in."

Casco and Baric are there, Neo thought as Britt

glared at him with confirmation. It was no shock to him that they would align themselves with whoever could provide them with the most power.

"Okay," Kaleb said, swimming back and forth in front of the weapons rack. "We need a plan…we need a plan." He paused in front of one of the spiked helmets that his father had loved so much. His lips quivered over his teeth, and his nostrils flared as the helmet mocked him with its clean and unblemished shining spikes. Kaleb ripped it off the rack, sending it spiraling across the arena, hitting into the impenetrable force field. He watched as it bounced back like a boomerang, tumbling into the sand.

"I have an idea," Kaleb said, looking over at Britt. "You are the only one able to cut through the force field. That's how you were able to get to all of us, and Tanis and Oliver were able to follow behind you."

"Okay…" Britt replied, nodding sarcastically with her arms crossed over her chest. "What's your point?"

Kaleb's lips parted but before he was able to speak, Yuri interpreted, leaving him with his mouth gaped open. "Wait, I think I know what he's getting at," she said enthusiastically. "If Britt can project a force field around all of us, we will be able to swim out of the arena unharmed. No one will be able to penetrate it unless Britt wants them to."

"Exactly," Kaleb said, smiling as he pulled Yuri in, and planted a kiss on her forehead.

Neo's nose wrinkled in disgust as he watched his brother's display of affection. *Ugh, I'll never get used to that,* he thought.

Britt's head snapped in his direction. "You won't have to if I burn you alive," she hissed with a wide-fanged sneer.

Neo squinted his eyes back at her and replied, "Cretinous Sea Witch!" pausing to lift his lips into a faux sarcastic smile. "Since you are going to hear me thinking it anyway."

"ENOUGH!" Yuri shouted.

Britt mumbled something under her breath as she crossed her arms over her chest and pouted. "Fine, it sounds like a decent plan. But I've never done that before. What if I can't?"

Oliver couldn't stand to listen to the quarrelling anymore. He had been biting at his fingernails and pacing back and forth as he waited for the group to concoct a plan that had even the slightest chance of survival. Every minute they wasted was another that Sadie was locked behind bars or worse. He shook his head, trying to stop a much darker thought creeping through his mind. "You're going to have to try," he said forcefully as he met Britt's violet gaze, then recoiled. His head bowed back down to the ground in submission, and he clasped his hands in front of him tightly, waiting for Britt to burst him into flames as she had almost done to Neo.

"You're right," Britt replied with a kind nod.

"I am?" Oliver said, slowly raising his head from staring at the ground as the peaks of his brows raised.

"Yes, I am going to try," she replied as her violet eyes scanned between Tanis, Oliver, Kaleb, and Yuri. "Everyone, move closer to me."

Tanis and Yuri each grabbed a sword from the weapons rack and then positioned themselves on each side of Britt. The three sisters interlocked their hands while Kaleb, Oliver, and Neo picked out their weapons.

When they were all huddled close, Britt closed her eyes and envisioned a giant purple light radiating from her chest and wrapping around them like a globe.

Okay, you can do this. The faint whispering sounds of the dolphins swept through her ears. *You seek protection. We can see. But the twin?*

Britt kept her eyes tightly shut as she squeezed at her sisters' hands. *Are you talking about Neo?* she asked, stressing each word.

Yes. Yes. Yes. Are you certain he is to be forgiven? Is he to be trusted?

Britt squinted, one of her eyes open. In front of her floated Neo, Oliver to his left, Kaleb to his right. Oliver stood out like a sore thumb next to the chiseled features of the identical twins. Their sculpted jawlines were as sharp as cutting blades, whereas Oliver's face was rounded and soft, a perfect oval. However, all three faces marveled at her with the same piercing look that one might find in the eyes of children at a circus, eagerly waiting for her next trick.

She shut her eyes again, squeezing so hard at her lids that her skin wrinkled around the edges. Deep inside, she still hoped this whole thing was a bad nightmare that she would eventually wake up from, but then the voices repeated themselves, slamming in her eardrums. Britt gripped her sisters' hands, taking a deep gulp of water into her gills before answering with her own thoughts. *I'm not sure, but there's no time to delay.*

A few seconds passed, feeling like a century as she gripped at her sisters' hands.

Please. She bent her head pleading with the voices that had gone silent.

You must want it. You must wish for it.

She focused her mind and pictured herself in front of a large plate of codfish, her mother's warm face peering over the mound of dead fish that she had brought her for her birthday. It was the last birthday that her mother had spent with her and the last time she had made a wish with true intent. Unfortunately, she didn't have any magic dolphins swimming in her bloodstream to keep her mother alive, but perhaps now, her wish would come true.

I wish there were a protective globe around all of us so that we cannot be harmed once leaving this arena, Britt thought, enunciating every word in her head. A few silent moments passed before she felt her body heat up, the warmth expanding akin to a bright ray of light.

"Ouch," she heard her sister Yuri say as both of her sisters yanked their hands from hers.

Britt counted to five in her head and then opened her eyes to find herself standing in the center of a translucent purple globe. The energy of her powers pulsed off her skin, and she wasn't sure how long her body could sustain this magic. Her sisters were still at her sides, but their heads were pointed up, admiring her work. Neo, Kaleb, and Oliver did the same, tracing the walls with their eyes.

There was a consistent shimmering that ran in waves down from the top of the globe, and unlike the King's invisible force field, it was apparent where their protection would end.

Neo extended his hand out, reaching his fingertips at the shimmering wave. *ZAP!* "Ow!" he cried, pulling his hand back from the globe and sticking his electrified finger into his mouth.

Britt glared over at Neo with a smug smile across her face. "Oh, sorry," she said sarcastically. "How silly of me to forget to mention to you that it keeps things in as well. I guess you won't be leaving anywhere unless I want you to."

Neo rolled his eyes as he popped his wounded finger out of his mouth, shaking it at his side. "Okay, so now what?" he said, agitated as he directed his gaze toward his brother.

Kaleb pointed at the arena entrance with an open palm. The whole situation was risky, and he wasn't sure how long this shield would protect them, or if Britt would be able to control her powers until they were somewhere safe. However, the alternative was to starve to death in an empty arena. "Now, we leave and hope for the best," he replied sternly as he puffed out his chest, preparing himself to take on whatever awaited them on the other side.

Britt stared down at the ground as Kaleb's words lingered on a loop in her head. *Hope for the best. Hope for the best. Hope for the best.*

"What's wrong?" Yuri asked, bending her head down to meet her sister's gaze.

"What if once we are out there, I can't control this force field anymore?" she replied as her lips quivered gently. She felt the choking of tears pulling at the back of her throat and swallowed hard, fighting the urge to cry.

Yuri reached for Britt's chin, raising her head up to face her. "I'm already so proud of how far you and your sister were willing to go to save me. This isn't all on you anymore. If the shield comes down, we will fight with everything we have, together.”

“Yeah,” Tanis chimed in, wrapping her arms around Britt’s neck. “We’re going to be fine. We are all in this together now!” She squeezed her into a tight hug.

“Let’s hope that’s true,” Britt responded as her violet eyes met the dark, hollowed exit.

Chapter 36

Athena swam back and forth in front of the arena entrance, her hands clasped anxiously into tight fists at her sides, as her long blonde hair chased behind. "This is taking too long!" she huffed, slamming her sequined tail into the seafloor.

A large portion of her mob had lost interest in keeping guard, and many dispersed into a slow fade, sneaking away as Athena's back was turned. The ones that remained chattered as they lowered their weapons in restless boredom. However, Casco and Baric had not given up trying to break through the barrier, even if every object they flung toward the force field was either propelled back to them or instantly disintegrated into ash. Baric lifted another boulder off the ground, circling to gain speed before launching it into the arena tunnel like a shot put. The boulder spiraled as it hit the force field with a loud SMACK, and then bounced back, nearly knocking Casco to the ground. He glared at Baric, and his lips parted to crudely scold him, but then he paused, noticing a purple glow from the corner of his eye. The tunnel was lit up, and Casco and Baric froze, peering inside, as shadows crept up the walls signaling approaching bodies.

"They're coming!" Casco shouted, lifting his sword.

Baric gave two test swings of his spiked club and

sneered as he waited for Marcus's orders.

Marcus had been still and silent, waiting with the patience of a seasoned warrior. His mouth twitched slightly on his stern statuesque face as he pulled a large metal sword from his holster and positioned himself at the front of the mob. "Ready your weapons!" He held his sword out in front of him. The clinking of metal weapons and shields echoed through the water behind him as the mob readied themselves for a fight.

Athena made her way to the back, carefully circling the sharpened edges of blades and clattering armor that hung on the remaining civilians.

She was willing to sacrifice them all if it meant defeating *the Inked* and making Kaleb pay.

The thought caused her mouth to curve toward her cheeks into a deceitfully innocent smile that would be considered charming in any other circumstance. She brushed her hair back behind her ear as she leaned against a boulder, waiting as if she had prime seats to a show.

Britt, Yuri, Tanis, Oliver, Kaleb, and Neo emerged at the end of the tunnel, trading apprehensive looks with one another as they paused at the mouth of the opening. In front of them, Baric, Casco, and Marcus held their weapons tightly in their hands, staring at them through narrowed eyes. Behind was a mob of twenty unrecognizable faces who wore mixed expressions of fear, anger, and adrenaline.

Britt grabbed at her sisters' hands and squeezed tightly at their palms. Once they crossed the threshold, they would break through the King's force field and only have her purple globe to keep them safe. She looked down at her tentacles; one more inch, and they would be exposed.

"It will be fine. We are in this together. You can do this," Yuri whispered from her right side.

Britt took a deep gulp of water, letting it fill up her lungs like a balloon before exhaling a parade of bubbles. She waited for the last to pass her lips and then swam forward, shattering the King's force field with her move.

Baric and Casco charged forward, ready to pierce through her protective shield with their weapons drawn forward. Britt pulled her chin back into her neck, wincing. Baric slammed his spike club toward her face. As the spikes hit Britt's shield, a purple electric current ran up from Baric's club and into his arms. He collapsed to the ground, dropping his weapon and writhing in pain.

Britt swam farther forward as Casco, none the smarter, propelled himself up over Britt's globe and stabbed down with his sword. As the tip of the blade hit above Britt's head, Casco was sent flying back with a blackened arm from the jolt.

Marcus' eyebrows furrowed, pitching at the center of the bridge of his nose as Casco and Baric writhed on the floor in pain. He held up his hand, signaling the mob to remain steady.

He couldn't afford to lose any more able fighters without a calculated strategy.

Britt advanced, fully revealing the protective globe and Kaleb and Neo within it. The tunnel stood behind them like the open mouth of a beast, leaving them vulnerable and exposed to the mob's prying eyes.

"They're BOTH alive!" a voice shouted from the mob.

"How can that be?" a merman in the front said, dropping his shield to the ground. The mob's eyes darted between Kaleb and his brother.

Kaleb moved forward, holding his head high. His throat felt tighten with uncertainty, and he swallowed hard before addressing the bewildered crowd. "We are still alive, and we are still your princes!" he shouted, puffing out his chest. "If you let us pass, you will be forgiven."

The mob seemed to freeze in place, except for twisting heads, glancing eyes, and whispering tongues baffled to see both the twins alive.

Marcus was just as perplexed, and his mouth hung ajar as his daughter stormed her way through the mob, bobbing and weaving her way through the puzzled crowd. Her narrowed eyes shot a dark, daggered stare at Kaleb before she turned to address her dwindling army of civilians.

"We can't let them get away with this," Athena shouted stomping her tail into the seafloor. "Your Prince, Kaleb, befriended our enemy and brought them into our home. Your other prince, Neo, disgraced himself before the King to save his traitorous brother. They are with *the Inked* now! We must fight!" Her long nails curved into her palms, digging into her skin as her nostrils flared from pent-up anger.

Kaleb cleared his throat loudly from behind. "You are welcome to try to fight us, but I can't promise you will live," he said, placing his arm around Britt's shoulder. "If her powers were able to bring back both myself and my brother, I doubt you'd want to see what else she could do."

Yuri, Oliver, and Tanis swam forward to join

Kaleb and Britt at the front of Britt's protective shield. Neo fidgeted behind them uncomfortably, his arms folded over his chest as he looked at his old friends Casco and Baric writhing on the floor. He paused for a moment, slanting his head toward the ocean surface, hoping that he would be pulled up by a fishing line, only to find Britt's globe shimmering in his view. There was nowhere else for him to go. He sighed heavily before swimming forward to join the rest.

Upon seeing Neo aligned with the rest, a burly-looking merman with a deep red beard and patchy chest hair came charging forward with an ax raised in his hand. "Traitors!" he shouted, swinging the ax toward Kaleb's face. The burly merman fell to the floor, gripping at his burnt arm as his ax fell to his left, nearly taking off his ear.

Britt's protective globe had flickered upon being hit, and she swayed slightly, feeling herself being slowly drained by her powers. A thin film had wrapped around her eyes, making everything cloudy, and a slow ringing seemed to echo in her ears. Her projection was consuming her, and she wasn't sure how much longer she would be able to protect them. She leaned into her sister Yuri on her left and whispered in her ear. "I don't think I can hold this much longer," she said, pressing her weight into her sister's side.

Yuri's eyes narrowed on her sister's violet globe. It was beginning to dim and lose its shimmer, and she hoped for their sake that the angry mob hadn't noticed its flicker. "Hold on," Yuri whispered back to her sister, placing her hand on her back. "You can do this."

Neo had also noticed that Britt was beginning to sway back and forth. There was an odd look of strain across her face as if every muscle in her body was working overtime. He couldn't help but think of how easy it would be to take her out in her weakened state. He gripped his sword tightly in his hand, feeling the cold metal handle dig into his palm as he swam behind her. Neo waited for a moment as her swaying became more noticeable and then reached out his hand, grabbing onto her shoulders from behind.

Britt jolted at his touch, jumping forward an inch.

"Hold onto me," he said, moving to her right side.

As the mob looked on in shock, he pointed the tip of his blade at the burly merman who lay passed out next to his ax, sprawled out with a look of roadkill. "Anyone else," Neo shouted, grinning in a cocky manner, helping Britt take another inch.

He twisted his head, nodding at his brother Kaleb who returned his wide smile with a matching one. For once, they would be on the same side, two twins united.

There was an uncomfortable silence for a moment as the mob shared confused glances, and then just like a dark cloud, they dispersed. The clunking of dropped weapons echoed, one right after another until the seafloor was left with the scattered remains of weaponry.

"Where is everyone going?" Athena shouted angrily, picking up one of the discarded shields off the floor and tossing it toward the fleeing mob. "Cowards!" She swam over to her father Marcus, who still stared at the two princes with a stone-eyed and stern face. Athena tugged at his arm as she whined. "We have to do something!"

Marcus turned his head to face his daughter and the vacant seafloor behind her. The once angry mob consisted now of Casco and Baric writhing on the seafloor with burns. They were outnumbered, and even more threatening was the fact that the two princes swayed in the water before him alive.

"Come, my dear," he said, placing his hand on his daughter's back. "Today is not our fight. We will have to regroup and form a real army."

Athena shot Britt and her crew one last scowling glance before allowing her father to escort her away. Her fingers balled into her palms and she squeezed them tightly as she promised herself that she would find a way to harvest *the Inked* girl's powers and rid them from the sea forever.

"They're leaving!" Oliver shouted once Athena's back was turned.

Kaleb nodded as he watched Athena and her father's silhouette fade into the distance. "For now," he replied sternly. They were leaving, but he knew better than anyone this wasn't over. Athena would stop at nothing, and it wouldn't be over until blood was shed and she had her way. He leaned his head against Yuri's shoulder as the globe around them flickered.

Britt collapsed into Neo's arms as the globe fell along with her unconscious body. He lowered her down to the seabed, a sour look of disdain crossing over his face as if he bit into a rotten sea urchin. "Well, there goes our protective shield," Neo huffed as Yuri and Tanis rushed to Britt's side.

Kaleb rolled his eyes at his brother. "I guess sensitivity is a learned skill."

Yuri and Tanis lifted Britt from the ground, bracing each of her arms over their shoulders. As soon as they got Britt up, her head drooped forward.

"We are going to have to take turns carrying her," Tanis said. "She's unconscious."

"Okay", Oliver said, taking it upon himself to lift Britt's tentacles. "But let's hurry up and get Sadie before they reassemble another troop."

Neo raised his hand into the air. "I second that," he said as a wide, sarcastic sneer crossed over his face.

Chapter 37

Sadie had awoken to find herself sitting on the floor of a dark cement cell in the dungeon of the kingdom. Her eyes were puffy and sore from crying and twitched as she examined her prison. An uneaten plate of fish sat in the center of the cell and was beginning to rot, leaving the water around it tasting like spoiled flesh. Across from her, outside the cell were two empty seats where she imagined guards would be seated and a pair of unguarded keys hooked above the empty chairs. She swam over to the bars and attempted to wiggle her tiny frame through its narrow opening. Despite pushing her shoulders in and contorting herself, it was no use. She sighed, dropping to the floor.

"Hello?" she called out as she wrapped her hands around the metal bars and pushed her head forward as far as it would go. Her voice echoed through the empty chamber, bouncing off the walls as if mocking her and her solitude. Starving to death in an isolated prison cell wasn't the way she wanted to die.

She pictured her mother at home, pacing back and forth, worried about her. She would be devastated to learn of her husband's death, but even more so if her daughter never returned. Sadie wrapped her arms around herself, cringing at the thought. After a few moments went by, she had an idea. *Maybe if I wiggle the bars from the base, they will loosen.*

She grabbed at one of the bars and pulled up until the veins protruded from her neck and she could not pull any longer. The bar was set in the ground firmly, and no matter how hard she tried, it wasn't budging.

"Damn!" she screamed, picking the plate of spoiled fish off the floor and throwing it at the cement wall across from her. The plate cracked as it hit the wall, and Sadie watched as the slimy fish guts dripped down the cement surface. She slammed her back against the wall on the opposite side of the cell and slid down to the floor. "I'm never getting out of here," she cried, sobbing into her hands.

Sadie jolted up from the floor. *Was that the sound of a door?* Her muscles tensed, freezing as she stared at the dungeon's double doors and the indistinct voices that chattered from behind it.

In a giant *boom,* the dungeon doors flew open, smacking against the side walls with great force. Sadie sprung back, lifting her hands into balled fists.

"Sadie!" Oliver cried out, bolting to her cell and clutching onto the bars. "Are you okay?"

Sadie recognized him right away. It was the boy from the stadium with shaggy blond hair and eyes that went wide every time he looked at her. Before she could answer him, Neo, Kaleb, Tanis, and Yuri swam through the dungeon doors carrying Britt's unconscious body in their arms like a ragdoll.

Sadie swam forward, looking past Oliver. "What happened to her?" she asked, pushing her face through the metal rods.

Oliver turned and grabbed the keys off the hanging hook on the wall behind him. As soon as he opened Sadie's cell, she sprinted past him and drifted over

Britt's unconscious body that they had laid out on the floor.

"She's drained from using her new powers," Tanis responded. "But we think she will be okay."

Neo huffed, slumping down in one of the guard's chairs. "Okay, we got her. Can we go now?" he said, tipping the chair back and rocking himself.

Kaleb gave Neo's chair a nudge with his tail and the chair fell back, causing Neo to hit his head against the wall.

"Ow!" Neo shouted, rubbing at the back of his head as he glared at his brother.

"Anyway," Kaleb said, choosing to ignore his brother. "It has been quite the journey here, but we really should be going. We would hate to outstay our welcome and don't know if anyone is going to come after us."

Neo murmured under his breath as he threw up his hands. "Literally what I said."

Sadie watched as Yuri stretched at her neck, circling her head on her shoulders and massaging her arms with her fingers. "I'm glad they were able to save you," Sadie said, placing a hand on her shoulder. "I can hold this side of Britt if you are tired."

"Thank you," Yuri said. "My arms are pretty sore." She traded places with Sadie who knelt by Britt's side, running her hands through her sister's soft pink hair. Yuri smiled and then looked up at Kaleb. He warmly returned her smile with a memorable cheeky grin. "What happens now?" she asked, staring into his deep green eyes.

Kaleb extended his arms and grabbed her by the waist, planting a kiss on her forehead. "I'm not sure," he said. "But be sure I will follow you wherever you go."

"Ugh," Neo said, shoving his brother and Yuri as he swam past them, pausing at the dungeon doors. "All right, lovey doves, how about we get out of here before we all end up locked in a cell."

Kaleb let his hands drop from Yuri's waist. He hated to admit that his brother was right, but eventually, Athena and her father would form a new army and come after them. They had to keep moving. "Okay," Kaleb said, grabbing hold of Yuri's hand. "Let's get out of here."

The group swam up the long spiral pathway, through a marbled foyer that led out to a small door connected to the castle's kitchen. Kaleb had been friendly with the help, but his father would never allow service people to enter through the jeweled double door of the castle. Those doors were reserved for royalty and heavily guarded.

As Kaleb turned the handle of the unmarked brown door, Neo scoffed, folding his arms over his chest. "I can't believe I'm going out through a service door, like a peasant."

When they had finally made it outside, it was clear that much of the kingdom had gone into hiding. The once-bustling empire of Atlantis had become silent and still as if an apocalyptic event was about to wipe out society. Guards and merfolk alike had retreated into their homes, their white shutters sealed tightly around their windows. They were terrified of *the Inked* girl who'd killed their King and now harnessed his powers.

"Wow, it's a ghost town out here," Tanis remarked, her eyes scanning side to side for potential danger.

Kaleb's teeth scraped around the edges of his skin as he nibbled on his fingernails. His eyes were narrowed and glazed over, and Yuri reached for his arm, entwining hers beneath his.

"This is good though, right?" she asked, looking up at him. "We will be able to swim right out with no trouble at all."

Kaleb paused for a moment as he squeezed Yuri's arms beneath his. They would be free to leave today, but at what cost? Commoners and guards alike were even more fearful of *the Inked* now that they had just witnessed Britt kill their King and topple some of their strongest guards. He knew the merfolk well; after all, he had been their Prince for all of his life. It would no longer be enough to ban *the Inked* from crossing into their territory. They would eventually come after them and eradicate them to save their children from the terror they believed to exist.

"Yes, of course," he answered Yuri, lifting his lips into a faux half-smile. There was no need to discuss his worries with her yet.

Neo, who had been eavesdropping, tapped Kaleb on the shoulder. "You know that's not the complete truth," he said, whispering in his brother's ear. "They will come after us as soon as they are ready."

"I know," Kaleb said, placing a hand on his brother's shoulder. "And I hope you will fight with us when that day comes." He gave Neo's shoulder a brief squeeze before letting his hand drop to his side.

Neo shrugged. "Well," he said as his face twisted into a half-grin. "You did make me a fugitive, so I'm kind of stuck with you and your OCTO-gang!"

Kaleb rolled his eyes, tilting back his head as he let

out a boisterous laugh. *Jackass.*

As they traveled forward, the large castle gates finally came into sight. Its shining golden bars crested at the top like a guiding North Star. As they drew closer, Sadie's heart raced and she sighed heavily, leaning her head against Britt's arm which was slung over her shoulder. Behind those metal bars was Sadie's broken-down home, and inside it, her mother who was surely pacing, worried about her daughter's return.

"Are you thinking about your mom?" Oliver asked as he swam up beside her. He studied her face, tracing from her furrowed worried brows down to her eyes that stared at the seafloor and then back up to her plump pink lips which parted as she spoke.

"Yeah, I guess I am. It's not every day you have to tell your mother that her husband is dead and her only daughter has become a criminal of Atlantis," she said sullenly as her eyes teared up. She lifted her free hand to rub at them, trying to hide how red and puffy they had become.

"I know the feeling," he replied. "I'm afraid to see my father. He was very loyal to the King."

Sadie let her mouth curve into an empathetic smile as she gave a slight nod in Oliver's direction. "I can imagine being the blacksmith's son came with a good deal of its own hardships, having to work for the King," she replied softly.

"About that," Oliver said, clearing his throat as he rubbed at the back of his neck nervously. "I just wanted you to know how sorry I am about your dad. I was there that day when he got fitted for his armor, and I wish I could have done more to help you...to help him."

Sadie looked up at Oliver, her lips slightly parted,

and just as she was about to respond, he continued. "Listen," he said. "I think you are courageous, strong, and just overall beautiful, and I thought maybe one day, we could spend more time together…like on a date."

Sadie's mouth fell ajar as her eyes widened. "Oh," she said, taken aback by his comment. "I think you are really nice too, Oliver, and I don't blame you at all for what happened to my dad. You and your father did what you needed to do to survive under the King, but I'm sorry to say you aren't really my type."

Oliver crossed his arms over his chest and looked down at the ground uncomfortably. His face flushed into a light shade of pink. "That's okay," he said, pausing before insecurity poured out of his mouth. "Is it because I'm not built enough?" He looked over at Kaleb and Neo who had the same muscular frame and broad shoulders and felt a tinge of jealousy. *Perhaps they are more Sadie's type.* He had always been on the slender side, unable to gain body mass like many of the other mermen his age.

"Oh no!" Sadie responded, grabbing firmly on his arm with her free hand, her fingers wrapping around his skinny bicep. "It's not that at all. You are rather cute for a merman, but I'm just not into *mermen*. Not at all. Not big ones or small ones! I'm so sorry. Now, mer*maids*…on the other hand…"

Oliver gave her a dubious look. "Oh?" he said, pausing awkwardly. His eyes widened as Sadie nodded and gave him a little wink.

"Oh, you mean…"

Sadie simpered. "Yeah," she said, giggling. "Britt's more my type."

Britt's arm was slung over Sadie's left shoulder

and her bobbing head had fallen to the side against Sadie's skin. Oliver couldn't help but feel a bit jealous as his cheeks blushed red with embarrassment and he looked down to hide his flushed face.

"Oliver," Sadie said, smiling as she raised his chin up with her palm until his eyes were level with hers. "I'm really glad that I met someone who would risk it all to save me. I would love it if we could be friends. You are really brave, and if I were into mermen, you would be my first pick."

"Of course, we can be friends," Oliver said, as his mouth rose into a cheeky half-smile.

The castle's golden gates stood few feet away, and the group had made it down the winding pathway from the castle uninterrupted. Yuri's arms were wrapped around Kaleb's side as his brother Neo trailed behind them. Yuri had been watching her sister Tanis and Sadie carry Britt down the pathway like fragile cargo.

Britt's head was slumped over onto Sadie's shoulder, but she didn't seem to mind.

It was good to have both her sisters back with her. "Let's go home," Yuri said, unhinging the lock on the unguarded gate.

As the gate swung open, Tanis beamed. "Fine with me," she said as she turned her head to look at Sadie and Oliver. "You are both welcome to come to our home, since we know you can't stay here."

Sadie smiled back. "Thank you. That's very kind. I just want to say goodbye to Mom first," she said as she turned to Oliver. "What about you? Are you going to say goodbye to your dad?"

Oliver's arms folded over his chest uncomfortably and he tapped at his arms with the tips of his fingers.

"No, I'm ready to go," he said, pausing as he looked over at his home that sat right behind the castle's gate. Its white pillars stood tall and proud, causing Oliver's stomach to twist in disgust. "My father will be in rage as he was very loyal to the King. I think its best if I just leave things for now, but I'll wait for you."

"Okay, I'll be quick," Sadie said as Yuri took her place at Britt's side, swinging her sister's limp arm around her shoulders.

"We will catch up," Yuri responded as she gave Sadie an encouraging nod.

Sadie returned her nod and dashed ahead, swimming down the familiar pathway to her shack-like home. Her green hair chased behind in mossy waves as the group watched her disappear into the pile of dilapidated scraps she had called home.

"And what about me?" Neo asked as they waited for Sadie to reemerge from her home. "Do I get to come too? I'm also a fugitive now, thanks to you all."

Tanis smiled grimly, twisting her head around to stare at him. "Well, you can come; we'll have to feed Britt something when she wakes up," she said sarcastically, looking over at Yuri and Kaleb whose lips curved into pointed smirks.

"So, is that a yes, then?" Neo asked as his eyes darted between Yuri, Kaleb, and Tanis.

Yuri whispered in Kaleb's ear. "Let him sweat a little."

Kaleb smiled, planting a kiss on the side of Yuri's temple. "Will do."

"Hello, are you all just not going to answer me?" Neo said, following behind them.

When the group had finally made it to the end of

the road, Sadie was waiting outside her home, sitting on the disheveled wooden steps that cracked and splintered around the edges. Her eyes were red and bloodshot, and she looked forward, carefully avoiding eye contact.

"You okay?" Tanis said, placing her free hand on Sadie's shoulder.

Sadie looked down as she rose from the broken steps that creaked under her lifted weight. "Let's go," she said, pushing Tanis' arm off her and swimming in front of the group.

Tanis glanced over at Oliver who shared the same worried look across his face that pinched at his brows, causing his forehead to wrinkle under his blond bangs.

"She'll be fine eventually," Oliver whispered to Tanis. "It's not every day you have to leave your family behind."

Tanis tilted her head to get a better look into Oliver's eyes, hidden under his bangs.

"And you, will you be okay?" she asked as she met his gaze.

Oliver shrugged. "What other choice do I have?"

Chapter 38

Athena swayed in the middle of the empty arena with Baric and Casco by her side. She pushed her long blonde hair behind her ears and listened to the silence once filled with a roaring crowd. Britt had unknowingly toppled the King's shield when she broke past the tunneled entrance, leaving Athena and her goons free to roam for any trace of power left behind.

Athena swam over to one of the weapons racks and ran her pointed fingers across the tip of an exposed metal blade. Her reflection glimmered back at her, beautiful but filled with anger. Her furrowed brows would surely give her wrinkles in the future. She opened her mouth, stretching her jaw into an O-shape, attempting to relax the tension in her face.

"Did you find anything yet?" she called out to Baric and Casco, both wandering around the arena as if lost children.

"Not yet," Casco responded, kicking the other weapon rack down with his tail as Baric let out a deep laugh that made him sound more like an ogre than a merman.

Athena massaged at her cheeks, still gazing into the reflection of the blade. *Morons.* From the corner of her eye, she spotted something sparkling from the King's booth. There, leaning against his throne was his golden trident. Its polished prongs were glowing, pulsing on and off as if sending out a Morse-coded message specifically for Athena.

She sprang up to the King's booth, knocking over the weapons rack with her tail, causing weaponry to tumble onto the seafloor. With her hand outstretched, she grasped her skinny fingertips forward, wrapping them around the trident's sturdy handle. Her body clenched tightly as a wave of energy ran through her palm and up her arms. She watched as her veins lit up. The King had soaked his weapon in the blood of the dolphins, and while it would be a limited resource, Athena would use it to get what she wanted. She tilted her neck back and let out a loud maddened laugh that caused Casco and Baric's heads to whip in her direction as they froze in place.

Athena held the golden trident up, pointing it to the surface as her eyes lit up. She smiled menacingly. She would have her revenge.

A word about the author…

Kristina Streva grew up in Rockland County, New York. As a chronic daydreamer she took up writing as a hobby and soon realized the magic in creating fantastical worlds. She loves museums, thrifting, movies, art, crafting, reading and all things creative. https://www.instagram.com/author.kstreva/

Thank you for purchasing
this publication of The Wild Rose Press, Inc.

For questions or more information
contact us at
info@thewildrosepress.com.

The Wild Rose Press, Inc.
www.thewildrosepress.com

CPSIA information can be obtained
at www.ICGtesting.com
Printed in the USA
LVHW081207240822
726588LV00003B/7